The Mist and the Wind

Jessica K. Stidd

Dedication

I'd like to dedicate this story to all who find themselves single as adults, whether at the beginning of middle-age, well into it, or beyond – and a wish to find happiness and gratitude for all that's good in your life, and for what life has brought you so far. Let you enjoy the magic of travel, of what makes you happy, and what inspires you. Even though it can be difficult to "go at it alone", let you live life with an open heart and know that love can find you at any time. For your path, too, is worthy and beautiful. And perhaps your ancestor of generations ago, part of the magic that led you to be here now, would smile upon your life with all its blessings of its own.

Acknowledgment

I'd like to acknowledge my brother, Sean C. Stidd, PhD, for his extensive research into our own family tree, and sparking my interest in his discovery of our great, great grandfather from Ireland. I'd also like to acknowledge Mary Adkins and her wonderful writing program, The Book Incubator, whose method of teaching to find the question at the heart of the novel was the key to making the story of Kayla's journey, an adventure foremost of self-discovery, and then her adventure finding truth linked to her ancestry and her spiritual and mystical connection to Ireland and love, that much deeper. A special thank you to Liz Pickart, whose debut young adult novel you can find under the name of E.C. Quinn, and Jennifer Barchi, fellow writers I was blessed to meet in Mary Adkins Book Incubator, for their invaluable feedback. And thank you to my mother, Karen E. Stidd, for reading an earlier version of the manuscript and her feedback on the writing and to "Auntie" Janice Baltrushes for being my first reader by audio book app and letting me know her feedback and impressions by listening to my novel. Another special thank you to Emma Dries from the Book Incubator for her editing of sections and insights on making more concise sentences and adding depth and suspense to my novel. And to all my friends and fellow students of the Book Incubator who showed great interest in the book, support, and shared ideas or feedback.

An especially warm thank you to all the lovely Irish tour guides at Turas D'Anam, whose trip in 2019, pre-Brexit, was the initial inspiration for my novel that also takes place in 2019. A time when Ireland, and indeed the world, was on the precipice of much upheaval from Covid and other geo-political dramatic changes in the world. A special thank you to Nóirín Ní Riain, PhD, for her invaluable feedback on the Irish language and to Cormac McCarthy for his great feedback on the story, and for reassuring me about the good dialogue that Kayla has with all the fine Irish people she meets on her journey.

Contents

Belfast
Lough Key
Shannon River
Lough Ree
Galway
Dublin
Lough Derg
Killaloe
Limerick
Cork

Prologue

I sat on the grass, above singers and seekers, hearing magic on the wind. Just the day before, Niamh, our spiritual advisor, had told us not to forget to tune into the hearing, and now, hearing the wind, I was feeling a new kind of profound peace and wisdom.

This was today's wind, yet all around, I heard whispers of its ancient past. The wind, trees, and grass had now claimed this circle, but in early medieval Ireland, somewhere in between 500 – 1000 A.D., this had been a busy fort and town. I had never felt so connected to the past in such a tangible way that also felt like a link into another dimension. It's as if spirits that had finally found peace were whispering to me to help release them. Or draw me in? If my heart was in the town of Killaloe, Ireland, a depth of my spirit that I hadn't yet fully explored was here at Beal Boru.

I first came to visit Beal Boru with a special tour group on my very first trip to Ireland. That was three years ago, and at the time, I hadn't ever imagined that I would be living here.

Since then, while living in Ireland, I found a group that visited different spiritual sites, and even though I had been coming back to Beal Boru by myself, I was happy to come here with the group to help expand my experience. At this point, we had all gone to meditate among the trees, where the ground was elevated in a hilly circle around where the original fort was, and have some silent time to ourselves.

The wind blew in a light, soft pitch: first, I just listened, and then, as I felt it pulling at me, I began to feel a bit lost in it. The wind truly sounded like it was communicating, and I wanted to know more about what it said.

My trance was interrupted by a friend – a new friend that I had just started to get to know from the group – Louisa, petite and dark-haired, a similar color to mine without the reddish hue.

"Kayla looks like it's time to go," Louisa tapped me on the shoulder and pointed to the group, who had begun to walk toward the entrance of the citadel. I just then longed for the singing I had heard at Beal Boru the first time I had visited Ireland on my tour lead by singers and storytellers. I could still feel the way the singing had made me feel – it was alive in my memory, like the wind.

I smiled at my new friend and walked with her toward the group that was leaving this beautiful, sacred spot; sad to leave but trusting what the wind was whispering to me: it was time to start my new life.

PART I

CHAPTER I

Living in Killaloe was like a dream come true – or maybe more accurately, like I was living in a dream.

I had found an apartment near the Cathedral Church of St. Flannan and loved hearing the cathedral bells ring and being able to walk throughout the town. Even though I hadn't visited Ireland until I was just 5 months shy of my fortieth birthday, as soon as I arrived, it felt beautiful, magical – and familiar. And when I first set sight on the town of Killaloe, I knew that I wanted to live there, though at the time, I had no idea how I would get from A to B. Somehow, by researching the links to my Irish ancestors and sharing with family and friends on how much I loved the place, my uncle had helped me get in touch with his second cousin, Miles Teague who ran one of the largest media companies out of Dublin. Through a lucky meeting, my uncle arranged while Miles Teague was in New York, I arranged a job writing weekend articles about County Clare and the west coast of Ireland for the Munster Post.

Most evenings like this one, I found myself at The Bean & Plover, a café close to the St Flannan cathedral on the opposite side of the street. In addition to working on articles for the Munster Post, I was writing about my time as an American in Ireland and all the discoveries I was making, thinking I might expand it into a memoir. I ordered a decaf latte, as I usually did when writing in the late afternoon, so I wouldn't have trouble sleeping. As I was trying to put down on paper my last visit to Brian Boru's fort with the Celtic Light group, and how it had opened up a brand new listening experience for me and the new ways I was hearing the wind, I saw a man enter the café. I found myself taking note of his interesting looks and energy. Nice and tall, an inch or two over six feet, it seemed, with a muscular yet lean build and very dark hair that was subtly greying on the sides. He glanced over in my direction and, gave me a sly smile, and then waved to another man that he was meeting. I smiled in which I hoped was a friendly, subtle way, but felt shy and looked down at my writing after making brief eye contact, just taking note of his grey-greenish-blue eyes that had an interesting intensity and sparkle.

He walked over to his friend, a man with sandy blond hair and at least half a foot shorter than him, and I liked the sound of his friend's medium-deep-sounding Irish brogue. I went back to my writing, yet there was only one table separating us, and I couldn't help but overhear what they were saying.

"Nolan, the concert sounds brilliant," the man with dark hair and intriguing energy said.

"Thanks, Declan. I think some jazz piano will add some flair to the vast array of classical that will be played at the festival." I looked up from my writing and noticed Nolan's mischievous and youthful smile.

"The acoustics in St. Flannan's are amazing, can't wait to hear your music there."

Suddenly, a large family came into the café, and it became harder to hear what Declan and Nolan were saying, and I also started to feel a bit like I was eavesdropping and put my will toward concentrating on my writing again. Through the woman talking loudly to her husband while two of her little ones were trying to get her attention and the other noisy sounds of the espresso machine and conversations around me, I just made out that they would be having a rehearsal for the concert at St. Flannan's cathedral next Tuesday. Not too long after that, the two men stood up, shook hands, and, with busy expressions, left the café.

Declan and Nolan. I visualized the greyish aqua eyes and black hair, and my mind wondered if the rehearsal was open to the public.

The next morning, the sun came up early, as it was late May, and the days were growing longer and longer for the "light season." I was still getting use to the very long days in the late spring and summer and the very long nights in the late fall and winter in Ireland.

The sun coming up early in the "light season" encouraged

me to rise a little earlier in the morning, too. The clock read 6:15 AM as I got up from bed, but the sun already seemed fairly high in the sky. As I started the hot water for my coffee, I remembered the Killaloe music festival was coming up. I wondered if that was where Nolan would be performing! Then my mind started wandering to Declan, his stormy eyes and black wavy hair… I was fascinated by him but couldn't exactly call it a crush from only seeing him once at the café. There was something about him…

After pouring myself a cup of freshly brewed coffee, I walked over to my desk with my computer perched by the window in my one-bedroom apartment that looked out onto the top of my café and its neighboring shops, with a sliver of the Shannon river in the background. As I scrolled through the online program for the upcoming Killaloe music festival at the end of May and beginning of June, I found an "emerging artist" concert on the evening of Thursday, May 28th, featuring jazz pianist Nolan Ó Donnabhain! Feeling like it was better karma to go ahead and buy a ticket instead of seeing if it was possible to crash the rehearsal, I went ahead and bought a ticket to the concert.

That same day turned cloudy and then very rainy, a hard Ireland rain that, even though it limited my outdoor activities, I loved because I knew it was what made the country so beautiful and green. Looking out the window out onto the heavy rain, I remembered when, on my first trip to Ireland, we visited the holy island Inis Cealtra, sticking to our itinerary rain or shine. The pouring rain made the experience more spiritual and other-worldly, even if I couldn't remember having ever been that soaked before in my entire life. The beautiful singing voices echoed in St. Mary's, the only covered structure on the island, with the rain pouring down outside all around us.

I gathered my laptop and notebook, planning to have a cozy writing session while the rain poured down outside at the Bean & Plover. I was just opening my front door to leave when my cell phone rang, and saw my managing editor's ID come through.

"Hi Kayla, this is Aiden, so glad I caught you! How is it going?"

"Fine, thanks how are you?" A mixed feeling of gratitude for my job and slight disappointment came over me, as I had been looking forward to a couple of hours of dreamy, no-pressure writing at the café while rain poured down outside.

"Good, thank you. The reason I'm calling is Liam wants to run your article about Flannan's Cathedral one week early, which means we will need it by Friday to run this weekend." I felt a little stress at the news of the sooner deadline, but a little excitement as I had been enjoying the article, and St Flannan's was one of my favorite places in Killaloe. The upcoming jazz piano concert flashed through my mind, too.

"Wow, ok, I can have it to you by Friday. Since I'm 'rained in', so to speak, today, I'll work on it this afternoon. Appreciate the heads up!"

"Great, will report back to Liam that you will have it to us by Friday."

As I grabbed my umbrella and headed out into the rain, I mused that as much as I tried to plan my life, there were always things that came up that made me readjust my plan.

The rain was heavy as I walked from my apartment onto the wet pavement below, and I had just walked a few steps when I heard St. Flannan's bells chime the time for 10 AM. I always loved the sound of the bells, but this time, I had an even deeper response and experienced them both as other-worldly and empowering. The bells ringing in the 10 o'clock hour led me on as I walked toward the cathedral.

Suddenly, as I was just a few steps away from St. Flannan's, I had a revelation wash over me as to how I would proceed with the day and complete the article and turn it in on time.

It was still raining hard as the tenth and last bell chimed. I proceeded on the walkway past the sign of the cathedral and a Celtic cross on my left and entered the cathedral just as the last of the ten o'clock bells chimed. I reviewed in my mind the parts of the cathedral I had already started writing about, and then visions started floating through my mind of what had been most fascinating to me about the cathedral – the Ogham Stone, the High Cross, and the East Window – but also somehow aware that a new discovery was waiting for me. Being a weekday, the cathedral was relatively uncrowded, with just a few tourists here and there.

I stared straight ahead at the Great Oak Screen that separated the nave from the beautiful chapel. Suddenly, I became unfocused and like I was observing not only all of St Flannan's but myself from a distance. Why had I felt I needed to come back to St. Flannan's before I finished the article? I thought I had known the reason when I stepped out…but now I just felt like a force had pulled me back to a place where I had been to many, many years before. Yet I had only visited Ireland for the first time three years before I moved there.

As I experienced this out-of-body sensation, time seemed to take on a mysterious and completely different character, and when I came out of the trance, I felt like I wasn't sure if it had been two or twenty minutes since I had been standing there, staring at the oak screen but really feeling like I was looking beyond it.

I felt like I was slowly returning to Earth as I felt my feet step by step walking toward the chapel past the Great Oak Screen. As I stepped into the chapel, I was struck by its beauty and spirituality and was transported back to when I heard the beautiful singing there on my first trip to Ireland. I knew then that I would have to write about the amazing acoustics of the room and the way it transformed sound magically.

Suddenly, it occurred to me that that was what I wanted to add to my article about St Flannan's Cathedral – the way sound transformed it and was so much a part of it – from the bells ringing on the hour to the way music added to the magic and the mysticism of the chapel.

***

I was three-fourths through my article at my favorite café when I heard a familiar-sounding voice. I looked up to see Louisa talking to a dark-haired man who looked familiar, but I couldn't quite place him. Then I remembered seeing him at a meeting at the paper. I stood up and waved to Louisa, trying to get her attention.

She spotted me quickly and waved back, looking very pleasantly surprised to see me. The man with her looked over at my direction with an expression that was very hard to read and then looked back at Louisa. She walked over my way, and he followed her over to my table.

"Kayla! Great to see you here!" Louisa said, with an expression like she saw me being there as a really interesting coincidence. Had they been talking about me? The man she was with looked at me, and it looked as though he recognized me right away. It was hard to tell by his initial expression how he felt about seeing me if anything.

"I was just telling Moley here that this is your favorite café," Louisa said. I wondered what they had been saying and how did Louisa know Moley?

"Wow, I just came to finish up my article for the paper." I stood up to hug Louisa and extend my hand to shake Moley's. "Hi Moley, I think I have met you some time at a Munster Post meeting?"

"Kayla!" He reached out and shook my hand, though it felt more like a friendly squeeze. "I have been contracting with the paper as a photographer."

"That's right!" I just remembered where I had seen him. "I remember you from the meeting about photographing Inis Cealtra."

"Yes, we will be doing the photo shoot there next Tuesday. Hopefully, it won't be raining like it is today," Moley winked at me, and I suddenly felt a little shy, having picked up on a rapport, if not chemistry, between him and Louisa when observing them walking over my way.

A flood of memories came over me then of the day my tour three years ago adventured over to Inis Cealtra in the pouring rain. I had discovered soon enough that it wouldn't work to take photographs with my non-waterproof cell phone, opting instead to take a few shots with my bulky DSLR camera, worrying if the pounding rain would soak through its case.

"I love Inis Cealtra. Funny you say that too, since the one time I've visited, it was pouring the Dickens out." Louisa gave me a funny smile, and I returned it as I hadn't expected to use the "Dickens" expression. Did they ever say that in Ireland? I looked at Moley then, and he was looking out the window, seeming like something had caught his photographer's eye outside.

"Do you both want to sit down?" I asked. I wanted to be friendly and polite, especially to my friend and colleague, though I was truthfully anxious to finish up my article.

"Just for a moment," Louisa said. I truly wondered if Louisa had been able to tell about me wanting to get back to my article. She sat down with her Americano while Moley stayed standing, looking out the window.

"How do you know Moley?" I asked. I was still curious why they had been talking about me, but maybe it was just because they were there, and Louisa, for small talk, mentioned it was her friend's favorite café…

At that point, Moley turned away from the window and sat down, seeming to have come back to earth. I noticed he was drinking tea, not coffee.

"My brother recommended him to take photographs of his wedding, and I'm going to be a "second photographer" – so we're the two official photographers, and he's showing me some tips," Louisa said. "I was thinking about the guest list, and we came here for a break, and I remembered I wanted to ask you if you'd received the invitation yet? Then I thought I realized I was thinking about you because I know you love to write here."

When they both left, I noticed Moley putting his hand gently on Louisa's back before he opened the door for her. So, I had picked up on it correctly – there was something a little more than friendly going on between them. I looked out the café window where I sat, seeing them walk off and then just looking out into the pouring rain, feeling caught up in it like it was bravely releasing its tears while I held mine back. Yet, at the same time, the rain was a comfort for how I was feeling. I remembered one of the last times I saw Danny before we broke up, four months before I moved to Ireland. He had been the first boyfriend I had (and not that I had had many) that both my parents really liked. After a year, which was also the longest relationship I had, other than one my last year of college, I had even thought we could be heading toward marriage. When he got a great job offer writing for the New York Times, I had greatly considered moving across the country to New York from California. Danny had already been living in New York City when my uncle set up my meeting with Miles Teague, and ironically, then I had a choice –

move to New York and disrupt my life, but be with the man I loved, or disrupt my life and follow a strong calling and new opportunity in Ireland?

Looking back, I see Danny may have been impatient that I didn't decide to move to New York right away. But when, just two days after my interview with Miles Teague, Danny said he thought we should "take a break," I walked alone heartbroken through Times Square, a rather surreal experience during the day, and as I walked and walked, somehow the pull of Ireland kept feeling stronger. Then Danny and I were on the road to a permanent breakup, and my excitement about moving to Ireland was the only thing that seemed good in my life. Even my parents seemed dismayed that such a good match, both journalists with budding careers, did not work out. At least Mom at last seemed happy for me to be pursuing such a unique opportunity in Ireland and a chance to learn more about my Irish relatives.

And I had moved to Ireland to start anew, lucky enough to have a work opportunity here. Still, at times like this, being single weighed more heavily on me. I pushed the loneliness away like I had the memory, had a sip of my latte, and focused on my article – back to the magic of music in St Flannan's chapel.

I stayed at The Bean & Plover until a quarter to seven, satisfied with my article and feeling ready to stretch my legs with a brisk walk, followed by a dinner someplace that didn't involve scones and espresso. I stood up and texted Aiden that I finished the article. He texted me right back that's great and that he would read it tonight and touch base with me in the morning.

Feeling happy to be done and ready to take the rest of the night off, I said goodbye to the friendly baristas Leah and Tori and stepped out. The rain had stopped after pouring down most of the day, and there was no sign of the sun setting as it was only about a month before the summer solstice, so it would be a while yet before it set.

I walked across the bridge over the Shannon River, which had become my favorite pedestrian bridge in the world, and headed toward Flannagan's on the Lake, a gastro-pub next to the Shannon River.

I ordered a glass of wine, their wonderful seafood chowder, and an Indian-inspired salad that I had come to love with pomegranate and a mint and yogurt dressing. It felt great to sit outside under a covered patio and breathe in the rain-kissed, fresh Irish air. It being a Thursday night and after a very rainy day, there weren't as many people as there often were, and as I scanned the tables, I noticed it was mostly groups of men and a few couples, mostly drinking Guinness, and I was amused once more that I still more often enjoyed a wine than a beer.

I wondered then about the upcoming summer and all the activities I had planned with the Celtic Light group. It was great that I had made new friends in Ireland, and even though I was looking forward to all the places we would be exploring, I still felt the call to spend more time at Bael Boru. Something about the sounds there, the echo from the past, that I felt. I looked across the Shannon river then and felt my eyes mist up a little – even though people surely still noted me as an American living in Ireland, I felt more at home there than I had anywhere else in a long time.

It was true that I had been feeling at a standstill in my life and career in California. When I decided not to move to New York and went back to San Diego, waiting to find out if I would get the opportunity in Ireland after my interview with Miles Teague, my day-to-day existence seemed out of place somehow. Every night, I pulled up Ancestry.com, and I couldn't stop wondering about the Irish heritage that was on both my mother's and father's side and what brought them over to America. On my mother's side, it looked as though her mother's mother came from England, but this great-grandmother's husband had Irish roots, yet I could not find out anything more about his Irish relatives. And how and when did my great-grandparents meet?

Having found myself in my forties and not having gotten to the place to have a family of my own, the more I had wanted to find out about my ancestors – like it would bring insight into my life that

I was longing for.

The waiter interrupted my thoughts and came to take my payment then, and I couldn't help but notice his attractiveness – dark hair and a nice smile, probably ten years younger than me? Like a younger version of the dark-haired man I'd seen at The Bean & Plover a couple of days ago – Declan.

CHAPTER II

I am standing in the middle of Brigid's church's ruins, rain pouring down on me. My jacket is on but not my hood, I can't remember taking it off but feel my soaking wet hair draped across my cheeks. I stare at the raindrops dripping from the archway, wanting to run through it and down to the lake's shore.

I reach the bargaining stone at the water's edge, and I finally see another person, his dark hair and sly smile beckoning me to put my hand through the opening in the stone. His face has stubble, and his hair is medium-length – he seems familiar, yet dressed like from a time long ago.

I put my hand through the stone to meet his; it's the only thing I've ever wanted to do.

"Brigid!" I hear a man's voice call from far away. How can his voice be calling from far away if he's right here, holding my hand? I release his hand, and as I pull mine out of the stone, my arm emerges covered in an old-fashioned, lacy sleeve. Through the misty rain, I see I am wearing a dress I don't recognize. Why does he not call my name?

I woke up, a sheen of sweat covering me under my nightgown. Both sad and relieved to be awake, I felt I had been so close to what I was supposed to know.

As soon as I had my coffee made, I checked my email and got confirmation that Aiden liked my article about St Flannan's and the magic of music and sound there, and wrote, "Great job!" I also received an email that surprised me:

Hi Celtic Light Family,

We will be starting our bi-weekly meetings one week later than originally planned due to Niamh attending a family wedding the first weekend of June. We are looking forward to starting Wednesday, June 5th, for our visit to the Brian Boru Heritage Centre and Saturday, June 8th, for our visit to the magical Inis Cealtra, or Holy Island. This will push our last day trip to August 4th. Please see the attached updated calendar.

Beannachtaí,

Meara Moran

Another wedding? A tinge of loneliness floated into me again. I took out my calendar to write the new dates down, to focus my mind on something else. Then, the image flooded into my mind of me shaking the man's hand through the bargaining stone.

Forcing myself to once again focus on the task at hand, I wrote down the new dates (still preferring to use an old-fashioned paper planner rather than a digital one), and I noticed that the Celtic Light Events being scheduled a little further out did free up more of my time the week of Nolan's concert at St Flannan's Cathedral and Louisa's brother's wedding. Looking at the wedding invitation I had stuck in the planner, I felt relieved that I wouldn't have to plan for yet another event with the wedding on Saturday and Nolan's concert just two days before on Thursday. And like the bargain I made with the man in my dreams, I made a deal with myself that I must not miss these two events.

***

St. Flannan's felt especially alive and magical as Louisa and I joined the line of people making their way through the entryway of the cathedral. I had decided to invite Louisa and had been very thankful when I did that tickets were still available.

Excitement was starting to bubble up inside me – I had heard beautiful choral, religious, and even New Age Music at St Flannan's before – but never jazz piano!

Louisa and I, without realizing it before we met up that evening, were wearing similar outfits – both form-fitting black skirts that fell right below the knee and patterned dressy blouses. Thankfully, our blouses saved us from being "twins"; mine was a turquoise blouse and white scarf patterned with a scattering of flowers, hers a deep, bright purple with ornate gold buttons.

Most of the people were dressed neatly but not too fancily, some seeming to have come straight from work. There was a distinct electricity in the air – the ancient feel of the cathedral mixed with the excitement and anticipation of something new. It was when Louisa and I were filing into the cathedral past the nave that I spotted him – dark hair, intense gaze from his sea-colored eyes on a nicely tall, subtly muscular frame, talking to a rather short, almost completely bald man who reminded me a little of a priest. The intensity of the feeling in the pit of my stomach after spotting Declan took me by surprise. Louisa was just a tad too petite to hide behind, but for a moment, I tried to just the same as the feeling was now warming my cheeks, and I was afraid I was blushing.

Louisa and I found our seats in the second row on the side to the right of where the piano, cello, and violin were set up. All the seats were filling up quickly – I realized then we had been lucky that there had still been concert tickets left for Louisa to be able to come too.

After a few minutes, the man who reminded me of a priest walked up to the front of the stage. I had been watching when Declan took a seat in the front, and they carried on talking to each other while the priest-like man remained standing.

"I'm Christopher Keenan, and I've known Nolan O'Donnabhain for many years since he was a student at University College Cork." He didn't sound like a priest. "I have been very proud to see my former student flourish, sharing his music and talent with Ireland and soon to make his debut abroad in Spain! It's my pleasure to be introducing Nolan, who I consider to be the most innovative contemporary jazz pianist I know – and his band, the New Irish Travelers! If I were a betting man, I would make you a bet that you will think so, too. But alas, I will let the music speak for itself. Introducing Nolan O'Donnabhain and the New Irish Travelers!"

Nolan, along with his cellist and violinist, had been setting up as Christopher Keenan wrapped up his introductions, and almost magically, Nolan started an upbeat piano solo, the sounds oozing from his expert fingers in such a lively and catchy way the audience instantly broke into applause. It was a shorter piece and a perfect introduction, and when it was over even more applause. Then Nolan's bandmates joined him, and they were on fire! I couldn't remember feeling this uplifted and excited by live music in a long while. Louisa was almost dancing in her chair and whispered to me, "This is so cool!"

The concert continued to be amazing, and the last piece Nolan broke out into got the audience standing up and cheering; and the cellist, a curvy woman with bobbed straight black hair, sang along, only the second time we heard her voice that night and it came out as smooth and soulful as any I could imagine. Nolan's playing aligned perfectly with her soulful voice, neither one drowning out the other, his riffs on the piano standing out and then smoothly flowing into her voice that picked up the tune on the perfect note. When the song was over, the audience broke out into loud applause and whistles, Louisa and I, of course, joining in with her expertly whistling.

For the encore, the band performed a perfect rendition of "The Wee Weaver," and when the show was all over, Louisa told me to follow her quickly so we could get close to the front of the line to buy CDs and get autographs. Thanks to Louisa's quick thinking, we were only fifth in line, and Declan was supervising the line along with Christopher Keenan – Nolan, and his two bandmates had yet to come out. Having already told Louisa about having spotted Nolan and his attractive friend at The Bean & Plover, and that's how I first heard about their concert, I looked at Louisa and talked in a low voice, just loudly enough for her to hear over the sound of the crowd, "That's him." "CUTE," She mouthed back.

Soon, cool, blond Nolan, the black haired-cellist, and the tall, slim, spectacled male violinist came out to sign CDs. When we got to the front of the line, Declan was behind the CD table, and I surprised myself by gathering up all three of The New Irish Travelers CDs for sale. I started reading the back of the first one in my pile when Declan spoke.

"That one is really great, it has several of the songs they played tonight."

"Great! I think I am actually going to buy all three." I looked up and finally had the guts to make eye contact and look into his grey-greenish-blue eyes, and felt warmed by his smile. "I can't remember the last time I enjoyed a concert so much."

"Brilliant," Declan said. "Hey, you know you look familiar – have we met?"

For some reason – maybe I was too shy to reveal to Declan that I was pleased he remembered me – I looked at Louisa then, and she gave me a quick, stern look before moving her gaze toward Declan, like an instruction.

I turned back to Declan, who had a puzzled yet very friendly smile. "Well, actually, I remember you and Nolan wandering into the Bean & Plover the other day…I'm there a lot, I…"

"She writes there all the time," Louisa interjected. "Kayla writes for the Munster Post."

"Oh… wow, small world. And excellent, great paper!" Declan said. "Well, Kayla, very nice to me you. And your friend?"

"This is my friend Louisa."

"Well, Kayla and Louisa, very nice to meet you both," He rang up my three CDs and then Louisa's two. "Nolan and his band will be happy to sign your CDs now – what you've been waiting for instead of just talking to me, his sidekick." Declan winked, and I didn't say just then what I was thinking, that I was very happy to have been able to talk to him. "Nice to meet you," I said, and Louisa and I moved past him to the CD signing table as Declan started to help the next customer.

Louisa and I both told Nolan and his bandmates how much we enjoyed the concert as he signed our CDs. I noticed a flirtatious rapport between Louisa and Nolan and thought about how recently I saw a similar rapport between her and Moley. In that moment, life seemed so full of exciting possibilities.

As we walked away with our CDs, I snuck a final look at Declan as he was still busy greeting and ringing people up at the CD table.

As Louisa and I walked outside toward her car after the concert, reality started to chip away at my elation. I had no idea how I'd contact Declan again – or when or where I'd see him again.

"What an amazing night! We've got to go see them the next time they're in concert!" Once again, Louisa amazed me with her ability to give me hope and see things in a positive light.

Later that night, I laid in bed, feeling sleepy and happy and a little bit lonely. I stared at my smartphone and tried to resist doing searches to see if I could find out any more about Declan. After coming back to my apartment and putting my purse and the program on my little kitchen table, I had started casually glancing through the program again and saw that at the end of it, in the "special thank you" section there was Declan Maloney, who helped coordinate communication between the Killaloe Music Festival and The New Irish Travelers.

Declan Maloney. So, despite myself, I laid on my bed with my head propped up on two pillows, searching for "Declan Maloney" and "Declan Maloney and Nolan O'Donnabhain." When I saw what appeared to be a link to Declan's Facebook page, I felt a tinge of excitement and relief that I could have a window into contacting him again. A couple articles also came up on the search that looked interesting, and Declan helped with the publicity of not only the New Irish Travelers concert at the Killaloe Music Festival but a couple of others that were listed, but sleepiness was starting to come over me. I chided myself a little for looking him up so soon and decided it was time to try to go to sleep.

I step into the cathedral in the very dim light. The candles are lit, as he said they would be. It's odd that he would invite me here at night, though I know in my heart I will come wherever he calls me. Then I hear the music, what sounds like an Irish lute starting slowly, hearing the magical sound through the flickering of the candlelight.

I can see shadows cast from the Ogham Stone, and then a shadow starts to come into shape ahead of me of a man emerging from the darkness. I stare at his hands, strumming the lute – or is it a lute? It looks and sounds so old, so beautiful. My eyes slowly rise up to his silky dark blue tunic, a silver belt that looks as old as the Ogham Stone, his strong chest, up to his stubbled chin, and long hair as dark as the night…I just need to see his eyes…

I woke up suddenly, and despite the shorter late-spring Irish nights, it was still dark. I fumbled for my cell phone on the dresser and realized it was still in my bed – I had dozed off with it. 3 AM. What a strange dream – the man seemed so much like Declan, and we were in St Flannan's cathedral again, but it felt different – much older. I placed my cell phone on the dresser and laid on my back, staring at the ceiling before I could fall back asleep again, longing for where I had been as much as I was perplexed by it. I didn't realize until I woke up hours later that it had been my second dream that took place long ago in the past…where I felt both like myself and someone else.

CHAPTER III

I arrived at Louisa's brother's wedding on the late side, but still with about ten minutes to spare before the ceremony began. I waved at Louisa as she stood next to Moley, consulting over a camera with him.

Lucas, Louisa's brother, and his fiancé Megan were getting married at Saints Peter and Paul Cathedral in Ennis, which was about a forty-five-minute drive west from Killaloe. It was also where Lucas lived. The outside of the cathedral had an old, serious presence to me, yet the sky had turned blue with friendly, white, puffy clouds, and cheerful yellow flowers were planted across from the front entrance.

I heard the beautiful organ music coming from within the cathedral while I was still outside. I remembered the last wedding I went to was my uncle's, and I had been part of the wedding party family – this one, besides for Louisa and a much lesser connection to her brother Lucas – I was just one of the many guests.

I entered the cathedral and was struck by its size and bright, welcoming light – a contrast to its dark exterior. Most of the guests appeared to be already seated. Louisa, herself having only one sibling, had told me that Megan had a large family and was the youngest of seven children and that most of the guests were on her side of the family.

The families of Lucas and Megan began to enter as the beautiful organ played continuously; once again, I admired the flower girls that I always found impressively adorable at every wedding I'd been to. I watched as Louisa came in and walked toward the right front area of the church near the small party of her brother's family and noted Moley on the opposite side of the stage from her for capturing the wedding from a different angle.

As the families of the bride and groom continued to file into St. Peter and Paul's, I barely suppressed a loud gasp as I saw a blond woman in a deep, shimmering purple cloak draped over a pink and white dress walking with two young teenage girls that I thought must be Megan's younger sisters. And right behind them, I recognized my spiritual guide from Celtic Light – Niamh.

So the wedding that postponed my tours and Louisa's brother's wedding were not just coincidental occurrences– they were the same. Niamh was here to see her niece Megan married.

I watched Lucas and Megan exchange their vows with heartfelt wonder, amazed at how the different people connected to my new life in Ireland were colliding.

After Lucas and Megan promised themselves to each other and kissed gently in front of the formal yet gentle-seeming priest who reminded me a little of Christopher Keenan at the New Irish Travelers concert, the organ sounded in beautiful celebration while the guests filling the pews clapped a whistle here and there, and Megan in her beautiful Ivory dress and Lucas in his handsome dark navy suit walked down the aisle toward the outside of the church, to start the rest of their lives together.

The reception was a short walk from the cathedral at the Old Ground Hotel. Niamh and I walked over together; she was pleasantly surprised as I was that we had both been attending the wedding. Louisa caught up to us, running up from behind us with her camera gear in tow.

"Kayla, Niamh!" Louisa walked toward us and caught up with us quickly.

"Hi Louisa, how did the photography go?" I asked.

"I think really well! I'm excited to see all the photos that Moley and I took."

"Excellent!" Niamh said. "And so nice to have both you and Kayla here to celebrate for my niece and Lucas – we're all becoming a family in more than one way now."

I smiled at that sentiment and felt both surprised and grateful – I could clearly see how Louisa and Niamh were family now, but I was touched by the mystery of why I was being included, too.

The reception was being held a short walk away in the beautiful Banner Suite inside the Old Ground Hotel. Niamh, Louisa, and I walked through a lovely room with a fireplace on the way to the hall, and Louisa was intercepted by Moley soon after we entered. And said that she'd see us later and went to talk to him. Niamh spotted the two young blond girls she had walked into the church with.

"Kayla, I'd love to introduce you to my great-nieces, Erin and Kayleigh," Niamh smiled and led me to where the two young girls were standing next to an attractive gentleman with subtle grey sideburns, reddish-brown hair splashed with grey, and smart black glasses. He looked to be in his sixties.

"Erin, Kayleigh – this is Kayla. She's a good friend of Louisa's and is also part of our Celtic Light group." Niamh introduced me. I noticed how similar Erin and Kayleigh looked to each other, Kayleigh with very light blond hair and Erin's hair not so light but more of a honey-blond color, and Erin had quite a few more freckles – but other than that, they looked so much alike, their hair both long and straight and parted in the middle, and had very similar features and bone structures. I wondered if they were fraternal twins.

"And Cormac, so good that you made it!" Niamh embraced the intelligent-looking, attractive middle-aged man.

"Ah, yes – it took some rearranging of the schedules, but so glad I'm here." Cormac turned to me then and extended his hand to me. "Nice to meet you, Kayla."

I shook his hand in what I hoped was both a confident and gentle grip. "You, too!" I was feeling a strange confidence like I was caught up with the momentous occasion and didn't feel quite like myself.

"Cormac is Megan's eldest brother in their big clan," Niamh said. "He's a diplomat and travels a lot."

"Wow, that sounds like fascinating work!"

Cormac curiously smiled at me. "I love it, thank you, Kayla, though it keeps me very busy – perhaps too busy at times."

We all walked together into the Banner Suite. The room welcomed us in a soft, enchanting light – the golds of the chandeliers and curtains and the white tablecloths and chairs in blue, gold, and white created an elegant and beautiful space. Thankfully, Cormac invited me to sit at his same table, explaining to me that with the size of their family, not all Megan's relatives would fit at the family table, and since he hadn't known until four days ago if he was going to be able to attend, he had expressed that other family members should have priority to sit there. I watched as Niamh and her two great-nieces walked over to the long table reserved for the bride and groom's family. Considering Cormac was Megan's oldest brother made me wonder if there was more to the story.

The tables, including ours, began to fill up rapidly, and I was happy that Moley joined our table, separated from Louisa, as she made her way to the long family table. Another older couple joined our table with their adult daughter.

The tables were just about all full when the room filled with applause and cheers as Lucas and Megan entered the dining hall, hand in hand – Lucas an average height with a lankiness that made him appear taller, Megan an inch or so shorter, slim and elegant in a beautiful ivory dress that showed off her subtle curves. Both dark-haired, with her skin tone a couple of shades paler than his, made them both a sweet and striking couple.

I spoke to Cormac a little more as everyone dined on the delicious three-course meal, learning that Cormac worked out of the Irish Republic's diplomatic foreign civil service, representing Ireland and the European Union in Northern Ireland. Cormac also introduced me to the older couple and their adult daughter at our table, the parents being Megan's older sister's Godparents. Fiona, their daughter, seemed shy and a little sad, yet kind and compassionate, and I instantly took a liking to her. She shared that she was to be in Northern Ireland like Cormac toward the end of the summer.

Before I could ask Fiona what was taking her to Northern Ireland, Lucas, and Louisa's father stood up and clinked his glass to get everyone's attention.

"Let's toast to the happy couple! I am so proud and happy for my only son Lucas to marry his sweetheart Megan, a lovely woman who I am so glad will be part of our joint families now."

It was good to see someone from Lucas' side of the family speak, since up until then, I felt like I had experienced so much more of Megan's side of the family at the wedding and with all the introductions. Yet I was there as Lucas' sister's guest.

After a few more speeches and toasts, dessert, and more drinks, it was announced that dancing and a DJ would start the festivities and that the two adjacent rooms would be available to mingle in while the floor was being set up. After the announcement, most everyone got up and started mingling with other guests, and also many exited the room to explore and mingle outside the hall while the dance floor was being set up. I noticed Cormac walking over to the long table to talk to members of his family, I presumed, and Fiona, after helping her mother up who used a walker, started exiting with her parents but inching more and more away from them, as if she were looking to branch out and find others to talk to. I finished the rest of my glass of wine and felt more spontaneous and relaxed but not quite tipsy.

I walked out of the room and peaked into the Poet's bar, which looked very cool and more Irish than the other rooms to me, and then went into the pretty room with the fireplace again and wandered around, observing the wedding guests, saying "Hi" to one of the groups as I walked by but not managing to get involved in the conversation… and mostly just observing and smiling politely. I looked around at the art and fixtures, finally making my way to one of the lovely little chairs by the fireplace.

Among all the lively conversation, there was a vibe in the air that seemed very similar to other wedding receptions I'd been to in the States, yet with an added Irish flair. I spotted Niamh walking in my direction a few minutes after sitting down. When she was a few feet away from me, she stopped to talk to two women who looked around the same age whom I hadn't met yet, and I wondered if she had seen me at all. Just as my mind wandered to life's possibilities in Ireland before me and how long I'd be single in them, Niamh's voice broke me out of my daze.

"Kayla! How are you doing? Enjoying the wedding?"

"Hi, Niamh! I am, it's just lovely! I feel so happy for Lucas and Megan."

Niamh sat down on the small, ornate loveseat caddy corner from my chair, on the side that was closest to me. She had an expression on her face like she was happy I was having a good time, but with an inner knowing that she wasn't quite getting the whole story about how I was doing.

"Glad you're enjoying yourself, Kayla, and yes, I am so glad to see Megan and Lucas so happy together. Have you been to the Old Ground Hotel before?"

"No, it's the first time! I've actually only been to Ennis once before since moving here, and I loved it. I've been wanting to explore more of the town here since."

"I'm looking to see if we can plan a day outing to Ennis with the group, a time after we visit Inis Cealtra."

The scene from my dream where I heard someone call Brigid's name while I grasped hands with the mysterious man through the bargaining stone suddenly flashed through my mind. Before I knew it, I was telling Niamh,

"I'm so happy our group will be visiting Inis Cealtra! To tell you the truth, I had a strange dream there recently that I can't stop thinking about; that makes me want to go back there even more."

"Oh?" Niamh said, looking into my eyes like she was expecting to find out just why she had been wondering how I had *really* been doing.

I continued. "It felt like I was there, except it was in the ancient past – or at least a long, long time ago."

"Ah," Niamh said with a tone of wisdom in her voice. I could hear the variety of conversations around us, but somehow, we had created a bubble there, sitting close to each other as we were both focused in on my words. "What happened in the dream?"

"What I remember is I was standing inside the ruins of St Brigid's church, and it was pouring rain out…I ended up running through the church's archway down to the lake, to the bargaining stone. A man then appears in the rain, he seems familiar, but I don't know why exactly – and we shake hands through the stone. I feel like I really, really want to do that – shake his hand through the stone - but then I hear a man's voice call out, 'Brigid!' But it seems like it's coming from far away, like maybe back at the church?"

I paused, trying to remember more about the dream.

"What an interesting dream, Kayla! I think you dreamt about a connection that is very real."

I felt that sensation of eerie tingles and saw goosebumps appear through my sheer peach-colored sleeves.

"Really!?"

"A real connection to the past."

"Oh yes, I now remember… what was also interesting is that when I released my hand from his and pulled it out of the bargaining stone, I noticed my sleeve…it was covered with old-fashioned looking lace."

Niamh looked at me as if she was waiting for me to realize

an answer I already knew.

"Do you think this could be a past-life dream?"

"I think that it must be – and I think you already knew that. What you want to discover is that if it's your past life or someone else long ago who you have a connection with. Either way, you still need to find out why you are connected – or more precisely, what is the reason you are remembering now, why this connection is coming to you at this time of your life."

I was floored. Niamh was one hundred percent right – I knew the connection had been real, more than a dream. My rational mind had kept trying to convince me that they had been "just dreams."

"Kayla, have there been other dreams like this one lately?"

"Yes," I said in barely a whisper.

"Niamh!" I was broken out of our bubble by the bubbly voice of Megan, who came up to Niamh and then temporarily separated from her beloved other half, Lucas. Megan sat down right next to Niamh on the other side of the loveseat, giving her an affectionate sideways hug. "I'm so glad you're here. I wanted to introduce you to a couple of friends before we cut the cake and start the bouquet toss."

"Lovely, sure, Megan," Niamh replied. "So happy for you, my dear. So you have met Kayla, right?"

"Yes, Lucas introduced us briefly – you're Louisa's friend, right?" Even though she seemed a bit preoccupied (understandably so), Megan seemed sincere and very friendly toward me.

"Yes, so nice to connect with you again! Congratulations, so happy for you and Lucas! I met Louisa in Niamh's Celtic Light group, actually."

"That's wonderful!" Megan said. "Do you realize we had wanted Niamh to marry us, but my mom so wanted a traditional Catholic ceremony. My aunt is the most spiritual person I know!"

I knew the Catholic religion still didn't allow women to perform marriage ceremonies, and I recalled Niamh gave spiritual weddings sometimes as an Ordained Interfaith Minister.

"Yes, thank you, sweet Megan, though it is what it is, and it's all good." Niamh was showing her true wisdom again.

Niamh turned to me again. "Kayla, before I go, I want to leave you with this: Look out in your life now, your waking life, for someone you know who can help you discover more about this connection that you have made through your dreams. You are not alone in finding the answers you seek."

I wandered around the rest of the wedding in a way like I was dream-walking – it all seemed make-believe compared to the truth Niamh pointed me to now that she had me believing that my dreams had been indeed more than dreams – a true connection to the past.

After I missed catching the bouquet (a red-haired young woman named Marguerite caught it, which I think I overheard was a second cousin of Megan's), I briefly watched a few people wander out on the dance floor – considering joining them but feeling in one of my shy moods and still contemplating the advice Niamh had left with me. I wandered out of the hall and into the Poet's Corner Bar. I walked up to the beautiful bar with its deep, rich, polished wood and spontaneously ordered an Irish Coffee. It wasn't until I paid the bartender that I spotted Cormac sitting at the end of the bar.

He was looking down at his phone, but almost as soon as I noticed him, he looked up and made eye contact. He waved and scooted his chair over just a little and then looked back at his phone.

"Thank you," I told the bartender while I took my credit card back, picked up my Irish Coffee, and walked toward where Cormac was sitting.

"Hi, are you enjoying the wedding?" I blurted out. He gestured to have me take the seat next to him.

"It's just lovely, though it seems like my work never ends – a work situation arose, and I'm having to book a flight back to Belfast tomorrow night."

Feeling fascinated at what could be bringing him back to Belfast, but like I didn't want to be too nosey, I took a sip of my delicious yet strong Irish Coffee and said, "It must be very important – I hope it's not cutting your time off short."

"A bit," Cormac replied, "But at least I was able to see my baby sister get married today."

"Is your work related to the Brexit situation at all?" I must have been getting more liquid courage the more I sipped on my drink.

"Why, yes, it does! Have you been following the situation?"

"Yes, well, as much as I can – I've gotten to reading the *Irish Times,* and it also gets covered in my paper, well, the paper I work for – the *Munster Post.*"

"Oh, you're a journalist?" He looked at me suddenly with more interest. "I'm familiar with the *Munster Post,* good solid little paper that is."

Sounded like a compliment except also pointing out that the *Munster Post* wasn't quite in the 'big leagues.'

"Well, yes, it's what I'm in Ireland to do," He smiled; the way he was looking at me with more interest now made me feel flattered yet self-conscious. I took another drink of Irish Coffee.

"Just a moment," Cormac told me, "Let me just finish this

booking for my trip back to Belfast." I looked at his wavy, reddish brown hair, a couple of shades lighter than mine (or perhaps that was just the grey streaks making it look that much lighter?) and his greying sideburns – and how his arm next to mine appeared muscular through his silky tan shirt. I'd guess he was 15-20 years older than me, but appealing and seemed like someone to learn a lot from.

After several minutes, he finished up with his phone and turned to look right at me as I turned to look at my Irish Coffee again.

"You know, Kayla, I'd enjoy talking to you more about the Munster Post and Brexit sometime," he said, taking a drink of his Guinness, "But we are at a wedding reception after all, and back to work soon enough for me! And what's a wedding reception without dancing?"

Before I knew it, Cormac stood up, finished off his Guinness, and reached his hand out to beckon me to come with him. Feeling surprised and flattered, I quickly said, "Ok!" and took his hand and let him lead me out to the dance floor.

With a very fast pace, Cormac led me out of the Poet's Corner Bar and, into the Banner Suite and onto the dance floor. It was already well into a fast-paced, lively reel, and as Cormac led me in a fun dance, I noticed Louisa dancing with Moley. She looked like she was having a great time and didn't seem to notice me when I looked over at them. Megan and Lucas were dancing, holding hands in a circle with the nieces Erin and Kayleigh.

I was completely enjoying myself and felt more a part of the wedding scene than I had all evening – more of a participant in the happy occasion instead of more of an observer like I had earlier. Very soon, the music turned into a slow tune, and everyone either started shifting into a slow couple dancing or walking off the dance floor to mingle or grab more refreshments.

"Shall we?" Cormac said, and I smiled shyly, and we began to slow dance. As he turned me, I noticed over his shoulder Niamh now talking to Kayleigh, who was no longer dancing, and Erin was a few feet away, palling up with a young boy around her age. Up to that point, I had felt grateful to have some male attention and happy and impressed with Cormac's dancing, but after seeing Niamh, my mind started drifting to thoughts of my dreams again and what their connection to the past could mean. And then I saw Declan's sea-blue eyes and black hair come into my mind's eye and fiercely tried to push the image away. And after that, the dance didn't feel quite the same.

CHAPTER IV

At 3 PM on the first Wednesday after the wedding, I waited for Louisa to come to meet me to go to the first Celtic Light group outing since visiting Bael Boru and the group's hiatus. I had just received Louisa's text that she was running a little late. As soon as she arrived, I would go down and meet her on the street; she had asked me if she could meet me at the apartment and walk with me to the Brian Boru Heritage Centre, as she wanted to talk to me about something privately before we met up with everyone else.

As I waited for her and made sure I had everything I wanted to bring in my backpack purse and went through my wallet to decide what cards to bring, I came across Cormac's business card again that he had given me as we said our goodbyes at the wedding. After the dance was over, he'd asked me to walk partway out with him, and when we'd gotten to the lovely sitting room with the fireplace, he gave me his business card. I hadn't contacted him yet, though it had only been four days since Lucas and Megan's wedding. Cormac had told me to keep in touch; he would be very busy this month with work but that we should continue our conversation about Brexit and the Munster Post sometime.

I received the text that Louisa was in front of my apartment, and I quickly put Cormac's business card back in my wallet, shoved the wallet in my purse, and went down to the street to meet her.

Louisa stood there in the street in front of my apartment entrance looking stylish yet flustered, in cropped navy pants with lace on the bottom rims and a white lacey lightweight sweater, her dark brown hair ironed flat yet a little wind-blown and designer sunglasses. "Sorry, I'm late!"

"Busy day?" I asked.

"Yes, but I just got away from work just in time."

"Yeah, we'll be ok. It's just a short walk from here," I said.

I walked with Louisa down toward the direction of the Shannon River, where the Brian Boru Heritage Center was located.

"So, the reason I wanted to talk to you before meeting up with everyone was to tell you that I have been in touch with Nolan O'Donnabhain again," Louisa said.

"Wow, really?"

"Well, what happened is I looked up the New Irish Travelers website and noticed they are having one more concert before they leave for their Spain tour, but it's sold out. I sent a message asking if it's possible to get on a waiting list, that I'm a big fan and my friend and I loved seeing them at St Flannan's…and then Nolan must have remembered us since he called me back personally!"

Again, I felt in awe of Louisa's ability to make connections and impressions on people and felt a tinge of excitement that this could mean I could possibly see Declan again. "Wow, that's fantastic! What did Nolan say? Where is the concert?"

"Nolan said he could probably work us in, and if we could meet him and a friend tonight at 7 PM at the Boruma Gastro Bar! We can meet them right after the Heritage Centre tour."

The Brian Boru Heritage Centre was a five-minute walk from my apartment, and we were almost all the way there after just walking past the Bean & Plover.

"What are the chances that it would be convenient for him to meet us right near the Centre?" I was really wondering what friend he was going to bring, but I thought I'd jinx it if I asked…

"Well, not sure how convenient it is…I told him I had plans in Killaloe at the Brian Boru Heritage Centre with the group, and he suggested we meet at Boruma's afterward."

Before much else could be said about it, we arrived at the Centre, and most of the Celtic Light group were already there. Niamh was standing hand-in-hand with all the others in a circle. The circle was her favorite way to hold gatherings with all the members; she said in a circle, everyone is equal – no one standing in front or "ahead" of any other.

Louisa and I walked up to the circle and joined in. Niamh opened up the circle and joined hands with me, so Niamh was on my right, and Louisa was on my left. On each side of me, the two strongest and caring female influences that were in my life then. A man named Grady was on Louisa's left, one of the only three men who had come to the outing that day. Ever since I joined the group, it had had a heavy feminine presence.

Niamh announced that now that the circle was complete, she would give us some history of Killaloe, the place where Brian Boru was born, lived, and ruled as "Ard Ri," or High King of Ireland. That during his rule, between 1002 and 1014, Killaloe was, for all intents and purposes, the capital of Ireland.

"Killaloe also has its origins in religion – as well before Brian Boru came in the 10th Century, the beginnings of Killaloe started with the monastic settlement of Saint Molua – on an island that is right next to us but that we can't see, can you guess why?"

Grady spoke. "Because it's under the water?"

"Yes – exactly," Niamh said. "We can't see it as it now lies under the river."

I wondered then about the many things hidden below in Ireland, whether under the Shannon River, deep in the lakes, or under Bael Boru.

"Everything changes, but the spirit endures – and rebuilds itself again and again. The monastic settlement moved to the mainland. Nearby is the sacred St. Flannan's cathedral, but it is not the first one to stand there either. The first St. Flannan's stood from the late 1200s with an oratory for the same Saint Molua. Destroyed by Cathal Carrach of Connaught in 1185 and rebuilt in the 1200s. The beautiful Romanesque doorway remains. So the truly profound and spiritual always finds a way to live on, to endure. And nothing completely goes away – it just transforms into something new. Like the Ogham Stone inside the cathedral, from 1000 years before Brian Boru! The ancient Gaelic was inscribed on it by a Viking – a Viking who himself transformed, having converted to Christianity. So people, like places, can also always transform."

When Niamh was done speaking, we all stood there quietly, and I could feel the profound energy all around us. Meara Moran, who had updated us on the new Celtic Light schedule that summer, then started speaking. "Now, we will leave you with this thought and give you some time to look around on your own. While you read about Brian Boru and the origins of Killaloe, try to visualize how it looked and felt way back then."

The circle then started to disperse and feeling already transformed, I started to walk toward the exhibition at the Centre, lost in my own thoughts. I was always amazed at how Niamh could bring so much meaning into any place we went.

I walked to the main building at the Heritage Centre by myself, still very much inside my own head, though several others in the group were headed that way, too. At the Centre's exhibition, as I read about the history of Killaloe, I noted its Nautical history, with the River Shannon and Lough Derg, the largest lake in the region and one of the largest in Ireland, being important waterways for transport and trade. I thought about the original monastic settlement of Saint Molua and how so much of the spirit of this town that I loved and was now my home was tied to the River Shannon and the mysteriousness of all its islands and lakes. I read that the island where Saint Molua Monastery was built is called Friars Island and how it had been flooded during a project for hydroelectric power in 1929. The history was buried, but the monastery endured – just moving to the mainland, but its essence living on.

When I had my fill of the exhibition, I walked outside and walked closer to the river and saw Grady standing on the edge of the shore, looking out onto the river a few feet from me. I walked a little closer to where he stood, and he spotted me.

"Hello, Kayla, right?" I felt it was nice he remembered my name, though we'd both been in the Celtic Light group since the late spring, so of course, he should know it by now. I just hadn't talked to him much yet and never had a one-on-one conversation.

"Yes, hello, Grady! I just came from the exhibition. Did you go in to see it yet?"

"Yes – well, I walked in for a short time," he said in his thick Irish accent in a way that sounded like he'd just seen nothing new. "I do like to see the updates – though I like to walk past here on my morning walks, so I just popped in and saw it last week; not much new since then."

Up to that point, I hadn't realized Grady was a local and lived in the same town as I did.

"I think they have done a great job since the remodel and the reopening," I said, looking out onto the Shannon, too.

"You know," Grady said, "The island Niamh was talking about with the monastery, Friars Island, is not always under the water."

"Really?"

"Yes, when the river recedes later this summer, by early September, a narrow strip becomes visible."

"Wow! But most of it is still submerged, right?"

"Yes, at that point still, about two-thirds is still under the Shannon."

"Do people ever go out to it when part of it surfaces?"

Grady laughed. "Occasionally. A couple of years ago, a pair

of mischievous lads went out with their dog onto the island but still got soaking wet and in a bit of trouble. A photo of it was in last year's paper.

"Which paper?"

"Oh, the *Munster Post.*"

"Oh, really? Before my time."

I turned my head to look at him then, and I saw that he had already been looking at me, no longer staring out onto the Shannon. He had a perplexed expression that turned into a look of recognition crossing his face.

"Oh, that's right! You write for the *Munster*, don't you?"

"Yes, I've been working there since I moved here."

An expression that was hard to read came over his face then – somewhat like he had a secret that he wasn't sure he should tell.

"You know, Kayla, you remind me of someone."

"Really?"

"Which is curious," Grady continued. "You being an American and all."

For some reason, I took no offense at his remark, but it made me feel like smiling.

"Well, my roots are Irish." I thought of my grandmother then and how I wished I had talked to her more about her parents and the Irish part of her heritage before she had passed away.

"And indeed they must be," he smiled back as mysteriously as a down-to-earth, rugged-looking Irish man could. "But who you remind me of lived in Ireland was part of my family generations ago."

As Grady and I walked back together to the group where we would have our closing circle for the evening, he told me more about his ancestor, who reminded him of me.

"So they call me Grady, but this turns out to be a nickname – my name is actually Sean O'Grady, but since my father is also Sean O'Grady, somehow the nickname my older brother Brian called me when I was a kid stuck to distinguish me from my pa – so Grady it is. Anyway, Kayla, when I was growing up, my Mother, Claire, kept a very interesting photograph of her grandmother in their bedroom. Her name was Cailin O'Grady, standing in front of Brigid's church. For the O'Grady's used to be all around these parts, a real nautical family."

"St Brigid's church, you mean the old church on Inis Cealtra?"

"Yes, that's right! When it was more than just the ruin, it is today. You look just like her."

The Mist and the Wind

After our closing ceremony and we said goodbye to Niamh, Grady, and the rest of the Celtic Light group, Louisa and I walked over the bridge to Boruma Gastro Pub together. We entered the pub and found Nolan and Declan talking to each other in the front reception area. My heart lifted when I saw Declan, and I realized I'd been so preoccupied with what Grady told me about his old relative who looked so much like me I hadn't been thinking much about whether Declan was going to be the friend Nolan would bring to the pub.

"Well, hello, ladies!" Nolan greeted us. We all took turns shaking each other's hands, and when I shook Declan's, he genuinely looked like he was pleased to see me again and gave my hand a little squeeze. Even though I was still feeling a bit in my own world, I felt my cheeks color slightly and that returning tingling feeling. Declan's grey shirt, navy blue jacket, and slacks fell on him in a way that made him look even taller and brought out the contrast between his black hair and greyish-green-blue eyes.

We were seated outside on a beautiful Irish summer evening; the temperatures had been warmer than average in the last few days. We had a lovely view of the bridge and the Shannon River. The warm sun on my face and the comforting breeze off the river were making me feel more relaxed and bringing me more down to Earth.

"So, how was your outing to the Heritage Centre?" Nolan asked.

Louisa answered quickly. "It was fun – very educational, and the remodel was really an improvement!"

"I've heard. I've been meaning to go back since it reopened again but haven't gotten around to it yet." I noted that I liked the sound of Nolan's mellow and friendly-sounding voice, his accent wasn't very thick, yet definitely still heard the Irish in it. I looked at his tan-colored shirt and white blazer; so far, I'd only ever seen him wear light colors. They somehow totally suited his pleasant, calming voice and his sandy blond hair.

"And Kayla, what was your impression?" Declan asked me.

"I…" I started to reply just as the waitress came to our table.

"Drinks, lovelies?" The waitress asked.

"How about a round of Guinness?" Declan asked.

"Sure," was coming out of my mouth before I realized it, despite my usual preference for wine.

The waitress left, and I continued, "It was very interesting – I hadn't known the whole history of Friars Island, how it was flooded, and the monastery was moved – or that it used to be the lock keeper's residence."

"And the whole history of Brian Boru is fascinating too, and how he lived and ruled right here in Killaloe," Louisa said.

"Yes, Louisa, so much history here," Declan said. "Kayla, you live in Killaloe, right?"

"Yes – I love it here. Even though I spent most of my life in the U.S., it feels like home."

"Lovely. There is an interesting walk, Kayla, that you can take – in fact, when I did it, we started at the Boru Centre where you were today – we went by St. Flannan's and St. Lua's Oratory – the one that you mentioned that was originally on Friar's Island. Then, through Ailebain Walkway, you can learn more about Brian Boru and his son, who was baptized at Tobermurragh well. And, of course, to Beal Boru."

"Wow, that sounds wonderful! I have been to most of those places but didn't know that about the well and Brian Boru's son – sounds like I need to do this walk!"

Declan smiled at me. "It was with the Historical Society, but you can find the same path we took and information about it online. And it's the best to do on Sundays when the Between the Waters Farmers Market is going on."

"Brian Boru's Fort is Kayla's favorite place," Louisa added. Just like at Nolan's concert, she was volunteering information about me to Declan!

The waitress came back to the table again right before I had to add anything about my fascination with Brian Boru's fort and found it a welcome interruption.

"Well, here's to Brian Boru!" When we all had our Guinness', Nolan led us in a toast to the honored and beloved old King of Ireland.

Our food came, and we continued to all talk to each other in between bites of food, laughing between swallows of Guinness. The sunlight that was still falling on my back into the evening and the slow buzz I was feeling from the Guinness was giving me a giddy escape from the intense thoughts of looking like an Irish lady of long ago, and it suddenly occurred to me if this could have anything to do with the mysterious dreams I'd been having. And having Declan interested to ask me questions about myself while he shared his friendly and a bit intense side with all of us made me feel even warmer.

Louisa also asked Nolan more about his next concert. I was completely amazed that Nolan invited us and gave us a spot at their sold-out last concert before the New Irish Travelers went abroad to Spain. Louisa gave him both of our phone numbers and email addresses so he could email the tickets.

When we all stood outside Boruma's to say goodbye for the night, Nolan kissed Louisa on the cheek. I stood there like a deer in the headlights for a moment, and then when I put my hand out to shake Declan's and said, "Nice to see you again!" he placed his hand on my arm near my elbow instead and drew me in for a friendly hug.

"Very nice to see you, Kayla."

When Louisa and I were walking back to my apartment and across the bridge, she sang a little tune softly, seeming very content and happy, and then she almost sang the words as we looked out onto the mighty Shannon: "I bet Nolan gives Declan your number."

Then, I did my best to hum her tune with her as we meandered back toward my apartment.

Later that night, as I got ready for bed, my phone alerted me that a text had come through. An excited feeling grew inside me, and then I inwardly scolded myself for thinking it could possibly be Declan texting me so soon.

Even though it wasn't Declan, I was still very surprised at who the text was from – Cormac from Lucas and Megan's wedding:

Hi Kayla, this is Cormac, I'm back in Belfast and have recently learned of something that I think would be an interesting story for your paper. Enjoyed talking to you at Meg's wedding. Please reply when you can – Cormac.

As I climbed into bed, I turned on Irish harp music on my portable Bluetooth speaker to try to soothe all the thoughts and feelings swirling through me. In between being intrigued by what newsworthy story Cormac wanted to tell me, to the mystery of me looking like Sean O'Grady's great grandmother, to Declan making a point to say goodbye to me with a hug earlier that evening – I pondered how there were now three new men in my life. And they all had their own sense of mystery – yet only one made me feel...

I fell asleep with these thoughts intermingling with the soothing sound of the harp, and when I awoke the next morning, the only dream I remembered was something to do with the vast, mysterious Irish sea.

CHAPTER V

Meara Moran was driving us all in a shuttle bus to the Inis Cealtra day outing as many members of Celtic Light were singing classic American rock. I had been discovering more and more how much the Irish loved American pop music, while I wanted to listen to more and more Irish music.

"Hey, maybe we should start singing some New Irish Travelers songs," Louisa said as we sat next to each other on the shuttle. I laughed as I bit into the scone I had brought from the Bean & Plover as my last-minute breakfast and took a sip of my lidded Americano.

"Actually, Meara said she liked them too, remember? On our way back, we should see if she'd like to play New Irish Travellers for everyone," I said.

"Yes, let's!" Louisa wholeheartedly agreed and gave me her characteristic "thumbs up" sign.

I was glad to be able to chat and laugh with Louisa on our way to Inis Cealtra – as inside I was very excited, and for some reason, I didn't quite understand a little nervous too. The day had finally come for our trip there. The dream I had of Inis Cealtra admittedly still haunted me since it was the dream I had most in mind when I had confided in Niamh about the strange dreams I had been having. And also since I talked to Louisa and Moley in the Bean & Plover before the wedding, the place was often on my mind, and I kept feeling irresistibly drawn to the place.

We arrived at the edge of the lake where we were going to go over in a boat, still to this day the only way to get to the Holy Island. After we walked a few steps from the van, it started to mist lightly; that morning there were some blue skies, but it had increasingly clouded over, now culminating in this mist.

"How ironic," I said. "It's starting to rain – like the first time I came to the island…"

"Though I doubt it will pour down the way you told me it did that day," Louisa assured me as we walked with the group toward the boat near the edge of the lake.

Louisa seemed to have a point. Instead of like that day of having pouring rain that I had avoided by staying in the shuttle as long as possible and then getting completely soaked through my windbreaker halfway to the island on the boat, today the mist was light and refreshing on my skin – yet also added a fitting mystery to the day ahead.

"Hello!" A man in a yellow rain jacket waved to us as we

approached the boat, and my eyes validated what I had already heard from his voice – it was Grady.

"Grady, hello!" Louisa called out enthusiastically, and I gave a big wave to him too. I had wondered where he was, and I had missed seeing his presence on the shuttle.

"So nice to see you, ladies! Looks like you both will be in the first boat to the island!"

Meara passed Louisa and me by then, her red hair blowing in the wind, her tall frame and pale skin looking even more commanding and standing out in the misty air. Niamh had not been able to make the trip to Inis Cealtra at the last minute, but instead of rescheduling like when she had the wedding put Meara in charge.

"Grady, I didn't know you were going to boat us across the lake today!" I said.

"I must be full of secrets, Kayla," Grady said to me and winked.

Meara, in her commanding yet friendly way, explained, "Grady has been boating groups across to Inis Cealtra for about a year now! He's also very knowledgeable about the island, so he is going to help me lead the tours today."

Grady was becoming more interesting all the time.

"Sounds great!" Louisa said. Then she turned to face Meara,

as more and more of the group started to gather around us, and asked, "Should we go ahead and get in the boat now?"

Grady laughed then, and Meara said, "Yes, Louisa, you and Kayla go ahead and climb in, and then I'll see who also wants to go in the first boat over."

I followed Louisa into the boat, and of course, she picked the very front of the boat. I felt excited, a little nervous, and at the same time comforted to be in the front sitting right behind Grady.

Unlike the first time I rode over in the pouring rain, trying to keep dry under my windbreaker, I noticed much more of what was all around me. Instead of the water being gray and rocky like I remembered it, the mist was starting to lift, and the water a mesmerizing blue-green color, its waves rolling in a seductive and mysterious way – who could tell what they would do next.

"So, Kayla, have you been to the island before?" Grady's voice broke me out of my trance. I saw then, too, that Louisa was talking to the third woman in our front row, a pretty blond lady who I knew had been in Celtic Light since it started and was old friends with Niamh named Katie. I hadn't noticed until now, mesmerized as I was by the waters of Lough Derg.

I answered to the back of Grady's head of silvery hair, atop his thick neck and broad shoulders, that still showed some honey color here and there. A vision of him long ago as a fair-haired boy came into my mind.

I raised my voice to try to make sure I was heard over the sound of the boat motoring its way toward the island. "Yes – once when I first visited Ireland a couple of years ago!"

"Ah, that's great!" He called back, his face still turned away from me, his voice echoing off the breeze and back to me. "I expect you'll see Inis Cealtra in a new way after today!"

"Wow – well, I did learn a lot last time, but I'm sure there is more to know!"

"Indeed," Grady called back. "I will enjoy giving away a few of its secrets today."

Already almost there, I looked out past Grady and across the lake to the shore of the island lined with shrubby trees that I remembered we would have to walk through to get to the ruins. I was ready to trace some old footsteps and set out on new ones. Before I replied to Grady, we had come to the boat landing.

"Time to discover its secrets," I said back to Grady, but it came out more quietly than I expected, and Louisa turned to me and said, "I feel like it's going to be a big day." And then it was her turn for Grady to help her out of the boat. And when Grady held out his hand to help me out next, he smiled, but I had no idea if he'd heard me or not.

Those of us that arrived on the first boat waited on the shore's edge near the boat ramp for a few minutes until the second boat with Meara and the rest of the group arrived. Then as a group, we all walked single file through the shrubby bushes.

Grady headed up the group, and Meara took the end of the procession. I emerged from the path to stand with Grady, Louisa, and Katie who had all been in front of me and saw the tower right before me, and scanned the view to see churches, ruins, and the island extend to touch the water on the other side. A small island where the most recent arrivals were buried in the graveyard among the Celtic crosses.

It was absolutely beautiful; the fog had turned to white, puffy clouds that were receding into the hills beyond the lake, revealing blue sky that was turning Lough Derg into the bluest I'd ever seen it. Even though the mystery and spirituality of the place were familiar, a new feeling of upliftment and peace struck me that I hadn't felt on my first visit.

"Welcome to Inis Cealtra!" Meara said, her voice once again snapping me out of my pondering. "The holy island that once you visit will always be with you. We will separate into two groups now – Grady will take the group that arrived in his boat and I will take mine – and we will meet up in one hour at the bargaining stone."

Louisa, Katie, me, and the other six people who came across

on the same boat gathered around Grady. I was happy and relieved to be in Grady's group; ever since I talked with him, looking out onto the Shannon river near Brian Boru Heritage Centre, and his revelation that I looked like his great grandmother, I felt like I had so much more to learn from him.

"Come with me ladies – and gent," Grady waved his arm for us to follow him, and I smiled to myself about there only being one man other than Grady who had been on our boat with us – other times I would have been disappointed by the lopsided ratio of women to men, but I hadn't cared about it all this time as my mind had been absorbed in the upcoming mysteries of Inis Cealtra and what more I would learn from Grady.

Grady led us toward St. Caimin's Church, a lovely stone church, the only one on the island that still had its roof, that at first sight was almost dwarfed by the impressive, tall round stone tower before it. Two ladies from our group ran up to the tower to get their photo taken by the one other man besides Grady in our group. Louisa and Katie were talking to each other again like they were on the boat, and I found myself separating from them at that moment and walking toward the small graveyard behind the tower. The gravestones were behind a short stone wall, and as I stood right up to the wall and looked over, I had the sensation I was looking for something but did not know what. My eyes rested on a tall Celtic Cross, and I wondered who was buried under it, and then my eyes began to drift to a much smaller headstone to the right…

"Kayla, come join us inside St. Caimin's now!" I turned to see Grady waving at me and the last couple of people from our group disappear into the church.

St. Caimin's – this was the place when we all sang on my very first visit to the island, with the rain pounding down outside. Today, as I looked at the ancient memorial grave statues, including two crosses in this sacred place, it had a lighter essence than it had that rainy day, an interesting contrast being drawn between the ancient grave memorials surrounded by discolored stone walls and the cheerful light streaming in through the doorway and windows.

I joined the circle that had already formed inside the church and saw that instead of standing in the center of the circle like Niamh liked to do, Grady remained part of the circle – standing next to Katie, and another woman named Maeve from the group who had recently started coming and who I hadn't gotten to know yet. Louisa stood to Katie's right. Behind Grady were the interesting windows, one arched and the other one more like a rectangle, and the light streaming in cast a flowing light on his dark blond greying head.

Grady began to talk about the history of St. Caimin's Church and the grave memorials from the 8th and 12th centuries. My mind wandered as I looked at the grave memorials, fascinated by how old they looked and why the Celtic crosses drew me to them so – and then was jostled out of my thoughts by something I hadn't heard before.

"St. Caimin's church was built at the beginning of the 10th Century by no other than Brian Boru himself," Grady was saying. Why hadn't I learned that the first time I was here? "Brian Boru's brother Marcan was also Bishop-Abbot of the monastery that was here at the time. In a sense, Brian Boru saved the island by defeating the Vikings who burned the monastery twice to pillage it twice before the 10th Century, in 836 and again in 922 A.D.

As Grady continued to describe how Brian Boru named the church after Caimin, who had been Abbot of the monastery for fourteen years and had made it into a thriving center of learning, I was struck by the lasting impact Brian Boru had made in this part of Ireland, and how I kept feeling a connection to places where it seemed his presence was still felt.

After Grady finished his lecture, he told us to walk around quietly inside St. Caimin's church and to look around at the grave slabs and memorials. I felt grateful that everyone was being very quiet, and as I walked around I found myself stopping at four smaller stone slabs, at least a third of the size of the crosses I was looking at before. There were four lined up next to each other, all with carvings of very different crosses on them, from ornate to very simple, with the one furthest to the right looking just like two lines or sticks placed into a simple cross shape.

I felt his presence right before he spoke, so I wasn't startled. "What are your thoughts about these crosses?"

"They're so interesting – maybe they are trying to tell a story?" The idea that they were telling a story hadn't occurred to me until Grady asked for my thoughts.

"The last two feel almost pagan to me."

"Pagan indeed," Grady said mysteriously. "If you're looking for pagan, off we go to St. Brigid's."

Grady gave us his arm gesture to again follow him, and we formed a loose line to file out of the church. I felt both excited and a little nervous to be going to St. Brigid's again.

As our group approached St. Brigid's, it became windier and, to my amazement, I thought I heard the sound of female voices singing! Was this my imagination again? We made our way through the rows of bars to keep the sheep out and into the roofless church ruin, where I spotted Meara and two other women in the group, Nora and Cassidy, singing in beautiful Irish Gaelic. I hadn't been the last to enter St. Bridgid's like I had St. Caimin's, and just as I was inside and others were still making their way into the church through the bars, the beautiful singing ended, and the group around Meara and the other two singers broke into a quiet, awe-struck applause.

"Wow, that was beautiful," Katie said as she came to stand beside me.

St. Brigid's was much more of a ruin than St. Caimin's, but paradoxically had an energy that seemed more alive that pulled to me. As I stood inside the ancient stones, I felt layers upon layers of history. And the past seemed very much still alive here.

I watched as Meara and Grady spoke private words to each other near the West Doorway, the archway to exit St. Brigid's. Then Meara exited out the doorway followed by the two women who sang with her and then the rest of her group. All of Grady's group had already come in by the time Meara's group exited, and when it was just our group left Grady turned to address us:

"Even though St. Brigid's seems much less intact and more of a ruin compared to St. Caimin's, its mystery, story, and spiritual significance make it what I find the most interesting structure on Inis Cealtra," Grady looked at me for a moment and then away back to the crowd, or perhaps to someone else in our group. "It too is part of the remains from Saint Colum's monastic settlement, like St. Caimin's and most of the remains on this island. Originally built in the 12th Century – but it is believed to have come into existence because of Saint Colean, who way back in the 8th Century wrote a book on St. Brigid's life."

I looked around St. Brigid's, the stone structure without a

roof, seeming to be a part of its surrounding island, the earth, the air, and the sky – but also separate, entwined with the story of its past. Getting closer to the stone wall to the right of the West Doorway, I saw fresh green plants growing out of some of the cracks between the stones. Just like at Brian Boru's Fort, nature brought fresh life to the old.

I wandered around the old church some more, pondering its structure, and as I turned toward the West Doorway again to see if it was time to leave, I felt a gust of wind on the back of my neck. The shadows cast from the shorter stone wall to my left, south of the doorway were growing longer, and I saw Louisa walk out of the shadows toward the doorway when the strangest thing happened. Her long, dark hair blowing back, flecks of gold light appeared, looking almost like a translucent gold cloak – and then I began to see sparkles, especially toward the top of her head like a crown – and for a split second, she turned toward me. But instead, her flowing dark hair, green dress, and flowing, translucent cloak were a different woman beckoning me forward.

Brigid?

I walked quickly toward the West Doorway and exited St Brigid's, and as I emerged on the other side searched the members of the Celtic Light group for Louisa. I finally spotted her several feet away speaking with Katie and Grady.

I ran towards them, and Grady was the first to notice me as I caught up. "Kayla, you're certainly in a hurry? Something happen?"

I was both pleased that Grady had been so attentive to me during the time on Inis Cealtra, and confused as to what I should say. I'd been expecting to just tell Louisa what had happened. At least at first. Pull her aside for a moment from the group…

"Um, yes – I saw something peculiar inside St. Brigid's, right when Louisa left…"

Louisa stopped chatting with Katie then and looked at me, and I was surprised to see she looked different – like she had more purpose, and I spotted a wild look in her eye.

"Maybe I should tell Louisa about it first," I blurted.

"I see. Well, we'll meet you at the bargaining stone," Grady had totally accepted this which made me feel more awed by and closer to him. Like he was someone I could trust. He and Katie walked ahead of me and Louisa.

Louisa asked, "So, my friend, what happened back there?"

"It…it's so strange, but one moment I thought I was looking at you – at the back of you as you were leaving – and then suddenly you had a glow around you, like the outline of a gold cloak and then someone else was looking at me…:

"Someone else? Wow, where did I go?"

"It only lasted a second, and then I blinked and you were gone, had already exited out of the doorway..."

"Strange, normally I'd think it might be a trick of the wind, but when I was walking away from St. Brigid's something strange also happened..."

"It did?" I was floored, completely not expecting this.

"As I was walking away from the church, I heard a sound, like a cross between a wail and a song – more beautiful than a wail but I guess haunting too. I turned to look back, and that's when I saw you coming out through the West Doorway."

I walked the rest of the way with Louisa to the bargaining stone, barely feeling the physical sensation of walking, my feet not seeming to make much contact with the ground. Louisa and I had both experienced – her by sound and I by sight – something otherworldly. A ghost? A portal into the past? I remembered then a painting I had seen of St. Brigid, long flowing dark hair, a gold cloak, and a green dress. Even if I hadn't recalled the painting, I knew back in St. Brigid's that I had seen Brigid when the apparition appeared to face me in place of Louisa.

When we arrived at the bargaining stone, the two groups had merged, everyone standing in a half circle around the stone close to the lake. Grady was intertwining hands with Katie through the stone.

"Who next dares to make an eternal bargain with me?" Grady called out, sitting next to the stone as Katie walked back toward the group – his Irish accent sounding thicker than usual to me.

And my feet still hadn't felt the ground.

"Me!" I jumped up and almost ran to the stone.

"Ah!" Grady smiled mischievously at me. "Very good! Brave lass."

"There was a spatter of laughter from the group, and I laid down on the opposite side of the stone as Grady and put my hand through the stone. I expected something magical to happen – like I had in my dream, but instead I felt his strong human hand intertwined with mine, and a slight tingling, yet grounding sensation – his humanity, wisdom, and a sense of secrets soon to be revealed – but no metaphysical vision like back at St. Brigid's.

After we "sealed our bargain" and pulled our arms out of the stone, I had no sense of how long we had been there. Expecting Grady to call out for the next brave soul to make a bargain with him, I was surprised to see him walk away from the stone, and Meara walk up to it.

As we watched one of the three males other than Grady who

made the trip over with us to Inis Cealtra that day make a bargain with Meara through the stone, Grady surprised me again by asking if I would take a walk with him, that he wanted to show me something.

"Now?" I was still processing the sensation I felt at the bargaining stone and coming back down to earth from the experience at St Brigid's.

"Yes, now or never." Grady winked at me, tapping my arm lightly and starting to walk steadily away.

"Now's good," I caught up to him, gladly following.

Grady and I were heading in the direction of the round tower.

"You know," Grady said, "The O'Grady's long ago use to live on Inis Cealtra, even before Brian Boru came. The O'Grady's and the O'Briens were also very close families."

"Really? How great, who knows possibly our old relatives knew each other!" It felt more grounding still to be told something to add to my own family research that could exist apart from my mysterious dreams and apparitions. A memory then came to me of a conversation I had with my grandmother when I was ten while my grandfather was out at the market picking up the ingredients for our dinner that night, an Irish stew pie. As I frosted cupcakes I had baked for dessert in the kitchen, I asked my grandmother, "So how Irish are we?" She had replied that their Irish heritage came from her father's side of the family, that her parents had come over to America from England, where her mother's family was from.

At that moment I wondered if my great grandfather, before he left Ireland, had ever been to Inis Cealtra, known any of Grady's descendants.

"The O'Grady's and the O'Briens were the most prominent families in County Clare at the time."

"Were the O'Briens at Inis Cealtra too?"

"Probably they came, though it was the O'Grady's that had a stronghold here. The O'Briens were very prominent in Limerick – and it was the O'Briens that granted them much land in the area."

Just as I was about to ask Grady to explain to me more what the O'Grady stronghold was like and what exactly having a stronghold here meant, we stopped and I noticed Grady had led me to the cemetery next to St. Caimin's church. Grady led me into the graveyard, and suddenly – like time stood still and now I was there – we both stood in front of the small, old gravestone of a Celtic cross atop a headstone. I was now close enough to read it:

Cailin Iona O'Grady,

Beloved Mother & Friend

Like the Wind, You Flew to Visit

The many people and places

On this Great Land

Not always understood,

But Alas Much Loved

"Kayla, this is the grave of my great-grandmother, the one that looks just like you." Grady said.

Everything I had already experienced on Inis Cealtra suddenly seemed both inconsequential and made sense compared to what Grady led me to discover – his great grandmother Cailin Iona O'Grady, the one that looked so much like me, called Inis Cealtra her final resting place.

I felt surprised – yet not – and a little chill ran through me. I noticed goosebumps appearing on my arms.

"Thank you for showing me," I said to Grady quietly. "You'll barely believe it, but I felt drawn to this grave when I was over here before we all went into St. Caimin's when you called to me to come in…"

"Kayla, I'm not surprised at all," Grady smiled. "Next time I see you I will show you Cailin's photo."

We stood by the grave a few minutes more, Grady telling me

he was doing some family research, and perhaps he could find some that could lead to more connections to the O'Brien's, too. Then it suddenly occurred to me, "Grady, back at the Bargaining Stone, we never said what our bargain was!"

Grady looked at me differently then – no wit or mischief this time – but with a serious and soulful look. "That's because, Kayla, we already both knew."

When we walked back to the river bank where we took the boat back, the others in the group were already all back, Meara loading up the first boat.

Meara, her fiery hair blowing all around in the wind that had picked up, called to Grady.

"Grady! So there you are! Giving Kayla a private tour, eh?" Meara said this in an upbeat way that didn't sound like it would rise any call to concern – or gossip.

"Something that was interesting to her family research into her Irish roots," Grady winked at me then – thankful for his plausible explanation, before it hit me that there could very well be truth in what he said. Could Cailin indeed be a distant relative of mine?

When it was time for the group that remained to get into Grady's boat, Louisa once again came to sit next to me. When we were on our way back across the water, Louisa was uncharacteristically quiet until she was not. Katie had gone on the first boat with Meara, so for the first part of the ride back I was a little perplexed why Louisa was so quiet, usually always one to pass the time with a conversation. I was very much within my own thoughts, however, so it bothered me less than I thought it would have otherwise.

Then suddenly, when we were about half way back with the lake all around us, she turned toward me and said, "I think you should contact Declan – I know you think about him, and I think he could like you too, but not sure how long it would take him to make the first move."

"What? You think so?" Where did this come from? Ironically, even though I did think about Declan sometimes, admittedly quite often, I hadn't been thinking of him at all just then, and not at all since Grady and I arrived at Cailin's grave. And just before Louisa interrupted my thoughts, I had kept going over in my mind the last thing Grady had said to me when we were still at Cailin's grave – that "we already both knew" what bargain we had struck silently at the Bargaining Stone. And did this bargain have anything to do with Cailin?

"I could…I don't want to scare him off though."

"He won't be – and if you're worried about that, you can always just ask him if he can give you a ride to the concert. Nolan wants me to meet him there early."

Louisa sounded different – and had ever since I saw her after my vision – the apparition – back at St. Brigid's. It wasn't like Louisa to nudge me in this way, be so straightforward – she normally was happy to do all the setting up, making things happen behind the scenes. Where was the Louisa who put together the plan for me to find a way for me to cleverly see Declan, bringing me early to the concert with her even if then Nolan wanted to see her alone?

It was almost like she read my thoughts. "It's time for you to take the initiative, make things happen in your life – before they just happen to you. And I have a strong feeling, Kayla, that a lot is about to happen."

This really was a new Louisa – sounding like a prophet! Had Niamh suddenly taken possession of her somehow? Niamh had decided she wanted to join us today after all, somehow inhabiting Louisa?

"Ok Louisa! I'll contact him for a ride…seems like a valid reason enough," My voice came out sardonically, and now I was reminding myself of Grady.

As Grady brought our boat to dock on the shore, I felt the connections with the spirits that had been with me on Inis Cealtra severed, whispering to me that there was much for me to do before I returned.

CHAPTER VI

The next morning, after preparing for the day and responding to work emails from Liam at the Munster Post over coffee, I received a new text on my phone. It was from Louisa, informing me that Moley had invited her to a photo shoot and suggesting I join them. She asked me to call her later for more details.

A sense of familiarity washed over me, reminiscent of the "old Louisa" I used to know. It felt reassuring. However, a realization struck me—I needed to respond to Cormac's text and contact Declan about the ride to the concert. Despite the text aligning with the Louisa I trusted, the recent changes in her made me believe she might have valuable insights. Perhaps, she hinted yesterday that I needed to take some initiative to progress with Declan. I couldn't afford to let that opportunity slip away.

I decided to reply to Cormac first, feeling less nervous about reaching out to him than Declan. I also owed Cormac a response regarding his idea for a story for the paper.

"Hi Cormac, good to hear from you! Apologies for the slight delay in replying; I was away all day yesterday at Inis Cealtra. I'm interested in learning more about the story idea you have for the Munster Post. Between 5-6 PM is usually a good time to reach me.

Hope all is well with you!

Kayla"

Later that afternoon, I attended a meeting at the paper. While driving to the Limerick offices, my thoughts oscillated between the meeting and when and how to text Declan about the concert ride. I also remembered I needed to respond to Louisa about joining her and Moley for the photo shoot. Navigating the roads on the left side of the road, my thoughts lingered in the background as I headed to the city.

The half-hour trip passed quickly, and I found myself driving through Limerick toward the Munster Post offices. Passing by a store named Sean's Shop, thoughts of Grady crossed my mind, prompting me to wonder if anyone ever called him by his given name. I parked in front of the office buildings and promptly sent a text to Louisa expressing my interest in the photo shoot. I stared at my phone, making a mental note to text Declan by the end of the day.

Entering the conference room where Aiden, Liam, and three other journalists were already seated, Liam briefed Aiden's team on new developments at the Munster Post. He then outlined the expansion of Brexit coverage and expressed interest in articles highlighting the significance of Irish Independence and peace with Northern Ireland. Thoughts of Cormac and his potential story idea resurfaced.

After Liam's briefing, Aiden met with me privately to discuss the next story assignment. He proposed that I cover the Montpelier Festival, celebrating the neighboring counties of Clare and Limerick connected by O'Brien's Bridge. The historical context, especially related to Irish Independence, would tie in well with the special Anniversary Edition. Aiden suggested exploring the bridge's history, given its connection to my namesake.

Aiden sounded, for this last part, like, in his way, he had a hidden joke, yet somehow sincere too, and suddenly a light brown lock of hair fell into his face, and a few moments passed before he pushed it back into place. "This sounds great!" I said, suddenly excited that I could mix in exploration of my family history while covering this story.

"The bridge has an interesting story architecturally too, and I thought with your interest in architecture you would enjoy that aspect as well," Aiden continued. "By the way, I really liked the way you described the history of the building of St. Flannan's in your last article."

When the meeting was over, I walked out happy that it had gone so well, and a surge of self-confidence came over me.

I went back to the car, sat down, and took my cell phone out of my purse.

"Hi Declan, this is Kayla. Hope you are well! I was wondering if I could possibly get a ride with you to the New Irish Travelers concert Saturday evening? Louisa is meeting Nolan there earlier for something. If you have time, thank you!"

I pressed 'send' before I could think twice about it, and then only after it was sent I felt some nerves in my stomach again.

Hi Kayla,

Nice to hear from you! No problem giving you a ride to the concert. You live close to the Bean & Plover, right? How about I pick you up there, say 5:30 Saturday evening? I have a meeting nearby that afternoon and can easily swing by and pick you up. ☺

Best,

Declan

I read Declan's text again as I sat with a latte waiting for him at the Bean & Plover. I decided to get there early, around 5 PM, and "relax" over some coffee – perhaps more like psyche myself up for meeting him than relax. I couldn't push back the thoughts going through my head – I am getting a ride with a man I've only met twice, three times if I counted the time I saw him in this very café? No, I couldn't count that first time I saw him – we didn't speak; in fact, he had no idea that I was there, or that I even existed at that point. And had we even had a date at this point? Well, yes, I think I could count our lunch at Boruma's with Louisa and Nolan as at least a double-date. But really, it was almost like Declan had thus far existed in my life in the realm of fantasy – with me more in my head... and it just hit me again – appearing to me in my dreams. Yet more the essence of him, appearing as someone from a different time.

And rereading his text somehow calmed my nerves. Declan came across as down-to-earth, kind, and at the same time a bit mysterious. I wondered what kind of "meeting" he had in my neighborhood near the café on a Saturday afternoon?

I had texted back, "Sounds perfect, thanks so much. See you there," and he simply replied, "No problem – see you soon Kayla."

I looked up from my phone, seeing that the café was filling up with more people, an interesting time of day as it was usually more crowded at breakfast or lunchtime, but sometimes it was a stop in the evening for people to grab a coffee or snack before heading to their Saturday night plans – such as I was doing. I overheard some American accents mixed with the Irish ones – as it was summer, and the height of tourist season – and mused how a couple years ago I had been one of them, a tourist too. Now I felt different, like Ireland was my home – even though I was still aware of being an American – albeit with two-thirds Irish roots – now too.

Just as I reached for my latte and looked down at my phone again, I heard a familiar Irish-accented male voice right near me.

"Kayla?" I looked up at Declan, making contact with his unique aqua-grey eyes.

"Declan, Hi!" I stood up, and before I knew it, he drew me into a light, friendly hug.

"How are you?" I felt more relaxed already seeing him in person, one on one – as much as he fascinated me, I felt more comfortable than I expected to now that he was here.

"I'm good! Thanks so much again for the ride to the concert."

"No problem at all – hey, good idea to get a coffee. Why don't you sit here for a moment longer and relax; I'll go order too and then we can be on our way."

"Ok, sure – sounds good! Thank you," I sat right back down, and he smiled a bit sheepishly at me. "I'll be right back."

I sat there feeling pleased by what came across to me as politeness and consideration, and watched him walk toward the coffee bar to order. I looked at what he was wearing – dark blue jeans, very new and stylish looking, and a navy blue jacket. A sense of style, but seemed like in a casual way. Even though it was at a distance, I noticed the petite, blond barista working there that day being especially friendly and upbeat, perhaps even flirtatious with him. Not surprising, he was a good-looking man. I resisted an urge to feel pleased that he was with me that evening.

It didn't take him long to order his coffee, and as he walked back toward me, I looked briefly at my phone again, self-conscious that he might have seen me looking at him.

When Declan got to my table, he sat down across from me, which surprised me as I had expected him to just signal for me to get up and follow him out, be on our way.

"So Kayla, just about ready to head to the concert? You know, I have to tell you this is a great place, love the coffee here. Top notch." It occurred to me then that since I had seen him here the first time with Nolan, he may have been coming before that?

"Sure, ready when you are! So glad you like this place. I probably drink too many of their lattes," I blurted out, but Declan looked amused not judgmental, like he "totally got it." I added, "Looking forward to the concert."

"It should be great! Excited for Nolan and the band to be going to Spain, but I'll miss him." My heart felt lighter, Declan would not be going to Spain with them! Then, hoping my relief didn't show too much, I realized it hadn't fully occurred to me before that Declan could be going with them – but felt relieved nonetheless.

"Shall we?" Declan stood up then, and I followed, both grabbing and putting the to-go cup lids back on our latte and cappuccino, and Declan came over to push my chair back in for me. "I actually told Nolan we'd try to get there a little on the early side."

I sat in the left front passenger side of Declan's darkinteriored sedan as a jazz piano played on the speakers, and Declan drove us to the concert. I looked out the window and saw the last of the town of Killaloe along the mighty Shannon, the town I lived in and loved so much. For reasons I didn't fully understand, I felt more at home in my adopted town and country than ever before, driving out of town with this both mysterious and inexplicably familiar man.

Before I could figure out how to engage Declan in conversation to find out more about his life, he started asking me questions about mine.

"So Kayla, how long were you working as a journalist in America before deciding to move to Ireland?"

Funny he asked this, as I had just been feeling so at home here, in Ireland – and now he wanted to know about my past in the United States.

"About nine years! I went to journalism grad school, and in 2009 got a job at the San Diego Union-Tribune."

"Wow, all the way from California! Thought I didn't

 hear a New York or Boston accent though."

I laughed. "Have you ever been to California?"

"Yes, actually twice – once in San Francisco and once in Los Angeles."

"That's great! For work or vacation?"

I was glad the conversation was turning toward him. I watched as the landscape outside was turning more pastoral, struck by how every shade of green kept expanding, more shades of green than I knew existed before coming to Ireland.

"Once for each – SF was a trip with friends after college. We first went to New York, then one of my friends had a brother we could stay with in San Francisco, so off we went. LA was for work." Declan once again was drawing me out of Ireland back to filling my head with images of the States.

"Do you work for the band?" I asked.

"I'm a music industry publicist – Nolan's band is my favorite gig by far but not my only one," He laughed good-heartedly then, and just like his speaking voice, I thought his laugh fit him perfectly.

"That sounds like a really cool job!"

"Thank you," Declan turned the music up a couple notches then, and we grew quiet for a while, Declan seeming like he was in his thoughts as I wondered what he was thinking. But I also felt comfortable with the break in conversation, enjoying the green pastoral scenery out the window.

Declan asked me suddenly after some time had passed, "So Kayla, tell me – why would you leave sun-kissed California for Ireland?" His question took me by surprise. I turned my head to look at him, noticing his ease with driving, him expertly scanning the road before him, his attractive subtle sideburns, mostly black like his hair with the slightest trace of grey and brown. I was pleased to find looking at him put me at ease, if not just made me feel a bit self-conscious about liking what I was seeing too.

"Seems like your career must have been going places in the States; I checked out your article about St. Flannan's and it was really good."

Declan made a point to read my article? I suddenly felt even more pleased but also a bit flustered.

Composing myself, I said, "Thank you, I appreciate you reading it! Well, I travelled here three years before I moved here, and just really fell in love with the place. I have an uncle who lives in New York, who is friendly with Miles Teague in Dublin."

"Miles Teague!? He's big time, the most well-known newspaper and media mogul in Ireland. What a connection!"

"And like they say, connections are everything…but what's interesting is how it all fell into place – I reached out to my uncle for ancestry research, then he talked to me about the paper, and he got me in touch with Miles…"

"And here you are," Declan turned his head to look at me then, with a sweet smile. Then suddenly, "And here we are!"

We had arrived.

Declan parked, and I looked around at the lot next to a large, impressive modern-looking stadium surrounded on the outskirts by quaint Irish houses. Declan got out of the driver's seat, came around the front of the car, and before I knew it was opening the passenger-side door for me.

I stepped out; Declan closed my door behind me and said, "Welcome to Páirc Uí Chaoimh, Cork!"

We walked together through the parking area, meeting up with the many concert-goers walking down the wide concrete walkway to the stadium.

"Wow, this is a fantastic venue!" I said. I had never been, not venturing south to Cork much since I moved here.

"It is completely awesome, Kayla. Did you know U2, Ed Sheeran, Prince – a lot of famous bands and musicians have played here?" I suppressed a laugh but couldn't help smiling at hearing him say 'completely awesome' in his Irish accent – an expression so at home in Southern California.

I was getting more and more excited, taking in the scene around us. People of all ages walking quickly toward the concert entrance, a fence separating everyone from pretty green trees and old attractive homes – yet the stadium itself not feeling too modern in comparison – more like a symbol of an exciting time had come in Ireland's lifespan. Ireland's day had come, and had come to stay.

Declan led us to Will Call, and before I could worry about my ticket, he retrieved mine for me as well.

"So, Nolan said to meet him backstage at 7:15, and it's about 7:10 now, so talk about perfect timing!" Declan touched my arm briefly, guiding me to follow him quickly.

Backstage!? Is this where Louisa was too, why she had come early? Becoming more excited by the minute, I followed Declan, keeping up with his quick pace.

"Isn't this place incredible?" Declan said as we continued to walk briskly across the inside of the stadium grounds. We walked past a burger grill, and on the opposite side of the grill large, wide windows looked out onto the stadium. So, it was an outside venue! Ireland was full of wonderful surprises.

"Yes, and cool it's an outside show! Great weather for it too," this summer, and the last couple of weeks in particular, the weather was warmer and clearer than usual in Ireland – with only occasional rainy days (which all the same I considered special, rarely having had experienced any rain during California summers.)

I followed Declan around a bend, and then he pulled out some keys to unlock a door, and I followed him through the door and up a staircase. We emerged three flights of stairs later to the backstage area, with a band I didn't recognize warming up on the stage, and Nolan, his band members, and Louisa standing in the back-middle area of the stage.

"Here we are," Declan smiled again at me, this time looking very happy and excited to finally be there. "Kayla, did you know Páirc Uí Chaoimh's motto is "Where Legends are Born?" He strutted over toward Nolan, and as I followed, I noticed, for the first time, Nolan looking wound-up and serious, a contrast to Declan's almost bubbly exuberance. Likely a reason they worked well together. "And one is about to be born tonight!"

Louisa came over to me then. "Hey Kayla, you're both here now!" I noticed her hand had been on Nolan's back – to help calm him? And she subtly dropped it when she saw us coming.

"Hi Louisa! Yes, it was a lovely ride over – the time went by quickly considering the trip was more than an hour…" I looked at Declan again, but his attention was now completely on Nolan and the band.

"So True Horizon ready to go on?" Declan asked Nolan.

"Yes man, and Michael and Eoin are all set to do the switch..." Nolan looked over my way then gave me a friendly smile, though looking preoccupied. "Hello Kayla, glad you made it!"

Louisa turned to me as Declan pulled Nolan aside to discuss more specifics, and said, "So, I had a good idea, no?"

I laughed, wondering if Declan would figure out what Louisa said had to do with him giving me a ride over, but he and Nolan seemed to be absorbed in their conversation.

"Yeah, good idea! I gave her a look that I hoped would communicate 'let's not be so obvious about it.' "And this is exciting; you were so secretive about us being able to be backstage!"

"Well, actually, I only just found out this morning when Nolan got in touch with me about where we would be meeting. He was so busy that he asked if I could meet him backstage, gave me brief instructions on how to find it and I had to figure out the rest! But it's ok, isn't this just completely awesome?" Louisa tilted her head up, turned her head to look around, and spun around. The stage looked spectacular, little lights the shape of stars strewn everywhere, two cut-out trees with exotic-looking birds (right away I thought they must represent kinds that are found in Spain.)

Louisa noticing me looking around said, "There is another set coming on to the stage when the New Irish Travelers come on – it's a beach and more, you will be blown away; it's totally spectacular!"

Soon we were all directed to go behind the back curtain, as the opening band was about to begin. Declan said something to

Nolan privately, and then they separated, Nolan walking toward his bandmates and Declan walking toward me. Louisa had walked toward Nolan and then off stage and out of sight.

"So Kayla, what do you think so far?"

I was getting more and more giddy and excited about it all, and for some reason just didn't want to stay "cool" and suppress any of it.

"It's fantastic! The sets, the stage – being here backstage."

"Totally agreed," Declan looked like he was seeing me in a new way, like my enthusiasm intrigued him.

The opening band started, and loud applause and roars of cheers filled the air. Declan stayed by my side through the first song, and the band was really good, better than I expected for some reason, being an opening band – and perhaps sounded better having Declan there experiencing it with me, subtly moving to the beat.

The band was good, different – unlike having the female presence in Nolan's band that his cellist brought, these were four men, swinging a beat with pipes, two flutes, a base guitar, and more danceable yet introspective.

A perfect band to introduce Nolan's music, waves of Irish-sounding flutes, flowing suddenly into a rock and roll guitar solo – then culminating in a jazzy, swinging saxophone! I started dancing when the saxophone started, and Declan moved a little more to the music himself before I spotted Nolan waving him to come over, and off went Declan to attend to Nolan and the band.

A couple of songs into the opening band, they played a slower piece with a dreamy, sexy yet wistful saxophone solo – and somehow even though mesmerized by the music, I felt my phone vibrate through my jacket pocket. I saw that I had a new text – from Cormac.

Hi Kayla,

Thanks for your interest. I will be in Limerick this Tuesday-Thursday at a meeting for the Embassy and remembered you're in Killaloe, plus the Munster Post's offices are in Limerick as well. Are you available to meet for lunch next week to discuss my idea? It will be great to see you.

Best,

Cormac.

So Cormac was going to be here next week! The concert wasn't so absorbing me to distract from my growing curiosity and excited anticipation for what Cormac's idea was. Then I looked up from my phone as I was trying to remember what days I was free to meet Cormac next week, to see Declan back, right next to and looking at me.

"Something important?" The face that was beginning to be my favorite one to look at lit up in the star lights and was giving me a look of a bit of concern and mostly curiosity.

"Hi again!" I said. "It's about work…someone has an idea for the paper."

"Excellent, would like to hear more about it sometime! Nolan and the band are about to come on. Follow me; I have a surprise for you!"

I followed Declan further backstage, down one flight of stairs. He opened the door, and we were suddenly in the first row, a wide area with both seats and a grassy knoll, an area to dance right in front of the stage.

"Welcome to the V.I.P. area – the best place to take in the show."

Louisa was already there, lounging in one of the V.I.P. recliners with a glass of champagne.

"Declan, this is so fantastic! Thank you!" I almost hugged him but held back.

"No problem!" Declan's voice was drowned out by loud cheers from the audience as Nolan, the raven-haired cellist Nadia, and the tall, lanky cellist Kevin came out onto the stage. Nolan waved at the audience, which brought on even louder applause, whistles, and cheers, and then sat down and began an epic piano solo – as a set came down behind them of a gorgeous beach and sunset, then star lights glowing ever brighter.

And it wasn't until that moment, of magic coming from the keyboard, wrapping me in its upbeat, otherworldly inspiration, and aware of Declan still by my side that I felt completely transformed.

And it seemed like as the magic grew inside me, the concert itself became more and more magical too. When Nolan was done with his solo, the lights dimmed until there was just a spotlight on his face, upper body, and keyboard – and he looked radiant and confident, all the tension of backstage gone. The cheers from the audience just got louder, and then suddenly the light expanded to show Nadia and Kevin, and the background exploded into a meteor shower, then a forest – the star lights still sparkling all around – then the projection behind them changed to luminescent fish underwater. And yet, it was the music that was the most magical of all – the soaring violin, the soulful cello, and Nolan weaving it all together with his incredible command of his keyboard – elevating their music to a new level, to a different dimension than I'd ever heard before.

Louisa had come over to stand with Declan and me after Nolan's opening solo and the main concert began, and a couple songs in she said, "Aren't they fantastic tonight?"

"Yes! This whole show is fantastic, one of the most beautiful things I've ever seen!" And magical, which thought I kept to myself.

The music continued, the keyboard on fire, the cello tugging at my soul, the violin making me feel like I was soaring. Declan disappeared for a little while through the doorway to backstage, but even though it was wonderful to have him near me, I was so transformed by the music, the magic of the whole concert – it felt like him coming and going just added to the magic and mysteriousness of the night.

During intermission Declan came out again, asked Louisa and me if we were having a good time (we emphatically said yes), and Louisa offered me a glass of champagne, "Courtesy of Nolan and the band." I took one but sipped on it slowly after we toasted the New Irish Travelers, not wanting to cloud my experience that night too much with alcohol, as I was feeling something magical already – yet real.

The magic continued, and it lasted a while yet still flew by; suddenly Nolan was announcing they'd do the second to last song of the evening. Dedicated to friends, old and new. I looked at Louisa then, and she looked elated yet with a touch of sadness – her feelings for Nolan had grown deeper I felt certain. She'd miss him.

The moving images in the background showed shooting stars

again, followed by beautiful Earth landscapes: forests, oceans, the sky and then images that looked like scenes from Spain.

Back to the music! So soulful, sounded like ancient Ireland and like the sweetness and sadness the Emerald Isle would share with the world in the eons to come. A guest flutist came onto stage then, creating a conversation with Nolan's keyboard – wistful, wise and soulful. I felt more and more elevated as it went on, almost like I was out of my body – all my hopes, sadness and desires carried by and then merging with the music.

Then suddenly I felt an arm around my shoulder, a warm, strong male arm, and as I turned my head to see Declan, a jolt went through me – beyond the strong attraction that I couldn't deny any longer.

The stars – in a universe, another night sky – I am in a clearing, a circle of trees surrounding me. A fort, a settlement is nearby. Or is it me? I see her, and I see him – but yes, I was already starting to float out of my body. An old woman approaches me briefly, a cloak over her head, and hands me a candle. He approaches me now – long black hair, an instrument that looks like a lute strapped to him, an unfamiliar dark beard but the same blue green grey eyes I know, have always known…

I'm back at the concert, Declan's arm still around me, and I lean into his shoulder. "This is beautiful, thank you." The words flow out of me. I feel an ever-so-subtle squeeze from him in response.

Then the song is over, the New Irish Travelers are performing their last song to screaming cheers. Declan takes his arm and moves his hand down my shoulder, and then the length of my arm, grabs my hand and starts dancing with me, gives me a twirl and then grabs Louisa's hand with his other, with a couple others then joining us to form a circle. Occasionally people break out of the circle and dance inside, Declan leading me into the center of the circle once – to dance and spin me around. A joyful celebration.

But what had I seen when he had first put his arm around me? I was both shaken up and elated; whatever I had seen, in "the real world" Declan was giving me attention, dancing with me, had put his arm around me.

Two encores followed, and Declan stayed with us, with me, for both of them. During the last encore, stars poured over the stage, both moving and still – Nolan played his piano to rapturous applause; Declan hugged me, Louisa and a couple other friends of the band. Declan seemed so pleased with how the concert turned out. And through my happiness, I suddenly felt myself shudder. I couldn't shake the feeling that I'd known him for so much longer than for the two months since I spotted him at the Bean and Plover – and like magic led me to be at this concert, and now a part of his world.

I rested my head on the back of the passenger seat and closed my eyes, the sights, feelings, and even the sounds of the amazing night swirling around in my mind. After the concert, Declan had invited us to celebrate with champagne at their conference room after party, where spirits were high all around at how well the concert had gone. Declan asked Louisa if she could drive me home, as he was staying with the band tonight so he could drive them to the airport tomorrow and see them off. Yet Declan didn't leave me feeling disappointed – just as we were about to leave, he thanked me again for coming and asked if when things calmed down a bit, in a couple of weeks or so, I'd like him to show me the Heritage walk around Killaloe – through Ailebain Walkway, that we talked about when we had all gone to Boruma's. He could also show me Tolermurragh Well.

So Declan wanted to spend more time with me! At that moment I let myself just float on the joy of it all, not letting the strange vision I had taken anything away from it.

Louisa also seemed to have been in her own thoughts as we listened to a CD Nolan had given her at the concert, but suddenly said, "Good idea for you to ask Declan for a ride, huh?"

Dreamily, having started to snooze on the way home after the exciting evening, I replied, "Thanks, my friend – you were so right. I'll have to find a way to return the favor."

Louisa laughed good-naturedly and then became quiet again. Her and Nolan seemed to be on very good terms and growing more affectionate at the after-party, and had even kissed goodbye. It must be hard to see him leave for Spain after things were starting to develop more between them. Knowing Louisa, she would be very excited and happy for him too. I felt hesitant on what I should bring up, as I wanted to be sensitive to Louisa's processing Nolan's leaving, but I had a feeling that their connection would endure the distance.

When we arrived at my apartment after the long drive, Louisa said, "So, I will see you for the photo shoot this coming Friday, right?"

Oh, yes, the photo shoot! It had slipped my mind. "Yes, so glad it's Friday, that will work perfectly with my upcoming work schedule next week! With everything going on tonight I hadn't had the chance to ask you yet where the photo shoot is?"

"I never thought you'd ask – Beal Boru!"

I was very surprised, though happy about it – but the excitement of the long night was leading me to feel more and more sleepy and ready to go into my apartment and call it a night. I thanked Louisa for the ride and wished her a safe ride home as I got out of the left passenger door, shut it behind me and waved goodbye.

So Louisa would have Moley around to distract her from Nolan being gone. And I would be going back to Beal Boru! Probably twice in the near future, as part of the Heritage walk with Declan too. And I needed to get back to Cormac about meeting him in Limerick. But just then I wanted to shelf thinking about these until tomorrow, and instead think about the next time I would see Declan. Walking in my new hometown with him, and what it would be like to experience this with him – especially at Beal Boru.

CHAPTER VII

I was running late to meet Cormac for lunch at Marco Polo restaurant, as a meeting at the newspaper was running longer than expected. After I had texted Cormac that Tuesday was the best day for me to meet him for lunch to discuss his idea for the article, he texted right back that he'd make reservations at one of his favorite restaurants in Limerick near the Munster Post offices, and the next day texted 1 PM at Marco Polo.

When I finally arrived, I was struck by the modern, cosmopolitan atmosphere and told the hostess I was checking in for a reservation for two under Cormac McBride. The hostess grabbed a menu and said briskly, "This way," leading me to a dining room with many shiny glass tables adorned with wine glasses, some empty and some full, a tall rectangular waterfall, and grey glassy marble slabs that seemed like windows until I took a better look at them.

I saw Cormac before he spotted me. His wavy, reddish-brown hair was combed back neatly, and he wore a dignified brown suit with a narrow dark brown tie – a suit it seemed to me he could pull off better than most.

Right as I was assessing him sitting there, the hostess and I were suddenly close to the table, and Cormac looked up and stood to greet me and thank the hostess.

"Kayla, good to see you!" The hostess had already laid my menu down and discretely left.

"Hi Cormac, good to see you too! Sorry, I'm running a little late," as I said this, he came around to pull my chair out for me to sit down. Another Irish gentleman.

"That's ok, Kayla, I'm sure you are busy – thank you so much for meeting me."

When we were both seated, feeling a little nervous, I said, "Wow, it seems like it's been a while since Megan's wedding. I suppose not that long…"

"Just a month. Though a lot can happen in a month," He was giving me a curious look; though friendly, it was also a little hard to read.

"Have you heard from Megan and how she and Lucas are doing?" I realized then that I hadn't yet asked Louisa this same question – whenever I was around Louisa, I seemed to be preoccupied with what was going on with her and Nolan – or her and Moley.

"I haven't heard much – though I talked to our mother last weekend, and she said they were having a marvelous time in the

Aran Islands on their honeymoon."

"Oh, wonderful! I haven't yet been – on my list, for sure. A lot of Irish still spoken there, right?"

"Yes, and it's one of my favorite places, actually," I detected a trace of sadness in his eyes then, but it flickered away quickly. "Family went there many summers when I was young."

"Reminds me of my family trips growing up – ours was to the Sierra Nevada Mountains when I was young."

"Oh, they are beautiful too – in California, right?"

"Yes – the California – Nevada border."

The waitress came back then, and I followed Cormac's cue and ordered just sparkling water right after he did. I looked at my menu for a few moments, which was an interesting mix of Chinese and Asian-inspired dishes with a few pub options mixed in like burgers and chips and fish and chips.

"Do you recommend anything?" I asked. I noticed he was looking at his mobile phone, and it reminded me of when I sat near him at the bar at the wedding reception. After just a couple of moments, he looked up at me, and I added, "I only work a block from here but strangely have never tried it."

"Glad to introduce you to it then, it's my favorite lunch spot in Limerick." Just then, I noticed his accent seemed just a tad different, I supposed, taking on hints of Northern Ireland. "Stick with the Asian dishes – I really like the Chinese Curry and the Thai Red Curry."

I read along and decided at the last minute to try their cashew chicken, familiar with that dish in the United States and curious if it would be any different there, and Cormac ordered the Chinese Curry (I was amused to see they both came with French fries in addition to the rice) and he also ordered vegetable spring rolls for us to share, saying they were also one of his favorites.

The waitress brought the spring rolls back very quickly, and over them, he asked me, "So Kayla, how is it going at work today? I'm really glad you had time to meet me."

"So glad it worked out too – I am able to work at home many days, but had another meeting today – so the timing worked out perfectly!"

"Another meeting?" Cormac asked, raising an eyebrow ever-so-slightly.

I hadn't realized I had said "another" until then, or at least that saying it would be interesting at all. "Oh yes – well, I had another meeting last week about the article I'm working on now. Today was just about some structural changes at the paper…"

"I'd love to hear about the story you're working on now, if

you don't mind?"

I told him about covering the Montpelier Festival, how I was enjoying the research and its history, and looking forward to going to it for the first time in a couple weeks – and just as I was going to mention O'Brien's bridge and possibly finding out more about ancestors that I think may have lived on the border between Clare and Limerick counties, our food was served – looking and smelling wonderful.

Right after the waitress left, we tried our lunches, and I said, "This is great, I see why you like this place! Oh, and about my article – I wanted to mention they want me to find an 'Irish Independence' angle – guess with Brexit looming, it's on people's minds what Irish independence meant and still means to Ireland…"

"Very interesting. In fact, that's a perfect segue to tell you about my idea for your paper."

"Oh? Great, I'm intrigued!"

Cormac looked a little surprised by my enthusiasm – though he did look pleased.

"My friend Douglas O'Donnell, strongly skeptical of Brexit and, is leading efforts in Northern Ireland to make sure a fair trade deal is secured, and to keep the peace between Northern Ireland and the Republic of Ireland and preventing a hard border. He is, however, taking this further than the common understanding of how there needs to be a good deal for Northern Ireland at the border."

"Oh?"

"Douglass O'Donnell is predicting that ultimately, Brexit will lead to a vote on Unity Ireland."

"You mean Northern Ireland becoming part of the Republic of Ireland?" In my heart, I had dreamed of this possibility and wondered if it were even possible.

"Yes. And Douglas O'Donnell thinks ultimately, the Irish will vote for Unity."

A sensation came over me then, a peculiar one of old happiness – like I was feeling something that wasn't quite coming from me, but like I was tuning into a collective feeling in the country, perhaps? "This – he – sounds fascinating."

"Indeed – though many are a little skeptical, or at least suspicious of why he can claim to be so certain. And, there are those – I suppose just like in the old days – that are even hostile."

I tried to remember then what I'd learned about the struggle for Irish Independence – and how the North had stayed a part of the United Kingdom – but many parts of it were fuzzy, and I made a mental note to read up more on it in the next couple of days. And even though my head was having a challenge recalling many details of that time – my heart was still tuned into that…collective feeling. And excited for the possibility of a United Ireland. It was perplexing to feel something that strongly in my heart while not feeling clear on the historical details.

Before I could express my interest in the story for the Munster Post and that I'd like to learn more, Cormac said, "I thought a good start is if you could meet Douglas O'Donnell – we could go together and meet him in Belfast."

Mist all around me, I walk through the cold air – alone yet feeling another presence somewhere nearby. I come close enough to see water next to my path on my right, subtly glowing through the mist, illuminated by a moon I am unable to see above. The air feels thick, yet cold. I feel myself shiver and quicken my pace.

I suddenly run up against a stone wall rising before me – feeling a little disoriented. Faintly, I start to hear the sound of the lute playing.

I look up, not quite sure why, and see just beyond the wall is a round turret of a castle. Seeing steps to the right of me, I walk over and begin to climb up them. As I walk up the steps, the music becomes louder yet soft and beckoning.

"Why did you make me wait?" The voice is deep and familiar, easily carried to me through the mist.

"Sorry, it was hard to get away…" I hear myself say, except now it is more like I am observing the scene. My hair through this mist looks different – a lighter shade of auburn-brown.

"You need to hurry to me now, every minute is of consequence for freeing Ireland."

A frame of a muscular, tall man emerges through the mist, his dark hair partially covered by a cloak. It feels like I am being pulled toward him by just the force of his presence, as a feeling increases in me, equal measures of nervousness, guilt and attraction…and then I get close enough to him to see his eyes peeking out from the cloak, greyish aqua like the sea…

I woke up suddenly, feeling damp and chilled – and restless. I turned onto my side and hugged my pillow, but sleep eluded me. It had been the same man in my other dreams, that much I was certain. But something had changed between us. I watched the early 4 AM summer sun cross through my window, and I rose with it. As I made my way to start the coffee and use the restroom, a strong desire came over to me to talk to Niamh again.

The feeling that I needed to talk to Niamh stayed with me all morning as I got ready for the day. Should I call her? I had never called her directly before. Somehow, a text didn't seem quite appropriate. Then, an overwhelming feeling came over me then that I wanted to talk to Niamh before going to Beal Boru again.

I finally decided to go to the Bean & Plover to plan the rest of my day and do some research about O'Brien's Bridge, and when I was almost there, a confidence came over me to just give Niamh a call.

Her phone rang a few times in my ear and then went into voicemail. 'You have reached Niamh Naysmith with Celtic Light, sorry I missed you, but please leave a message and number to reach you. I look forward to connecting with you soon.'

I heard myself say then, "Hi, Niamh, this is Kayla. I'm looking forward to our outing to Lough Gur coming up soon! Actually, there is something I would like to talk to you about before then if you have time… I feel it would really help me to get some insight to speak with you before I go to Beal Boru – I will be there again this Friday. I've had some more dreams since we last spoke. Thank you, hope you are well." I hung up then and walked to the front door of the Bean & Plover, and when I stepped inside, I was very surprised to see Megan and Lucas standing in line right near the front entrance to the café.

"Megan! Lucas! How cool to bump into you here." It seemed like a sign somehow, seeing them right after leaving a message for Niamh.

"Kayla! So nice to see you!" said Megan, and without hesitation, giving me a warm hug. Lucas, always the more reserved of the two but equally warm, said,

"Hi Kayla, what a pleasant surprise."

"What brings you both to Killaloe? When did you get back...how was your honeymoon?" Restless, though seemingly good-natured customers continued to cue up behind us, so I walked a bit more briskly toward the front of the line, with Megan and Lucas following suit behind me.

"Oh, we got back three days ago...and guess what? We are actually looking to move here!"

Very surprised, I couldn't wait to find out more, but then it was Lucas and Megan's turn to order.

After we all ordered, me getting my typical latte and Irish soda bread with eggs (when I was craving a 'real breakfast,' more than my other usual of a latte and one of their famous raspberry scones), we all walked together to one of the last available tables.

After we had settled into our table and started in on our breakfasts, surprisingly, Lucas was the first one to speak. "Killaloe seems like a great place to live, Kayla! How do you like living here?"

"It's great! I love being near the cathedral and the river – lively yet a not too hectic pace of life. So you and Megan are looking for a place here?"

Megan spoke then. "Yes! About nine months ago, before the wedding, Lucas and I were spending a lot of time at my apartment in Limerick, and a couple of months ago, Lucas got a new job there – but we are a little tired of city life."

"I commute to Limerick – when I'm not lucky enough to be working here on my laptop. It's not too far at all!"

"That's what we were thinking," Lucas said. "That's right, the Munster Post offices are there!"

"Lucas got a job as an energy engineer there. I'm really excited for him to land it after completing his degree last Spring," Megan chimed in.

"That's great!" I was touched then by the happiness and excitement Megan and Lucas exuded as they started their new lives together.

"So you'll be looking at some places today?" I asked.

"Yes, we were just on our way to look at a cottage house. It's a couple blocks from Flannagan's."

"Oh, on the other side of the river then, in Bellina! Very nice over there, too."

"A friend of Auntie Niamh is leaving on vacation for two months and looking to have a house sitter – we thought we could use it as our home base while we look around for something more permanent."

"We'd also be taking care of two very large dogs," Lucas added, making Megan laugh.

"Sounds like a great plan! Hey, how about later? We celebrate your move here by meeting up at Flannagan's." Suddenly, I pictured myself not at Flannagan's but at Boruma's, sitting across from Declan. I then thought to mention Boruma's as an option, too, but then Megan began to speak again.

"That would be fantastic, Kayla! We could invite Niamh too. I'm missing her lately, since getting back."

"Oh, have you seen Niamh since getting back?"

"No – it turns out she left for a trip to Iona in Scotland. Oh, that's right…she said if we talked to anyone in the Celtic Light group, to say she would be returning the night before the Lough Gur trip, so she will see everyone there!"

I felt my heart drop a little – how strange to bump into Megan and Lucas, thinking somehow it was a good coincidence having just left a message for Niamh – only to then find out I would miss talking to her about the dreams I'd been having before I visited Bael Boru again.

Megan and Lucas had to leave soon after we wrapped up our conversation about the housesitting near Flannagan's for their meeting at the cottage there. I watched Megan and Lucas leave out the front door of my favorite café, my second workplace and home away from home, feeling happy for them starting out their new life together. At the same time, I also felt a little sad and wistful that I, to that point, had been missing out on that part of life. I set up my laptop then, getting ready to do more research on O'Briens Bridge and The Montpelier festival, looking at my empty latte cup and deciding to order another, when my cell phone rang. Excited, thinking it could be Niamh calling me back already, after all (would she call me from Scotland?) I picked up to say hello but heard a low, Irish male voice instead. For a split second, I thought of Declan, but my brain registered quickly that it wasn't Declan's voice.

"Hello, Kayla! It's Grady here."

"Hi, Grady! What a nice surprise! How are you?"

"I'm fine. I wanted to see if you could meet with me today, to see Cailin's photograph, and I also uncovered some family history I think you'll find interesting."

I had asked if Grady could meet me at the Bean & Plover, but instead, he asked me if I could drop by his house as there were some family heirlooms he wanted to show me too, and then also told me his sister was home, and they also had to resume an important project after he talked to me. At first, I wasn't sure if I should go to Grady's house alone, though after spending time with him at the banks of the Shannon River at the Heritage Centre and our deep experience at the graveyard at Inis Cealtra, I simply just felt like I could trust him. And true to this morning of strange coincidences, it turned out Grady's house was also on the other side of the river, near Flannagan's! I wondered if I would perhaps run into Megan and Lucas, though Grady wasn't available until 12:30, and it was still just shy of 11 AM.

After getting off the phone with Grady, I had about an hour to work and do research. My research and writing went well. The café had morphed into the perfect spot conducive to getting work done. At noon, I left the café and headed toward the bridge that crossed over the Shannon River to the other side where Grady's house was. It was lightly misting, which fit the contemplative mood I was in. As I walked across the Shannon River on what had truly become my favorite footbridge, my mind started to wander to another bridge, which I had just learned about in my research – O'Brien's Bridge, which I would see soon at the Montpelier Festival. I had already decided that I would make sure I had plenty of extra time there to explore, wanting to take in the canal, walk along the Old Barge Loop trial with the old canal path that long ago was used when horses pulled the barges up the waterway.

It was also fascinating to learn more about Turlough O'Brien, who built O'Brien's bridge in 1506. I remembered hearing my uncle talk about Turlough O'Brien, our distant relation who was the first Earl of Thomond, his brother becoming the Bishop of Killaloe. Yet strangely, I didn't remember him ever mentioning O'Brien's Bridge. Also fascinating, which I knew I would have to incorporate into my article, was that the bridge was at the ancient river-crossing that was believed to be the same as the Ath Caille, the "Ford of the Wood" which was one of the three fords from the Triads of Ireland from around the ninth century.

My mind was wandering and contemplative, lost in my thoughts, as I crossed over the bridge to the other side in the misty, light rain. It felt like I was somehow crossing both of these bridges simultaneously: pondering both the exploration of O'Brien's Bridge, linked to my ancestry, for my article, and my present identity tied into the bridge I had just walked over.

Now that I had crossed bridge, I turned onto a main road that went toward small shops, restaurants and the neighborhood that forked off from the small road that ran parallel to the river, on the banks of the Shannon with Flannagan's and its outside patio with a view of the river. The Shannon was so wide there, that sitting out at the Flannagan's patio had always made me feel like I was experiencing lakeside dining.

A slight fork in the road took me to the right and away from the river and Flannagan's, and the street it led me to became completely residential. I found myself walking slightly uphill, the houses lovely and quaint, and just as I rounded the first corner I came to, I spotted Grady's address on the left. It was a small to medium-sized house with a roof divided by two pointed triangular sections with a flat part in between, each of the triangular parts having small round windows near the top. The house was painted pale yellow, with wide square windows at the ground levels of the two pointed parts of the house, with a covered doorway in the middle, flatter part that had two beams that gave the impression of supporting it. It had a big, grassy lawn of lush green with just a hint of gold to its color, the grass longer than in many suburbs in America but not unruly.

Starting to feel more nervous, I walked briskly up to the door and knocked, wanting to get the initial greetings over with. I hoped once Grady opened the door, I would be so curious about what he had found out about Cailin that that would overpower any nerves.

Now psyched up to see Grady, I was instead greeted at the door by a stocky woman with a straight, whitish-blond bob, a rose blouse and a straight brown skirt, who had an interesting contrast of looking both boxy yet gentle, her smile welcoming and the flats she wore on her feet sparkly and glittering with rhinestones.

"Ah!" She greeted me, "You must be the Kayla girl Sean is expecting! I'm Ide, Sean's sister," I had guessed right away she was his sister, not only because Grady had mentioned to me she'd be home, but because of her solid build that resembled his and especially her honey-colored eyes that were almost exactly like his, except with a few less noticeable wrinkles. What surprised me was not that she was his sister, and not even that she was the one who had opened the door, and more than how it had amused me her calling me "Kayla girl" when I was in my early forties, but the most surprising was that she called him Sean. Everyone in Celtic Light called him Grady – and I recalled Grady telling me that he grew up being called Grady to distinguish him from their father, Sean O'Grady senior.

I followed Ide into a dimly lit yet cozy living room where a grey cat slept curled up into a ball on the far left side of a rose-colored couch, a couple of shades darker than Ide's rose skirt. After noticing the cat, I looked back to Ide, wondering when Grady would make his presence known, and saw her staring at me with a look of surprise and wonder coming more and more over her face, like a wave of recognition.

"Oh my goodness, you do look so much like Cailin!" Then, as if on cue, Grady emerged from the adjoining hallway.

"Kayla, welcome!" Seeing Grady made me relax, and I let out a deep breath, not realizing that I had still been nervous. I looked away from them then, feeling self-conscience while at the same time so excited that I would finally see Cailin's photograph, my eyes back on the cat who at the moment woke up and looked at me, and I walked over and gently pet the cat's head, who stayed on the couch but rolled over and stretched, and then hopped off the couch and walked toward Ide. I stood myself up straight and looked back at Grady and then Ide again.

Grady then said, "And you see, Ide, what did I tell you? Kayla, even though distant, I think we have all just discovered long-lost family."

"Really? I can't wait to hear what you found out!" I couldn't believe I had found Irish relations this easily without having to seek them out – just finding me like they had.

"Follow me into my office, Kayla…oh, and I see you met Oscar, our old cat. He seems to like you." I laughed, as I hadn't quite been able to tell, though he certainly wasn't scared of me. "Ide, can you put on a spot of tea for us?"

With that, Grady turned back toward the hallway he had come from, and I followed him with Oscar at my heels until Oscar changed his mind right before I got to the office doorway and ran back toward the kitchen where Ide had gone.

Grady had left the office door open behind him, and I walked in to see him already sitting at a desk in front of a computer, and he gestured for me to sit beside him on a comfortable-looking blue chair that seemed like it had purposefully been pulled up to be closer to the desk.

"Kayla, make yourself comfortable." I sat down and facing me, standing up on the desk, was a photograph that could have so easily been of a distant grandmother of mine – or even me, but dressed like an Irish lady of generations ago.

The photograph was sepia-toned somehow, the hint of red still suggested in the woman's dark hair, blowing out behind her like she was facing a strong wind. She wore a pale dress, and her darker, silky jacket was starting to fall off one shoulder. I guessed her necklace to be silver, but how could I know, with what looked like a Celtic cross pendant?

I blinked several times, more and more seeing her resemblance to me – her face shape, her eyes and brows. Could her eyes have been the same green, golden-flecked hazel as mine? The only thing that struck me as different was her mouth and the expression she conveyed with it – a smile secretive, defiant, and just a little bit smug. I doubt I had ever looked like that like I held the kinds of secrets she did, and I was entirely positive I never looked so much like I had the upper hand – even with the wind blowing fiercely at her.

She was standing in front of the water, in what seemed to be early twilight, on some kind of landing – a small boat of some kind in the background, giving the impression of bobbing up and down in the waves created by the wind. Some kind of building was reflected on the surface of the water, looking to be a pale gold in this sepia-toned world. The further back from where Cailin stood in the photo, the darker the water looked, the reflection being cut off in the shadows and also seeming to sink underneath where she stood on the plank.

"What did I tell you?" Grady's voice startled me out of my total immersion in the photograph like I had entered another world years ago, in a trance seeing a woman who looked so much like myself. And even where she stood near the water looked familiar.

"She really does… look like me! What a fascinating photo, too, with her hair blowing back on the wind like that and the sparkling water."

"Cailin was a fascinating woman – in fact, the more I find out about her life, the more fascinating she becomes."

All of a sudden, my curiosity turned into something much stronger – a real yearning, a real need to know – to understand my connection to her. "Grady, you said we have some kind of distant family relation – how exactly are we related?"

"Ah, well, it looks like I have uncovered that late in the 19th century, let's see…in 1884, Dennis O'Briain married Martha Gallagher." He pointed to his computer screen for me to look along with him to a family tree that showed Dennis O'Briain and Martha

Gallagher and then lines beneath them pointing to the left to Sean O'Briain and Cailin O'Briain.

"So they are Cailin's parents? Interesting the spelling, O'Briain…is it an Irish spelling?"

"Yes, O'Briain is the Gaelic spelling before it was Anglicized into O'Brien. So I wanted to do some further research to make sure it looked like it was the same ancestral line."

"To…my O'Brien relatives?"

"Then the family tree gets very interesting," Grady said, not answering me directly. "Cailin O'Briain – yes, the same woman you see in that photo – married Neil O'Grady, my great-grandfather, and my grandfather Sean was born in 1929. Cailin's brother, interestingly also Sean (named after his uncle), married a British woman named Eliza Fitzgerald."

"Oh my goodness!" My heart leapt. "This totally fits my ancestry. I am part English! Eliza…the name sounds familiar…"

"The furthest I get into Sean and Eliza's story is that that after they married, they moved to England and then two years later moved to America."

"Oh my goodness – yes, that's right, my grandmother told me when I was young that her mother came from a well-to-do family in London, and they never really accepted the Irish man she married!

It wouldn't have been so great for them back in Ireland, still under British rule and the economy still not very great at that time in Ireland. I'm forgetting some of the details about what she said about them not wanting to move back to Ireland. So they left one night, left a note and made their way to America!"

"It was harder for me to find out more after they left the United Kingdom. I'm thinking that the change to the spelling of O'Brien happened when they went to America. Sharing your story with me just confirms my thinking that Sean and Eliza O'Brien are your great-grandparents and are connected to the O'Grady's by Sean's sister Cailin, who married Neil O'Grady. This makes you and I distant cousins."

Grady showed me some more of his family tree then the branch that extended from Cailin and Neil and their three children, Liam, Sean (Grady's grandfather), and Connor. All boys! Then Grady pointed to the branches of his parents, Sean and Claire, and their four children, Sean (Grady), Ide, Mary and Eoin.

"In this photo," I looked from the computer back to the photo of Cailin, once again mesmerized. "Do you know if she was already married when this photo was taken?" I didn't know exactly why I wondered that, but it felt significant, more than mere curiosity.

"No – I don't think so, I believe that was taken in the North – when she was getting involved a bit too much with the Anglo-Irish war – she had a love interest – gads! – up there, but it was after the war in 1923 when she married an O'Grady from the South and settled down. She was late to marry in those days, already 34 years old. Her youngest son, Connor, was born in her early forties, I believe!"

"Interesting! Wow, she just keeps getting more and more fascinating to me." Grady smiled at me then in his curious way. "So Cailin was in her early thirties in this photo?"

"Yes – see, if you look at the back," he reached over and turned the photo around. "It's dated – April 15, 1921 – just three months before the war was over."

Grady decided then it would be a good time for a break, to relax and contemplate this discovery together – and to celebrate finding "his American relative."

He stood up, gesturing to me in his familiar way to follow him. I glanced at Cailin's photo one more time and was struck again by how familiar it seemed to me, yet I hadn't ever been to Northern Ireland, not yet – though soon I would meet Douglas O'Donnell with Cormac there.

"EE-DA!" Grady called toward the kitchen as I followed him down the hallway, drawing out the two syllables of Ide's name. "How is that tea coming along?"

I followed Grady into the kitchen, where Ide busily carried cups and saucers to their kitchen table. Irish biscuits, jars of jam and plates with butter were already set out on pretty, flowery dishes.

"Miss Kayla, please take a seat – you are our honorary guest here today, after all," Grady said.

I sat down and noticed Grady was now looking in the refrigerator for something, closed it, and then came over to sit to the left of me at the table. Ide followed him with a tea kettle wrapped in a light green cozy and sat down across from me.

"Kayla, it's so nice to have you here, our long-lost relative from America."

I smiled at her, a little amused since lately, I had been feeling like my home was in Ireland now, though I still felt my ties to America strongly – it had been my home until eight months ago. And I knew, at least when I opened my mouth to speak, that the Irish thought of me as American, too.

"I'm happy to have made this discovery too," I said as Ide poured me tea, then Grady. "Grady showed me how Cailin's brother Sean married a British woman – Eliza. I'm so excited to further explore my own Ancestry chart now! My grandmother, Mary Ann, told me some about her mother, who left England with her Irish husband for America. I always thought it would be harder to then find out more about my great-grandfather's Irish relatives. It's just so amazing that we made this discovery by Grady and I, just happening to be in Celtic Light together.

"The Celtic Light group is a spiritual group, is it not?" Ide said.

"Yes – it's great because it isn't like a religious group – all faiths and beliefs are welcome, and you don't have to even be religious, just have a sincere desire to learn about the spirit and the spiritual origins of Ireland, ancient Celtic knowledge…"

"So, no wonder Grady spends more time with that group than going to church," Ide said, and Grady laughed and then took a bite out of his tea finger sandwich.

"Well… I can see that," I said. I was feeling an even deeper kinship with Grady just then, as I hadn't fully dedicated myself to a single religion either – sometimes I wondered if that was due to my upbringing, having an Episcopalian mother and a Catholic father, who never made me decide which faith to choose.

"So you see Kayla, it is from spiritual callings that we make the most interesting, magical connections – and I'm sure it is not a coincidence that you and Grady were called to the same group. Really, no one we meet – and especially if we feel drawn to them – we meet by chance. Everyone drawn into our lives is connected to us in some way."

"My sister takes this belief further than I do," Grady said. "I think the people in our lives are probably a mix of both – connected and just completely new to us, even random. Though I do agree that Kayla it does seem like too much to be a coincidence we were both drawn to Celtic Light," Grady looked at me when he said this.

The tea with Grady and Ide went differently than I expected, less about delving more into the family tree and how we were related, but more about the meaning behind why we were related and how we found each other, more philosophical on what it meant to find family connections and pondering the discovery that we had all made now. After about forty minutes, Sean told Ide they better start getting to work, and I just then remembered Grady had told me earlier he had something to work on with her.

When we finished up the tea, I asked, "Oh – I was just curious, why do you call Grady Sean?"

Grady answered me before Ide could. "My sister here and our late mother were the only ones who called me Sean. My mother said she wanted to call me by my given name, and with Ide being the second oldest, she was also calling me Sean before Grady stuck…"

"Sean, did you also show Kayla the photograph of Cailin in front of Brigid's church? Since you both went there recently," Ide said.

"Oh, of course, Kayla, let me show you before you leave."

I somehow felt like there was a little more to the Sean/Grady story than what Grady had said, and Ide abruptly changing the subject confirmed these feelings in me even more. But my thoughts were now turning to Cailin again, and just then remembered when I talked to Grady that day near the Shannon when we visited the Heritage Centre, he had mentioned a photograph of Cailin in front of St. Brigid's! Until that point that afternoon, I had been thinking I had been looking at the photograph he mentioned that day, back in his office. But he had talked of her in front of St Brigid's, we had been talking of St. Brigid's that day…strange how the mind worked.

I followed Grady down the hallway, past his office on the right to the very end of the hallway, where he opened a closed door on the left.

"I don't go in this room very often, it's my late mother's Claire's room." I hadn't known until that afternoon that Grady's mother had passed away. I felt a little sad then, sensing Grady's sense of loss. I realized that it was good to be quiet then, letting Grady have his space and quiet for contemplation as we entered his late mother's bedroom.

The room felt as though no one had slept in it for a long time, yet still had a trace of a soft, almost ethereal energy. Grady led me to the nightstand next to a queen-sized bed with a flowery comforter.

The Mist and the Wind

There was Cailin again, this time her hair not blowing fiercely back in the wind but long and dark and still, looped over her shoulders and hanging down in the front. A light, lacy-looking shawl that did not obscure her lush hair was wrapped loosely over her head. There she was, right in front of Brigid's church, though at the place I always thought of as the exit. The church looked more intact than when I had visited, yet the way the light hit the inside of the church through the archway it seemed to still have no roof. The tower of St Caimin's church could be seen in the background to the left, the place where Cailin's gravestone would lie years later. The sky in the photo looked dramatic – big clouds in a sky that I imagined held traces of blue in this black-and-white, grey-shaded world. Cailin stood right where Louisa said she saw me outside the church after hearing that mysterious sound, like a cross between a wail and a song. Yet, in this photo, Cailin looked like she was posing for a photograph. She could be any sightseer to Inis Cealtra, except perhaps for that unique knowing look in her eyes. That look was still there but much more subdued than in the photo of her near the water that I had seen in Grady's office. I sensed that it had to be a different photographer who had taken this photo.

"A different look in this photo, eh? This was taken by her husband after they were married and had their first child, Liam."

Amazed that Grady had clued into my thoughts so well, I asked, "Interesting, do you know who took the photo you showed me in the office?"

"No…well, I never knew for sure who took it – we found it years later, in Cailin's old keepsake and jewelry box – years after she had passed away. I have always wondered if it was taken by that Northern Irish chap she got into some trouble with up there."

Ah, so I had tuned into her being in much different moods in each photo. And I just knew Grady had to be right about it being taken by "the Northern Irish chap" – and that if he had gotten Cailin in some trouble, he also made her come alive.

When it was time for me to leave, it was raining much harder, and after receiving sweet hugs from both Grady and Ide, Grady insisted he call me a cab to take me home, even though I said I had an umbrella and didn't mind walking in the rain. Grady, though, insisted, and my rational brain told me he was probably right (and remembered how soaked I had become the first time I visited Inis Cealtra in the rain!), but part of me yearned to walk alone in my thoughts, contemplating all these new discoveries. It wasn't until I walked out to catch the cab that was parked in front of Grady's house, the rain pounding down hard on my umbrella, that it flashed into my mind why the photo of Cailin with her hair blowing in front of the reflective water in Grady's office had struck me as so familiar. The reflection, the landing, the boat – I had also seen a glimpse of the same reflection, and it hadn't just been one of a building but of a castle!

And I had just seen that same reflection last night in my dream.

CHAPTER VIII

My thoughts were a mix of excitement and wonder about the ancestral connection I had discovered with Grady and the dream I had that occurred in the same setting as Cailin's photograph in front of the water - mixed with the fact in one hour, I would be having my first date with Declan. Finally, picking which outfit out of three that I had laid on my bed to wear (a good task to bring me down to earth from all the thoughts and feelings I was having simultaneously), I turned on some light jazz music for a soothing soundtrack to it all as I got ready.

After returning home in the pouring rain the day I had visited Grady, I had decided to stay in the rest of the afternoon and evening and work from home, and also to journal toward discovering more about my ancestry tied to Grady's and the uncanny dream I had when at about 6 PM I got a call from Declan. When I looked at the number coming through as Declan's from our previous text communication, I was surprised. For some reason, I thought he would still be tied up with the work of wrapping up the tour…

Declan had said he was just about caught up with all his work and loose ends, and if I wanted to do the Heritage walk and farmer's market Sunday! He said he could use a relaxing day off. But nothing about it being "convenient" for him like he would be in the area anyway. He was coming to spend the day with me.

All that week after I spoke to Declan, I'd been thinking about what it would be like to explore the Heritage tour and Killaloe with him, and now the day was here, Sunday morning, just an hour and a half before I was to meet him. I decided on the outfit I would wear, a yellow blouse, a white scarf with little green, purple, and yellow stars scattered all about, and black pants and comfortable short boots suited for all the walking we would be doing that day.

Declan suggested we start at the farmer's market at 11 AM and grab a snack and coffee before we set out to do the walk. That way, we could get some "fuel" in us for the walk before starting out and be sure we didn't miss the market since it was only open from 11 AM – 3 PM.

I arrived right at 11 AM, and even though the market had just opened, it was already bustling with a lot of people and activity. I'd been to the farmer's market twice before – it being recommended as a not-to-miss in Killaloe, though the second time I'd been called away just a half hour after getting there by Aiden calling that I do more research on the story I was covering at the time. The market seemed more lively to me this time, maybe because of my excitement for the day before me.

Declan had texted me when I was on my way out the door of

my apartment that he was running a little late, but he should be there by 11:20 and to enjoy myself, and he would meet me in front of the Marie Berry coffee stand.

I figured I had about twenty minutes to find it, so I just wandered leisurely, taking a look at the vegetables, fruits, and then cheeses, which I couldn't resist sampling a delicious goat cheese from St. Tola Goat Cheese farm northwest of Killaloe in Ennistmon. I then noticed the coffee stand at the end of the row next to a stand with beautiful sunflowers. As I walked toward it, I glanced at the sky, thankful that the heavy clouds that looked like they could go either way were breaking up, revealing patches of blue here and there. It looked like it was turning into great weather for our walk.

I arrived at the coffee stand and noticed on the opposite side of the sunflowers was a perfectly situated pastry stand. The coffee smelled divine, but Declan still hadn't arrived. A jewelry stand on the other side of the sunflowers then caught my eye, and I was drawn to a set of turquoise earrings, a bracelet, and a necklace set in silver – the dangling earrings in the shape of waves.

The woman running the stand had been talking to another customer – someone she seemed very friendly with like she knew – and then, as she started coming toward me, I heard a familiar voice over my right shoulder.

"Those would look lovely on you." A little startled, though

not sure why since I expected him, I turned to see Declan, looking more rugged in a handsome way, with some new stubble on his chin, wearing jeans and a cream over shirt that contrasted well with his black hair and blue greenish-grey eyes, that at that very moment reminded me of the changeable sky above him.

"Declan!" before I knew it, I was greeting him with a warm and slightly reserved hug, and I felt him returning an affectionate squeeze before releasing me.

"Kayla, how are you? Looks like we are going to have a nice day for our heritage walk adventure," Declan said.

"Indeed." The saleswoman walked up to us then. "They are on sale, only €25 each or all three for 70." She looked at Declan when she said this, and I felt my face flush. I was flattered that she would think we were perhaps a couple. But I also didn't want to start my first date, well our first outing where it was just me and Declan, with him feeling pressure to buy me something.

"I think I'll just take the earrings, I love the wave shape and the interplay of silver and turquoise..." I said.

The saleswoman adjusted her pitch perfectly. "So true, they are my favourites!" Then, looking at the Declan, "She has good taste."

So grateful for the smooth and tactful words of the

saleswoman, Declan then set the start of our time together in an even more positive light. "She does – I never doubted it."

I thanked the saleswoman again and asked her for her card. Cathy Malloy – Illuminating Designs.

As we walked toward the coffee stand, Declan put his arm on my back and said, "Coffee is on me. A latte?"

Touched that, he remembered my drink, or at least what I drank when I met him at the Bean and Plover. At the same time, I suddenly felt adventurous. "Lattes are usually my favorite, thank you, but how about you surprise me? I'll have what you're having."

Wondering if he'd order us both cappuccinos, it surprised me when he handed me a lidded cup and when I removed the lid, I saw a latte-art heart.

"Try it," he smiled at me.

It smelled wonderful, nutty – and when I tasted it, a wonderful, subtly sweet flavor of real hazelnuts pleased my palette.

"They are famous for their hazelnut latte," Declan said.

"Excellent! Truly tastes like real hazelnuts."

We wandered over to the pastry stand then, and before I could buy anything, he bought two large, luscious-looking cream scones. I followed him to one of the tables that were set out in front of a tented area next to a small stage, where it looked like music would be playing later. When we sat down, Declan handed me my scone, and just as I thought to ask him if he knew how Nolan and the band were doing, he surprised me by taking out a map.

"Oh, you brought a map of the heritage walk?" I asked.

"Indeed," Declan said, smoothing the map out on the table between us. I noticed below the map, which was an illustrated one with the Shannon River going through the middle, each point on the tour was numbered. There was also a description of each stop under the map.

"As you see, we started in the middle, the first stop is usually the Heritage Centre – but we can make our way back and then around."

"Sounds good, I liked your idea of starting out at the farmers market."

"Good, glad you are up to the adventure."

I laughed and then looked closer at the original sequence of the walk's path and saw if we traced our steps back from the farmers market, which, to my surprise, was originally the ninth stop, we would be walking through the Canal Bank to Beal Boru! I hadn't expected Beal Boru to be so soon into our walk, another surprise as I had thought I'd be seeing it with Louisa and Moley before experiencing it with Declan. It turned out that Moley had been called to another photo shoot, and Louisa said he had to reschedule for the following Friday. So here I was, being called to the fort with Declan – 'out of order,' which seemed to be the order of things as of late…

"Now, from here, we are close to the bridge that takes us to Belina, but I thought to go back to the first steps, see them in reverse order – but doing this walk twice before, that order will still make a lot of sense."

"Sounds great to me too – I've been wanting to get back to Beal Boru, and I see then right to Tobemurragh Well, the well you told me about," I felt self-conscious then, wondering if he even remembered that part of our conversation at Boruma's.

His response was mysterious. I truly couldn't tell if he remembered the conversation either way. "Ah, Tobemurragh Well is definitely one of my favorite spots on the tour. St Flannan's as well – love it." A little chill went through me then, that feeling of the familiar. It felt like we had both been in St Flannan's cathedral before, long ago. Well, we had in my dream if he had been the man in my dreams, but it couldn't really be him, it was so long ago! At that moment, I really wished I'd already had a chance to talk to Niamh again.

"I'd say a penny for your thoughts, but your thoughts look worth at least €100," Declan said, and my chills turned into gratefulness for his humor and a surge of attraction. I took a swallow of my latte before answering.

"I had an interesting dream about Saint Flannan's – it has been on my mind again after my article came out…"

"Ah – well, how about we get going if you're finished too? We have a long walk ahead of us. You can tell me more about it on the way."

With one last swig of my latte, my scone already gone (and realizing how un-self-conscious I had been eating in front of him), Declan led the way through the farmers market, stopping at one stand where he said I had to try the strawberries that he always made a point to get there in June. I then told him I loved the goat cheese at Saint Tola's stand, and after getting the strawberries (which he said he was happy to buy for me, too), we went to Saint Tola's stand so I could buy the two cheese logs I had tried earlier, the original and the one rolled in ash which had been surprisingly smooth and good. Declan, after sampling a couple of the cheeses, decided to buy the ash log.

Now, walking with our strawberries and cheese in tow, we came to the end of the rows of shops. We reached a small stone brick building, which reminded me of a large hut, and then turned left on a walking path with green grassy hills to the right, and on the left, homes could be seen in the distance that looked similar to the ones I saw in Grady's neighborhood.

"So up on the road here just a bit, we will hit the old canal bank at the Shannon River," Declan said.

"A long time ago, it was used for navigation, right – to avoid the rough rapids on the river?"

"Right now, it looks like it is an ideal part of the river for upscale waterfront cottages and yachting, but indeed, it originally served a greater purpose," Declan said in a subtly cynical way.

"It stopped being needed – I learned about not too long ago about a hydroelectric power project – was it that which made the canals unnecessary?"

"Exactly right, Kayla – for the hydroelectric station, the water level of the river was raised over the rapids, so the canal was no longer needed for navigation."

I suddenly remembered my conversation with Grady at the banks of the river near the Heritage Centre. When the water was raised, it had buried Friars Island, and the monastery flooded and had to be moved to the mainland. And something Grady told me about how, in late summer, a small strip of the island became visible again…

We reached the water's edge and then, to our right, beautiful stately homes, one in particular I found charming of stone brick and bright yellow doors; reaching the canal by crossing a narrow paved street, by a stone wall with Irish green moss growing on it, making our way to the steps leading down to a walkway made of wooden planks. Colorful motorboats were nestled up against the walkway, on the opposite side of the canal of the stone wall and homes.

"Did you ever hear about the water receding late in the summer, so part of Friars Island becomes visible?" I asked Declan, who had crossed over to the other side of the walkway and stared out onto the Shannon River, where I saw a large yacht sailing in the distance.

"Hmm, well, of course, the water does lower at certain times – but Friars Island has been underwater for a long time."

"I learned about the monastery, St Molua, how it had to be moved when the river was flooded for the hydroelectric project – a friend told me that some kids went out on a strip of the island when the water receded – the story runs in the Munster Post before I worked there of course…"

"Interesting! Somehow, I missed that…" Declan still sounded a little skeptical, though not like he dismissed the possibility entirely. I walked a little closer to him then and noticed he was intently watching the yacht out on the river.

"Now seems like your thoughts are worth at least €100," I said, surprising myself with what seemed bold and flirtatious, using his line on him – at least for me.

Declan laughed, a sound I was enjoying more and more. "I'm surprised to see that yacht out there is all – it's one of the ones I usually am out on in Lough Derg by the Dromineer Yacht Club."

"Oh wow, do you sail?"

"Indeed, Kayla – you should come out there on the water with me sometime," I felt my insides melt a little, Declan wanting me to come yachting with him!

"That would be nice," I said, feeling some of my shyness come on again.

"Come, let's keep on walking so we can fit as much of the walk in today as possible. So what you were saying about the monastery we'll be visiting Saint Lua's Oratory right before we get to Saint Flannan's, it's the Catholic Church that was originally on Friars island. Funny about progress – the canal was built so the ships could pass, only to become redundant and unnecessary when the river rose for the hydroelectricity. Making possible good living and frivolous – though fun – activities like yachting."

"I suppose progress isn't linear. Like life?"

Declan looked at me like I had surprised him but was anything but displeased. "You are a good thinker, Kayla."

"Oh, thank you," at that moment, Declan started walking up the wooden-planked path.

The clouds had cleared way even more than back at the farmers market, and a bright and deep blue sky reflected on the water, everything looking especially beautiful as we progressed down the walkway in between the canal and the river, the greens on the land and trees looking rich and bright, standing out among the homes of brown and white with an occasional yellow or blue.

"Have you walked this way to Bael Boru before?" Declan asked me.

A strange feeling came over me when he asked – it felt so familiar, yet…

"No, I actually have taken the main road the last two times by car – it's great to be discovering new ways of seeing my own 'backyard.'"

The familiar feeling I was having made me think of the dream I had started to tell Declan about at the farmers market, and the most recent one I had that I remember looking like it was in the place Cailin's photograph was in front of the water was taken! So why would Declan remind me of the man in those dreams, if anything, that must have lived in Cailin's time?

Feeling like I didn't know what Declan would think of these dreams and perhaps overwhelmed by their possibilities myself, I changed the subject to one based on the real world that had been on my mind.

"Do you know how Nolan is, and the band – any interesting updates on the Spain tour?"

"Oh yes, cool that you ask. Nolan and the band got there fine. Their flight was held up in Madrid due to some unexpected plane maintenance, so I was a little concerned when Nolan finally texted me. They're all fine now, their first concert was last night, and the reviews have been fantastic!"

Declan pulled out his cell phone, found what he was looking for and handed his phone to me.

"I read Spanish just ok, so I used the translator on it," Declan said. I scanned the page for reviews, four out of five stars, five out of five stars – and read the translation of the first two reviews.

"This is so awesome – I wish we could have been there!" I felt so happy for Nolan and the band, and I couldn't wait to tell Louisa – though because I was pretty sure she and Nolan still had something between them across the miles, she very well may already know. She certainly would be interested in keeping track of their tour.

"Me too, Kayla. Maybe the next one." Emotions I felt during Nolan's last concert came back to me, experiencing it with Declan – I then looked at him, realizing that now I didn't have all the other friends and concert goers around me – at the moment, it was just me and him.

And we had reached the sign pointing to the path to Brian Boru's Fort.

We walked together along the long path lined with tall hedges to our left, Declan telling me more about the New Irish Travelers' concert schedule in Spain. Interested in what Declan was saying, both excited and nervous to be about to share this sacred place with him, I didn't notice the wind whispering through the trees until we reached the informational plaque in front of the entrance to the site of the ancient fort.

Declan stood in front of the plaque, looking like he was concentrating a lot on what he was reading, which I thought was great and came to stand next to him to read alongside him. I loved how the description of the fort was first written in Irish, then English. I found myself wondering if Declan could read the Irish language? It flashed through my mind that there was so much I still didn't know about him.

After the Irish (which I was really interested in learning), the English described that "this great earthwork" was originally a large ringfort – a habitation in the form of a circle that was common in early medieval Ireland, surrounded by a round outer ditch. A castle had replaced the ringfort after it was destroyed in war in 1116.

"These are great drawings of the original ringfort," Declan said. "I've always wondered if this was really the birthplace of Brian

Boru."

"Hmm… come to think of it, I have thought to find out more about why that is believed," I said, "It makes sense to me since Brian Boru was based in Killaloe in his later years."

"Yes – he definitely lived in Killaloe," Declan agreed.

After spending a little more time reading the plaque, we walked to the entrance of the fort – and a family was walking out and we exchanged friendly hellos. Then I saw that no one else was there, I was now alone with Declan at Beal Boru.

"Whenever I come here, it's so peaceful I start to forget I'm in an archaeological site – it feels more like an enchanted forest," Declan said.

"I agree it does feel enchanted! The remnants of the old fort below us, but I always feel something here – like the nature of the present and the spirits of the past alive as one."

Declan led me to the center of the fort, where a circle of stone and twigs was the only noticeable remnant of human activity, the rest of the place filled with the greenest of grasses and trees.

"Interesting how what was once a bustling fort is so peaceful now," Declan said.

We walked up the slope to the top of the bank. Declan leaned against one of the many trees that grew on the upper ridges around the bank, and it reminded me of when I had visited Bael Boru for the first time since moving to Ireland, I had spent a long time resting against one of these trees, alternating leaning against it as Declan was now doing to putting my hand up to the trunk, something Niamh had told us was a way to communicate with the tree, to tune into its energy.

"These trees here have amazing energy," I said.

Declan laughed in his good-natured way. "So Kayla, what was your dream about that you started sharing with me earlier?"

So it would be here, it had to be here – I would tell Declan about my dreams. It struck me then that I would have to explain to him about how it wasn't just one dream and how the man reminded me of him. I didn't want to scare him off – just when it had become clear that Declan wanted to spend more time with me.

Three trees grew close to each other, forming a kind of close, lopsided circle, and I rested my hand against the tree closest to Declan. He watched me as I leaned my back against it like what he was doing on his tree.

"Yes, about St Flannan's – the dream, I mean," I was trying to draw energy from the tree to feel more grounded, more confident. "You see, I've been keeping a dream diary lately. I've been having a series of dreams where it feels like I'm transported into the past."

"Wow! So what happens in the St Flannan's dream?"

I closed my eyes for a few seconds and heard the wind blowing and whispering, encouraging me to continue. I opened my eyes and then began telling – alternating between looking Declan in the eyes and the third tree next to him and the enchanted, beautiful Irish green trees and grass all around us.

"I wandered into St. Flannan's at night. It seemed like it was very late – at least midnight. 1 AM? I was meeting someone, someone who had invited me – I…I had expected the candles would be lit…"

"A man?" Declan was looking so intently at me, in my eyes then, and I felt like I was getting very warm, and he was on the verge of taking my breath away – so I looked away and continued.

"Yes, he was a musician – well, I began to hear a lute playing beyond the flickering candlelight. I remember seeing the Ogham Stone, and the shadow of him slowly start to take the place of the stone's shadow – actually more like merge into it. So beautiful…" As I told Declan about the music, it seemed the wind picked up and was making that beautiful sound – like whispers from the past – that I only heard the wind make here. "So, the man definitely had clothes on from a different era – blue tunic, silver belt, and he had long hair…"

"And?"

"Oh!" I realized just then it had been a shorter dream than it had seemed, the feeling of it perhaps only really known to me.

I laughed, feeling like lightening the mood, and the sound of the wind seemed more erratic then, too, like it was laughing too but not letting me off the hook. "You know, I woke up! I wanted to see his eyes then, but then I woke up."

"Hmm," Thankfully, Declan seemed like he was thinking but not disappointed. "So, the other dreams? Is it the same man?"

"Yes – well, before this dream, I had one at Inis Cealtra before I went there with the Celtic Light group." Carried by some unseen force, I walked over to the tree where Declan was leaning and stood next to him. "And I held a man's hand through the bargaining stone – and then I heard a voice call out Brigid – for St Brigid perhaps? But oddly, the voice sounded like it was coming from far away, like from St Brigid's church. (It was the first time I thought to pinpoint where the voice had been coming from in that dream.) "Oh – and I was in old fashioned, lacy clothes – and then a recent dream I was in Northern Ireland near a castle, by the water."

"And was the same man there, too?"

I reached my hand out and put it on the tree then, right near Declan's shoulder. "Yes – oh, Declan – it's getting so strange. In the dream, he said something like I shouldn't be late, that every moment counted in freeing Ireland. So, I think I was dreaming about the Irish

War of Independence! And then – I met a long-lost relative in the Celtic Light group. I can hardly believe it – he said I looked like his great grandmother – and then I saw a photograph of her near the water – and it looked so much like the setting of my dream!"

What happened next completely surprised me. Declan put his hand over mine on the tree and held it there for a few moments. As his hand was on mine, I watched the beautiful branches and leaves of the trees blowing in the wind and felt the wind's cool, gentle breath on my face and on my arm, and I sensed Delcan felt it, too.

"So any idea why you keep seeing this same man in these dreams?" Delcan took my hand in his then and gave it a gentle squeeze, and we held hands for a brief moment…

"Well, in the last dream – in Northern Ireland – I did see his eyes, they – well, looked like…" The wind made a loud whistling sound then, and as it blew the leaves wildly in the group of trees, through the gap in between the other two trees in our circle, the misty shape of a woman appeared – the wind calling out as a misty extension of her reached in our direction for a split second – then disappearing back into the trees and wind – then everything became still.

No longer holding hands, and I had no idea who had let go first, I asked Declan, "Oh my, did you see that?"

"That was really odd. It got so windy all of a sudden, and it sounded almost like a human sound – then it just suddenly stopped. This is the quietest I've ever experienced it here, though think the wind is just picking up again."

I heard it too – the light whispers of the wind returning – but alas, Declan had heard the sound but hadn't seen the brief, misty shape of the woman. Maybe it was my imagination. It had happened so fast. Nonetheless, I felt a presence like Brigid's here.

"How about we walk on now – we have a few more stops today. And we have been blessed with the spirit of Beal Boru now," Declan winked at me and started stretching out his legs, preparing for the next leg of our journey.

"Sounds good, Delcan. It… was good to experience this with you."

"Yes," Declan said as he began walking down the embankment, and I caught up and walked by his side. As we walked toward the end of the sacred space where Brian Boru's old fort lay, just before we reached the pathway that led to the entrance with the plaque describing the historical site, Declan said, "So who did the eyes in the dream remind you of?"

"Yours." All I could do then is plainly tell him – hitting me that I hadn't directly told him yet, and there was no escaping doing so now.

Declan stopped walking, laughing a little in a nice way, and said, "Interestingly, Kayla." And then he took my hand as we walked along the path together. All I wanted to do at that moment was to spend more time with the real Declan, the one who was blessing my waking life, and learn everything I could about him.

PART II

CHAPTER IX

Declan and I stood across from each other at Tobemurragh well, our hair blowing in the breeze as we chatted, laughed, and took turns peering down the brick well. The place of Brian Boru's son Murrough's baptism was so different from Bael Boru – sparse trees, tall tawny grasses mixed with the green ones. Cows slowly grazing in a pasture down the sandy dirt trail leading to the well.

"Funny, I've never been here before," I looked back up at Declan and saw that he was peering down the well, but looked up after I spoke.

"I always liked this place – it's not technically a spiritual site or considered a holy well, however."

"Interesting, even though a descendent of Brian Boru was baptized here?"

"Yes – perhaps since it was well after that it supplied Killaloe with water before the town was connected with pipes."

"Ah – interesting how the practical and spiritual... do a dance for attention here," I said, and Declan walked over to me then, stood behind me and gently placed his strong hand on my shoulder as he peered over it into the well. I looked in with him for a moment, not much to see but an interesting pattern to the stone bricks, covered here and there in gold and green moss and a barely visible water line below.

"Sometime I will show you the holy well – the Well of Segais. Quite the mythical and supernatural history there, drinking from that well gave Finn ma Cumaill wisdom from the otherworld as the story goes – you would relate." I turned to face Declan then, who had seemed to be gently teasing me while at the same time further connecting with me. He put his hand that had been on my shoulder on my face, then leaning into kiss me, and all I wanted to do is get lost in his kiss…

I woke up suddenly to the sound of the conductor making an announcement, "Two more stops to Lisburn, then on to Belfast," and the whir of the train coming to a stop. This time – my first dream on an Irish train, maybe my first dream on a train ever? And I hadn't been dreaming of a time long ago, with a mysterious man of the past who reminded me of Declan, but of the last time, I saw the real Declan, the dream very close to my real memory, up until the time when he leaned into kiss me.

True, I had wondered if he possibly would have kissed me – he had been a total gentleman when he was with me so far, yet increasingly affectionate. The dream I just awoke from just revealed that I had wanted him to. In reality, as we had been looking down the well with his hand on my shoulder, he started telling me about the Well of Segais, I looked up at him and his hand had slowly left my shoulder as it gently caressed my arm and he moved closer to me…and then his cell phone rang.

As my train gradually came closer to Belfast, no longer in the Republic of Ireland but crossing through the border and now in Northern Ireland, my heart was just starting to miss Declan again as I had been going over the memory and thoughts around the last time I saw him.

Nolan had been the one that called and interrupted us at the well, there was a problem with the venue for the Barcelona concert falling through for security reasons! A possible terrorist attack, with him and the tour manager trying to arrange to play at the Plaza Catalunya instead, and them needing Declan to help with the new press releases and publicity.

When Declan mentioned to Nolan that he was with me at the well, I could hear Nolan apologizing through the phone and telling Declan that he said hello and that he and Declan would both make it up to me. So our Heritage walk had been cut short, as Declan said he really had to get to work on it right away, so we headed back toward Aillebain Walkway, between the canal bank and the picturesque homes – but instead of turning toward St. Lua's Observatory, the next stop on the walk we'd originally planned – the oratory that use to stand on Friar's Island and where we would have walked together to St Flannan's next – we crossed the road instead back to the Farmer's market where Declan's car was parked.

The vendors were busy closing down their booths when we got there, and I checked the time on my phone and it was already 3:30 PM. Declan offered me a ride home, and even though I could have easily walked, I accepted – admittedly, to spend a little more time with him now that our day had been cut shorter than expected.

When we arrived on the street in front of my apartment, Declan said, "Great spot you live in – a short walk to 'The Bean' and Saint Flannan's."

"Thanks – think so too – it was great to explore what we could today – gave me a fresh and special perspective on my 'own backyard.'"

"So sorry it got cut short – let's do St. Flannan's soon, have you been on the top to see the view of Killaloe?"

"Oh yes – they took us there on my first trip to Ireland – but just love it would go back any day."

"Well, I do believe Nolan will, too – but regardless, Kayla, I will make it up to you. Had a great time today."

"Me too."

And then Declan had said he'd call me when he had the

concert situation figured out and gave my hand a squeeze – and even though I had a sudden urge to kiss him on the cheek, somehow my reservedness at the moment it didn't happen – and so I had just dreamed of a kiss that may have come close… but never happened.

The sound of a text coming through on my phone interrupted my thoughts, and my heart leapt, thinking it could be Declan – but then seeing it was from a different Irish man made me scold myself a little and that I needed to get back to reality and stop dwelling in my fantasy world.

Hi Kayla,

I just arrived back in Belfast and will definitely be on time to meet you at the station when your train comes in. Looking forward to showing you around and introducing you to Douglas O'Donnell tomorrow!

Yours,

Cormac

As it was summer, it was near nearing 6:00 PM and there was still light out, though overcast when I looked out the train window – the weather adding to the mysterious feeling I already had about my trip to Northern Ireland. Cormac's text had come through right as we arrived at Newry Station, and as I gathered my thoughts, I looked out the window as the green rolling landscape with sparse buildings – I guessed it was farmland – became a watery one, a bay coming almost right up to the tracks, with trees nearly growing out of the water.

I was grateful Cormac was meeting me right at the station in Belfast – it would be good to see a familiar face there, especially being my first time in Northern Ireland.

The rest of the train ride seemed to fly by – stopping at Portadown, Lurgan, Lisburn, and then Hilden – the views becoming more residential, giving my mind time to be in work mode, thinking about what I would learn when I met Douglas O'Donnell, who I had since read up on as being considered a "radical Sinn Féin" by some, a future leader of the party by others – and how our interview would be received by the paper.

"Next stop, Lanyon Place Station. Welcome to Belfast!"

Alone in my compartment at that point since the passenger sitting across from me had gotten off at the Lurgan stop, I gathered my overnight bag, coat and purse and started walking toward the train exit.

When I stepped off the train, the first thing that struck me was how modern it looked. Though, what did I expect? Belfast was the capital and largest city in Northern Ireland! A new excitement coming over me, I scanned the busy station for signs of Cormac, and as I walked toward the platform exit, my phone rang.

"Hello?"

"Hello Kayla, so glad you have arrived! How was your trip?" Cormac said.

"It was good, went very smoothly! Are you here at the train station?"

"My apologies, Kayla, the embassy contacted me about a half hour ago – had to stop by, so running late. I'm happy to do so if you prefer, but how about instead of meeting you at the station, we meet at Holahan's at the Barge – very close to the station with great views of the river. Then you will have my undivided attention. We can take a little tour of Belfast and I'll make sure to get you to your accommodations."

"Oh sure, I think meeting you there would be ok."

"It's a lovely spot, a comfortable place to get yourself a drink and relax, take in some of Belfast – will be there as soon as I can."

Before we got off the phone, Cormac reassured me that he would send me directions, though Google Maps should get me there "just as well." At this point, being a single woman in the country for a while now, and a journalist at that, I was used to finding my way around new places on my own – though I had been picturing in my imagination Cormac being right at the train station when I arrived, and it being my first time in Northern Ireland, I felt a little bit of nervous energy. Funny how it was a couple of degrees less than my very first trip to Ireland when I had flown into Shannon airport, which now seemed so small and comforting compared to where I was now.

After I got off the phone with Cormac, some of my tiredness from my train trip caught up to me, and I felt both worn down and excited to be in Belfast for the first time. It occurred to me then I could let Cormac know I wanted to rest and call it an early night before our drive to meet Douglas O'Donnell on Saturday, but my excitement won out, and I looked up Holohan's on my phone and it looked like the perfect place to take in the Belfast waterfront, order a drink and appetizer and refuel for the Belfast adventure.

I made my way through the train station – again struck by how roomy and modern-looking it was inside, and called a cab. The cab came in just fifteen minutes, and I was on my way to the Belfast Barge and Holohan's.

The cab driver was very friendly.

"Hello, misses! You just come from Dublin?"

"Yes, how did you know? Though my starting point was Killaloe, took the bus to Dublin, then the train to Belfast."

"Oh! You sound American – you live here now?"

"I do."

"Never been to America - but I have driven around so many Americans, I think it would seem familiar if I go someday."

"Ah yes, lots of American tourists here."

"Usually tourists – not as often expats." Being referred to as an "expat" made me feel old, but then he added, "Especially not ones as young as you." Often, people thought I looked younger than being in my early forties, but truly, I wasn't young either, yet felt like I was in a whole new stage of my life, discovering anew who I was. This made things seem fresh and new in my life.

"So you off to the barge?"

"Ah – yes – well, I'm meeting a - a friend at Holohan's at the Barge."

"Ah – great place! It's the restaurant on the old barge."

"Oh, it's right on the boat?" For some reason, I hadn't quite pictured it on the actual boat, though knew it was right on the water.

"Yes, it's a great spot – a popular place for tourists to go and see the museum too." I began to see a view of the river in the distance in between tall buildings, the cabbie telling me it was Waterfront Hall, where you could catch top music and entertainment, and great comedy too, and then he stopped on the road near the park, across the street from a red brick building. I could see the walkway that led to the barge on the river a short distance away.

"Since you are new to Belfast – here is my card," he said as he got out of the cab and got my small suitcase out of the trunk for me. He was about my height, 5'9 and very broad, so seemed almost twice as wide – not very overweight but very large-boned. I looked at the card he handed me, 'Belfast by Cab - Discover the Heart of Belfast.'

"I also give cab tours of Belfast with my partner."

"Great – I'm only planning to be here for a long weekend – I'm actually researching something for work – but if not this trip, I'll be back and sounds great! Thank you, Brian," as now I knew his name from his business card.

"And your name, lovely?"

"Kayla."

"Well, Kayla, enjoy your weekend in this great city, and hope we hear from you soon for a tour," Brian tipped his cigar-colored cap and was back in his cab, driving off in what seemed like a heartbeat.

I walked along a pathway toward the barge, to the right, by trees that lined the small park and to my left, the river. Seagulls cried above, and several groups of people stood in front of the barge from casual to very dressed up. I looked at my phone for the time, and it was almost 9:00 PM – still seemed earlier to me with the long Ireland summer days, and the sky was just starting to get that pre-twilight look, the clouds and sky a suggestive goldish blue pre the sun going down. The tall lamp posts were already lit up on the walkway.

I felt like two people then – part of me wanted to explore the whole Marina, linger outside and listen to the guitarist that was playing a few feet down the walkway from the barge, but the other me was feeling tiredness and some aches set in from the long journey, and couldn't wait to sit inside Holohan's with a comforting drink.

As I walked closer to the Belfast Barge, I saw it had another name – CONFIANCE – its true name, I thought, and then the entrance to the ship said, "The Barge," with information about Lagan Legacy to the left and a poster for the Titanic exhibit on the right. Another poster for the Maritime Museum was hanging up close to a life preserve. The Titanic museum would be interesting, but at the moment, I felt more intrigued by this multipurpose barge I really knew so little about.

I wandered into the barge and followed the signs for Holohan's, delighted when I passed by one of the barge's round nautical windows that looked right into the restaurant. Right down the Hall, the other way was to the museum, and the thought occurred to me to see if Cormac would like to take a look at the museum later.

What a pretty, cozy, relaxing restaurant, I thought.

Cozy – yet busy on a Friday night. I saw one available table, a raised one right next to the window.

"Good evening, welcome to Holohan's! Do you have a reservation?"

"Uh – no, well – unless there is one under Cormac McBride?"

"Oh! Are you American, then?" The young man who looked in his late teens asked me.

"Yes – I live in County Clare, though."

"Oh! Welcome to Belfast," I noticed his accent was a little different than the ones I was used to hearing in the South. "You look Irish, you have family there in Clare, then?"

"Well – yes," I thought of Grady and Ide then, sitting in their kitchen having tea.

"Oh, we are busy – but you are in luck! Cormac did make a reservation for 9:30. You are a little early…"

"Yes – he let me know he's running late…"

"No problem – it's reserved for a table for two. Right this way," the young host led me to the table I had spotted near the window with a view of the river and bridge.

It was a lovely view, a pre-twilight glow starting to show in the sky and reflect on the river. Just then, an image popped into my mind from a storybook I read long ago when I was very young, my favorite for some time after my mother had given it to me for my birthday – featuring a young girl who enjoyed hot soup inside on a ship during a storm out at sea. I felt cozy like she did – and somehow like I was in a storybook, too. As much as I was interested in Douglas O'Donnell's vision for a reunified Ireland – which also was coloring my first experience in Belfast for sure – I also kept thinking about the dream in the same setting as Cailin's photograph – that I was almost certain was at Carrickfergus Castle. I would plan to go straight there after our meeting with Douglas tomorrow.

My cell phone rang then, and suddenly feeling part nervous and part let down, expecting it to be Cormac with possibly another delay. But I saw instead a different familiar number, though I couldn't quite remember who it belonged to.

"Hello?" I was still wondering if perhaps Cormac was calling me from a different phone number from the Embassy.

"Kayla, my dear – it's Niamh."

I hadn't expected to hear from Niamh this weekend in

Northern Ireland!

"Niamh! So good to hear from you! Are you still in Iona?"

"I'm still in Scotland but am leaving only the day after tomorrow from Glasgow. I'm calling you from Oban, a lovely town en route back from Iona. I'm sitting here on a balcony– looking out at the sea – and you came into my mind."

"Sounds lovely – hope to get up there to Scotland in not too much longer – would love to see it and Iona."

"Oban is lovely, a lot busier in the summer, but it really is a small town. You would love Iona," Niamh said. "What is your impression of Belfast so far?"

"I love it – a different feeling from the south – I just arrived, so I haven't seen that much yet, and came right to the Belfast Barge so, being soothed sitting by the water. I'm meeting Cormac soon – I'm at Holohan's."

"Cormac just told me last night he's going to introduce you to Douglas O'Donnell."

"Oh – nice you talked to Cormac!"

"I called him – you have both been on my mind – and I wasn't quite sure why until he let me know you were coming to Belfast to meet him."

"Oh?"

"I feel like – you are going to be more vulnerable – that you should take extra care of yourself – the veil is going to be thinner between you and this realm you've been connecting to in your dreams."

"Oh my goodness – really? Do you know why I'm having these dreams?"

"You are connecting to someone real who lived a few generations ago – that's the sense I get. The connection is very strong where you are and during your time in Northern Ireland. I think something happened with this person in 1918 during the War of Independence. Then, when I talked to Cormac last night, this feeling became stronger."

"Oh, Niamh! I just recently discovered Grady and I – Grady from our group! We have a common ancestor, she's the sister of my great grandfather – his great grandmother! She has something to do with my dreams – I saw an old photo of her in a place I swear I dreamed about!"

"Ah – this makes a lot of sense," Niamh said, and just then, the waiter came over and brought me the wine I had ordered, and I wondered if anyone in the restaurant had overheard my unusual conversation with the woman with the American accent on my end. I so wanted to talk more to Niamh about my dreams if only she had called me when I was not in the busy restaurant, like back at the hotel.

"You think so too?" I just wonder why it's happening." Another call started to come through on my phone – Cormac's cell.

"Niamh, Cormac is just now calling on my other line. Can you hold a moment?"

"Dear Kayla, tell Cormac I say hello, and to take good care of you this weekend. I'm travelling tomorrow, but please call if it's important. Should let you go now – sending you a blessing from Oban."

"Ok – Bye Niamh, safe travels and thank you for calling," and then I suddenly was connected to Cormac.

"Cormac, you still there?" I asked into the receiver. I had switched over to his call too late but saw that he left a voicemail.

"Hello Kayla, sorry to miss you. You were probably on a call. So sorry I'm running a little late – I'm almost there, but wanted to say – go ahead and order whatever you'd like since it's getting late – my treat! Since it's late, I think I'll just have a drink with you and drive you back to the hotel. I have some exciting news about our day tomorrow with Douglas, too! Oh – and order the crispy prawns, I'll share a few with you – not to be missed. See you soon, Kayla."

As I tried to call Cormac right back, the waiter came back and, per Cormac's instructions, ordered the crispy prawns and the

Irish cheese plate (thinking I could share that with Cormac, too, even if he originally said he'd just have a drink)…and plus it would go with my glass of wine. I then ordered a house salad, and the waiter left, and I was suddenly famished. I hoped Cormac arrived soon and I wouldn't eat too many of the appetizers before he arrived.

After the waiter left, I dialed Cormac's phone number, and it rang a few times on my end before I noticed him appear at the restaurant's reception area.

Cormac caught my eye right away and gave a small wave, and even from the small distance of the restaurant, he seemed to be a little worn out, a long day.

"Hello Kayla, my apologies for being late," Cormac said when he got to my table a few moments later, and I stood up and he gently shook my hand. As we both sat down, him across from me glancing out the window looking like he was appreciating the view, the waiter came back and brought the appetizers.

Cormac thanked the waiter and then said to me, "Oh, excellent, Kayla, thank you for ordering already!" And then ordered with the waiter an Irish hot whiskey.

"No problem! Something important came up at work then?"

"Yes – it's tied up in Brexit – even though it hasn't happened yet! Again, I apologize for my lateness."

"It's ok, I actually got a call from Niamh – your aunt – before you arrived, that's why I missed your call…"

The waiter returned with Cormac's hot whiskey already, and it looked and smelled surprisingly wonderful, with slices of lemon floating on it and scents of clove and honey.

I looked at my wine glass, now empty and then at Cormac's warm, inviting drink and he asked me, "Would you like one?"

"Sure, thank you!"

"One for the lady, too," Cormac said. "So Niamh called?" Did she seem well? She called me last night too, actually – had a wonderful time in Iona – and she also told me to take care of you while you're here!"

"Oh, she told me to take good care of myself too…"

"I thought it was very protective of her, yet you being a journalist and independent woman, you gave me the impression of being able to take care of yourself very well," at that point, the waiter arrived with my Irish Hot Whiskey and salad, and I took a bite of the crispy prawn and then a sip of the hot whiskey which had a brown-sugar sweetness, tartness and lingering spice – strong but delicious.

"I do pretty well looking out for myself," and took another sip of the whiskey. "You are right, these prawns are delicious – the

Irish Whiskey, too.”

“It's a good drink after a long day,” He held his out to clink on mine, “Cheers for your first visit to Belfast and Northern Ireland! And you are in good hands.”

“Ah, never doubted it,” and was suddenly feeling more calm and confident in Cormac's presence.

“So I talked to Douglas earlier, and he suggested we meet for breakfast tomorrow and then head to Carrickfergus.”

I could hardly believe what I was hearing. We would be going to the town where the castle was that I suspected was the location of my dream.

“How…did Douglas O'Donnell know about my interest in Carrickfergus castle?”

Cormac chuckled and took another bite of crispy prawn. In a moment, he said, “He asked me what he could do to thank you for agreeing to interview him. We talked soon after you told me about your interest in Carrickfergus Castle and that you were going to try to get there this weekend – so he said he loves it there and could be a good tour guide for you, too.”

“Wow, that's amazing! Thank you – so we will still meet him in Belfast for breakfast and then drive to Carrickfergus?”

“Yes – and Sunday, I can show you more of Belfast before

you catch your train back to Ireland."

We spent about an hour at Holohan's and then walked to Cormac's car together, him pointing out to me the statue that looked ethereal, beautiful and almost ghostlike, just a short walk from the barge at Thanksgiving Square – the female form, her arms outstretched holding a ring – symbolizing hope, peace, and reconciliation. Standing on a globe – a symbol of respect for all cultures and a happy existence for all.

"This statue is especially beautiful at night – like a dream for humanity reaching out of the darkness."

The first time I'd heard Cormac express something so poetically. I looked out at the water then, glad we had stayed out late enough to see the Belfast lights shimmering on the River Lagan.

I was grateful it was only about a ten-minute drive to the hotel by the City Centre, and Cormac dropped me off at just ten of midnight. As I stepped into the lobby eager to check in and get to bed, feeling excited to be going to Carrickfergus Castle and to be finally meeting Douglas O'Donnell, and musing how neither Cormac or Douglas knew the real reason I was intrigued by the castle.

CHAPTER X

The next morning, Cormac picked me up at 9 AM from my hotel, and we were on our way to meet Douglas O'Donnell.

"How is your stay so far? Did you sleep well?" Cormac asked me as we drove off.

"I just crashed out," I replied honestly. I was already craving coffee despite helping myself to the Irish Breakfast tea in my hotel room as I was getting ready.

Soon, we were driving next to a wall with colorful and stunning murals combined with graffiti.

"Is this – the Peace Wall?"

"Yes – a fitting place for me to introduce you to Douglas, eh? We are meeting him at The Foundry. It's right around the corner…"

I studied and admired the art and writings on the long wall that stretched out as we drove by. Two hands grasping through the bars of opposite jail cells, black and white armed soldiers, even what looked like a monk with doves flying overhead, next to him a circle of different faces, several looking familiar and would have liked more time to study.

I had never seen so many different stories and feelings conveyed in one place. It was a little jarring.

"This area has a history of being Unionist, but it's more nuanced and complicated than that," Cormac said.

Cormac found a place to park near the corner of Glenwood and Shankill roads, and as we got out of the car, I admired a mural of a field of flowers, yet somehow, the overall industrial feeling and grittiness of the area made me miss and long for Killaloe and the softer aspects I was familiar with there and in the South.

It was a short walk to the Foundry, and as Cormac and I entered, I was struck by the contrast of the dimly lit interior and the light streaming through the big windows that nearly covered one wall of the café. Cormac waved to a man sitting at a table in the corner of the café between the window wall and the ordering counter.

When we got to Douglas' table, he was already well into his cappuccino, with a newspaper, *The Irish News*, spread out before him.

I had only had a fuzzy image of what Douglas would look like – more of an impression – and if his real appearance matched my impression at all, it would be a larger-than-life one – my version almost like it had been just a shadow of the real Douglas O'Donnell.

"Hello, Cormac!" Douglas greeted Cormac, patting him fondly on the back. "And this must be Kayla!" He stood, I would guess, 6'5, with curly brown hair and stocky shoulders, the tallest man I had met so far in Ireland, with a medium to broad build. "Honored to meet you!" Douglas shook my hand, and his was warm, firm and welcoming in mine. "Thank you very much, Kayla, for meeting with me."

"You're very welcome. I was looking forward to it!" I said as we all sat down, and perhaps what was most intriguing to me was his broad face and lively and intense dark eyes under thick brows. How could a face look kind and just a bit dangerous at the same time?

"If you want to eat light now, there is a great restaurant I recommend in Carrickfergus, so we can spend more of the day there and can fill you in more about Carrickfergus castle on the way ."

"Sounds good! I'm looking forward to our interview, too and hearing your insight on reunification of Ireland."

Douglas and Cormac both laughed then and for a moment, it felt like I was missing out on an inside joke.

"Kayla, get ready for Douglas to talk your ear off."

After enjoying croissants, lattes and cappuccinos and light conversation about ourselves – plus Cormac asking Douglas about how his wife and family were doing – we set off to Carrickfergus, Douglas leaving the newspaper behind and me grabbing it before we left.

"It won't take us long to get there, only around a twenty-minute drive or so!" Cormac said. He had suggested Douglas and I sit in the back seat so we could more easily talk to each other and 'discuss matters.'

"It's a lovely drive too along the coast," Douglas added. I was sitting on the right behind Cormac so Douglas could have the most legroom with the front passenger seat pushed way up – though Douglas still looked a bit squashed to me, though he didn't seem to mind.

"It's the first major attraction we will come to on the Causeway Coastal Route," Cormac added.

As the coast came into view and the landscape turned to rolling hills and pastures, I began to relax and feel more in tune with my surroundings and the familiar peace Ireland gave me. It was not so different here…

"So Kayla, what's your understanding of the history of the conflict between the Irish Republic and Northern Ireland?" Douglas asked me.

"Well…" Where to begin? "It has been peaceful since the

Good Friday agreement, with both countries part of the European Union, with Northern Ireland part of the U.K. still while the Irish Republic is an independent nation."

"Yes – in a nutshell," Douglas said. "Today there are people in Northern Ireland that see themselves more as Unionists, but more and more people are asking themselves what being part of the Irish nation could offer them, for their lives."

"And Brexit is probably making people see this possibility – of being part of Ireland, in a new way? The possibility of Britain and the U.K. leaving the European Union?"

"Exactly," Cormac said from the front seat.

"Yes, that is the issue at hand," Douglas added. "But did you know this struggle, this back-and-forth between self-rule and British rule, goes way back in Irish history? In Northern Ireland, too. Even Carrickfergus Castle itself has a history of Irish rulers wanting to have autonomy from British rule – control their own trade and defense – and even though being taken by the British, the ruling of the castle changed hands several times."

Just then, Cormac said, "Look, Kayla, Carrickfergus castle!" And I looked out between the gap in the back seats to the front window of the car and gazed out the window across the waters of the Belfast Lough to the great castle, a large central rectangular structure surrounded by a great castle wall, with glimpses of round, smaller turrets.

A chill ran through me then, feeling like it was coming from some unknown place that was both long ago and present. It washed over my thoughts about what Douglas had just said, that the independent spirit and struggle for Independence of Ireland was very old, far pre-dating the War of Independence and the years leading up to it.

I didn't quite feel like my usual, go-with-the-flow self when I heard myself say, "Can we visit the castle first, before lunch? I'm not too hungry yet."

"Of course," Douglas replied. "This visit is for you."

"Very well," Cormac said as he pulled off the residential stretch of the Antrim Coast road and onto a side road, going toward the dock and the entrance to the castle.

Cormac parked, and Douglas scooted out of his seat quickly and came around to open the car door for me, and as I thanked him, I thought of Declan, when he opened the door for me when we went to the concert in Cork.

But then, a very different kind of familiar feeling came over me as I looked out across the water to the castle.

Any question I had in the back of my mind that perhaps my dream had not taken place here was gone. And even beyond that, noting the boats floating in the water and resting on the land in front of the castle, I felt I stepped into the perfect synthesis of the present meeting the past – both were here now, simultaneously.

I suddenly noticed that, unlike the abandoned feeling I had had in my dream, there were quite a few people around – yet, like in the past, there were people dressed like another era – from what I could see, there were knights with bows, a man with a kingly red coat – though surely dressed for a time period before Cailin's lifetime!

"People dress for Medieval times, get into the spirit here," as if reading my thoughts – or probably just my expression as I looked at the costumed visitors – but to much my surprise, it was Cormac who had spoken and was now standing beside me, and I didn't see Douglas. "You never told me where your interest in Carrickfergus Castle came from – is it related to the paper, a story you are researching perhaps?"

I laughed then, realizing I had been projecting a different picture of my life to Cormac than all that had been going on inside me.

"I – no, actually – it's more related to my recent ancestry search, discovering a relative of mine in Killaloe – Grady, who also attends Niamh's group…"

"Oh?"

"And, a dream I had…"

Douglas passed us then, seeming like he was hurrying and now in front, facing us.

"Beautiful day to see the castle, isn't it? I just remembered something I must show you," Douglas gestured for us to follow him, and we quickened our pace to catch up with him.

As we walked with Douglas, he led us closer to the water and castle, and the sensation came over me of being in the past and present simultaneously. Clouds started to gather overhead, blocking the sun – even if just temporarily – bringing the present day just a little closer to the darkness of my dream.

"So there is a chamber that is very worth seeing, in the east tower – that is believed to have been the castle's chapel," Douglas said.

And there I was – near the water, but instead of being alone at night, being beckoned by the mysterious sounds of the lute – I was with two interesting and real (or at least present-day) Irish men. And other visitors to the castle milling about. But the water seemed familiar – it was the same water in my dream, on the right of the path leading to steps beyond the stone wall.

We walked up the steps, and instead of the sound of a lute, a solo cellist was playing beautiful medieval-sounding music. I walked over to him and dropped 2 Euro in his open cello case. I then turned around to see Douglas looking at me appraisingly and Cormac reading the informational sign near the castle entrance.

"Kayla, thank you again for agreeing to meet with me and do the interview," Douglas said.

"You're very welcome – I'm very interested too! When are you thinking…"

"So after we see Carrickfergus castle, I thought we could do the interview in town. I know a café in Carrickfergus that has outdoor tables that are never too noisy, conducive to talking."

"Sounds perfect."

"Ready to see the chamber?"

"Lead the way."

We walked up to Cormac, who nodded at us and then proceeded into the castle first. Right before I entered, Douglas said, "You do have an air about you like this place is familiar to you. You've never been here before, though, right?"

"No, my first visit – at least in person – I've…"

"I'll follow you in now, Kayla. Let's catch up to Cormac – I hope you tell me about this familiarity you're feeling later."

I followed Cormac through a passageway, and we entered a

lamp-lit room facing an ornate Romanesque window. Unlike where we had just been outside, I didn't have the same kind of familiar feeling like I'd been here before.

"I get the greatest sense of the layers of the castle's history in this tower," Douglas said.

My mind began to wander as Douglas described more of what he knew of the history of the tower and castle, catching only some of what he was saying about the curtain wall surrounding the castle dating back to Medieval times, and then suddenly, I thought I saw one of the lamps flicker. I looked away, scanning the room, noting Cormac studying the chapel more closely and Douglas looking at me. Suddenly, I was startled by a cool breeze on my neck (why would there be a breeze inside the castle?) and saw a light reflecting on the glass part of the Romanesque window – and quickly pulled out my camera to snap a photograph.

Suddenly, I felt an arm on my shoulder, and I turned around startled, completely in the moment expecting to see someone else.

"Oh, sorry, did I startle you?" Cormac asked, a look of caring concern mixed with a tinge of surprise.

"Oh – yes – I guess I was lost in my own thoughts."

"Douglas would like to show us some more of the castle now. Are you ready?"

With Douglas now in the lead, we walked through the corridor and met up with narrow steps that we climbed up and around. When we reached the last step before the door, where I could see the sea beyond the castle wall when Douglas opened it, I felt the breeze on my neck again, but not from the direction of the open door, but unmistakably behind me on the back of my neck – and as I was about to take a step out the door to the landing I heard a voice:

"Fi… Ah…"

Fire? Fionna?

I sensed the light again, but when I turned back to look, I only saw Cormac standing there, looking curiously at me, and then two small children ran out the door.

"Did you hear that?" I asked Cormac when we were outside on the landing. The young freckled mother had caught up to her children then, though I was convinced I hadn't heard her voice, as she had called after Isaac and Lily, and I had heard an f-sound…"

"What did it have to do with the kids?"

"I don't think so – it was like someone said "fire," perhaps? So strange, then it felt like a wind on my back – though it really at first sounded to me more like "Fi-ah.""

"Hmm – I didn't hear that, though maybe a whistling of the

wind when the door opened."

As Cormac and I stood on the landing, Douglas was already climbing up the next flight of stairs leading to the top of the sea wall. Instead of directly following after, I noticed Cormac walk up to the big cannon that was pointing out to sea and then walk toward the gap in the castle wall, staring out to sea. I was drawn to go stand by him, but then I saw him turn around and look my way. I turned to spot Douglas way up on the top step, and I started to climb up the stairs. When I got to the top and saw the dramatic view of the sea through the gaps in and beyond the sea wall, the feeling of familiarity washed over me again.

I walked along the sea wall, peering through the gaps, feeling like I could be in many places at once – a timeless feeling and one of déjà vu.

The unmistakable sea air now blowing on my face and through my hair, I felt more at ease, even invigorated, as I ran my hand across the rough stone of the castle wall toward where Douglas was standing, seeing Cormac out of the corner of my eye walking a diagonal path from the stairwell toward Douglas.

When I arrived to where Douglas stood, he was in front of the most dramatic view at the top of the sea tower that I had seen yet: a sharp drop to the lower landing that was enclosed in its outer castle wall, plunging to the rocky depths of the castle below me, and several feet straight ahead the sea and the harbor in the distance.

A feeling of vertigo overtook my exhilaration, and I stepped back and leaned against the castle wall to the right of Douglas to steady myself. I looked up and a dramatic castle tower came into my view to the right of the sea.

Cormac was there now, too, standing to my left and a bit back from Douglas, like we made an interesting three-person circle.

"Did you know that many believe Carrickfergus Castle to be haunted?" Douglas began, and that familiar feeling mixed with chills came over me, though at least my logical brain was very surprised Douglas was telling us this now by the dramatic sea wall. "A soldier named Robert Rainey was stationed here in the mid-1700s. He lived a rough and tumble life and no stranger to the drink, but he fell madly in love with a lass named Betsy Baird, who he swore he'd give up drinking and gambling if she married him. Betsy said yes, and they were both overjoyed."

"However, Betsy was also being wooed by another admirer, and she was not decided after all and did not dismiss the other man's attentions, who was the brother of the constable of this very castle. Robert became consumed with wild imaginings and jealousy but held back until the two men came face to face one day on the road into town. Robert then attacked him, stabbed the man with his sword and then returned quickly to the castle to cover up any evidence that he had left the castle that day."

I just stood there, enthralled with the story while I leaned against the castle wall – while Cormac said, "So it's the man he stabbed, the constable's brother, who now haunts the castle?"

"Actually, no…there's a twist! It turns out that when the constable's brother was discovered, in his last breaths, he said that it was another man, another soldier named Timothy Lavery, who had killed him – Timothy looked very similar to Robert, and in the darkness, he had mistaken Robert for Timothy! Timothy Lavery was then convicted, found guilty and sentenced to death. But before he was executed, he swore he would haunt the castle forever." Douglas paused then, looking first at me and then to Cormac, and then said, "If we dare, we can go see the place where Timothy's ghost has often been spotted – near the dark and deep well in the castle's basement."

We then all agreed that we would go see the basement next, Cormac descending the stairway first, followed by me and then Douglas. When I was just a couple steps down, I turned my head to the right and took in the sea view again, taking note of the color of the sea now taking on a more glistening-grey color as more clouds gathered.

Then, as I descended a few more steps, I felt the wind on the back of my neck again and the sound of the breeze, "Finnnnn…"

Fin? And when I instinctively turned to try to see where the sound was coming from, I felt my foot slip and started falling…

Just as I felt my arms flail out in front of me to try to catch my fall, bracing for the worse, I instead felt a strong male embrace, hands digging into my armpits and shoulders, not minding the sting and a feeling of being forever grateful came over me that I was saved from something much worse.

"Kayla, are you ok?" Cormac's voice sounded distant, yet I knew he was there, supporting me. I briefly felt the vertigo feeling again and noticed then we were no longer on the steps but on the ground next to the last step, on the level with the canon and the lower sea wall.

"I…think so," I stood up straighter, now Cormac's arm supporting me on my right shoulder.

"Kayla, you took quite a fall there – lucky Cormac was there to catch you," Douglas said, descending the last step of the stairwell.

"Thank you, Cormac, I am so grateful," I stood with Cormac's support a moment longer and then slowly pulled away from him to see if I was capable of standing on my own at that point. I noticed then a dull pain in my foot and ankle. "So strange – I don't remember how I – how we got to the bottom of the stairs."

"You lost your step and started falling forward, and

thankfully, Cormac had turned around just in time to catch your fall. Then he guided you down the steps," Douglas said.

"You seemed to lose – faint briefly, Kayla," Cormac added.

So strange not to remember this. "Wow, so sorry…"

"Oh, lass, no need to apologize!" Douglas said. "Thank goodness you called out when you did."

"I called out?"

"That's what made me turn around," Cormac said. "You called out right before you missed your step and started to fall. That's why I was turned around to you. And Kayla, looks like you are having a little trouble standing now. I think we should go someplace. Let you rest – we can explore more of the castle later."

That sounded good to me, especially good to me at this point. And I already experienced something supernatural anyway – so I wouldn't miss that experience if we skipped the basement today, I thought wryly.

"Cormac, when I called out…what did I say?"

"It sounded like 'Finn.'"

With a promise from Douglas that we could explore more of Carrickfergus Castle another time, I walked a little way with Cormac toward the harbour while Douglas brought the car around so I didn't have to walk as far and could rest my ankle. When

Douglas arrived with the car, Cormac looked down and asked, "How is your ankle?"

"Sore, but don't think it's swollen."

"Oh good, yes, doesn't look swollen. I'd have it checked out if it continues to bother you."

We arrived at the restaurant with the great outside seating Douglas recommended, called the Dancing Goat (which turned out to be exactly my kind of place!), and as I sat with my hot latte, goat cheese salad and cup of tomato soup and two attentive Irish men, I could almost forget about my ankle, slightly throbbing – but starting to feel better.

When we were almost done with our late afternoon lunches, Douglas said, "So how about we start the interview over dessert? Kayla, does this seem like a good time?"

"Yes, we can definitely do this now," I reached into my purse for my notepad.

As Douglas was ordering some of their signature tarts to share, Cormac got a call and excused himself and walked away to take his call in private.

Our desserts arrived, and the tea that Douglas recommended would go well with it. He ordered in decaf when I said I should probably avoid having any more caffeine, and Douglas went right to it,

"Kayla, do you know the *Munster Post's* view on Irish Nationalism?"

So Douglas was starting the interview by asking me a question!

"I think most of them tend to be open to it – ironically, I'm not exactly sure where Liam, the editor-in-chief of the paper, my boss' boss stands, but your interview seems to be very good timing! Liam announced the Munster Post is expanding its coverage of Brexit at our last meeting and having a series of issues that come out about what Irish independence and peace in Northern Ireland means to the Irish."

"So pro-peace, but not sure of their stance on Unification?"

"Honestly, Aiden, my editor, advised me to go ahead and interview you, write it up and then he'd pitch it to Liam. But Aiden did like the idea!" I decided to hold back on telling Douglas how Aiden advised me to pitch it in a way that wasn't overly political and stay fairly neutral, not too pro-nationalist or pro-unionist.

"So Douglas, I did write up some questions. Can we start with them?"

"Of course, Kayla." Douglas reached out his tea cup to do a 'cheers' with mine. "Thank you again."

I read off my first questions to him. "So, how recently has it seemed to you that Irish Unification is a real possibility?"

"Well, of course, Irish Nationalists have had their eye on the prize of a united Ireland ever since the War of Independence, when the Republic of Ireland was formed, with Northern Ireland, of course, staying in the U.K. But in modern times, really, it's been since Sinn Féin in called for a referendum when the U.K. voted for Brexit in 2016."

"That leads into my next question perfectly! Which is, how much is Brexit a factor in the movement toward unification?"

Douglas laughed ironically. "It's the catalyst – it's what led to Sinn Féin calling for a referendum on a United Ireland – as now a possibility of a return to a hard border between Northern Ireland and Ireland, which almost all people in both places would like to avoid, especially not to return to any violence like there was before the Good Friday Agreement."

"And also, it would mean Northern Ireland would leave the European Union if they remained part of the U.K., right?"

"Exactly. This has brought many more Protestant Irish Nationalists into the conversation."

I interviewed Douglas for about forty minutes, even more fascinated than I realized I'd been to learn more about the probability (a high one, in Douglas' opinion) of unification and the challenges of the vote for Ireland to become one nation.

As I was about to wrap up the interview, Cormac came back to the table, and not until then, so absorbed in the interview with Douglas, had I noticed Cormac had been gone for that long.

"Cormac, welcome back!" I said, looking up from my interview notes.

"I didn't mean to be gone quite that long, got an important call from the embassy."

"Everything ok?" Douglas asked.

"It's – complicated. I think we'll work it out. I'll go order another cappuccino – don't want to interrupt the rest of your interview."

"We're almost done," I said.

In a moment, I turned back to Douglas. "So Douglas, when do you think a vote for Irish Unity will happen?"

"The time for Sinn Féin to bring along the majority of public opinion is coming. The pending Brexit is worrisome to the Unionists and what will happen to trade and national security, among other concerns, and paving a path for the unification of Ireland to be seen as a more appealing possibility to once those who were staunch Unionists. I think this will all come to a head by 2027, and the vote for Unification will prevail."

***

The darkness of the alley is palpable, the only light coming from the tall street lamps illuminating the foggy mist all around me. It's also eerily quiet until a shout that sounds like it's coming from a boy comes through the mist. I walk forward toward the sound, not sure how far away the sound has come from.

"I will never give up my Protestant and British heritage. I feel like I don't even belong here anymore!"

"The Catholics aren't the ones who are betraying you! It's England who has pulled out of the EU!"

The voices increasingly becoming louder, I now face four Irish teenagers – a rather short, freckled lad with a baseball cap standing on one side by himself, and a teen boy a few inches taller than him facing him at a distance, standing next to an even taller boy on his right and a pretty, tall and slender girl with dark hair on his left.

"Come on, let's not give this radical Catholic Nationalist any more of our time," the tallest boy said. "We have some serious protesting to do," he said as he held up a large, sharp uneven stone.

None of them seemed to notice, or at least take any interest in, my presence there until the dark-haired girl looked into my eyes.

A kind but also a warning look…

Suddenly, the mist gathers around me so thickly I can barely see them, and I hear the girl saying, "Come with me." A soft hand takes mine, and we start running, her pulling me along.

I hear glass breaking among loud shouting, a car horn followed by an explosive sound like a loud firecracker. A siren in the distance coming closer…

Suddenly, I'm in a hospital room. A gentle, fair-haired nurse stands next to a boy in a hospital bed, and the same dark-haired girl is with me, but now she looks a bit taller, her hair longer and straighter.

"Poor Billy," the girl gently says to me, and just then, I reach out and feel a hard, invisible barrier – there is some kind of barrier separating us from Billy and the nurse. What on Earth? And did those other boys hurt Billy among all that commotion? Yet he, like the girl, looks different – his face more hallowed out, a little older…

The early morning sun was just starting to light up the dawn sky as I awoke, and I shivered before I noticed I had broken out all over in a cool, damp sweat. I pulled the blanket over me, yearning to get warmer and also wash off not only my body but the feeling from the dream. As the sun steadily rose in the Eastern Sky, now shining intensely through my hotel window, my realization grew that this hadn't been a dream like the others of the past but one of the future.

After I showered, dressed and helped myself to my first cup of coffee of the day from the hotel brewer, I noticed two new messages on my phone. Louisa and Declan! They had both decided to leave voicemails rather than texts.

"Hi Kayla, I hope you're having a fabulous weekend in Belfast! Can't wait to hear more about the interview with Cormac's friend. I wanted to see you soon after you get back, within a couple of days if possible! I'm going to be leaving for Spain in five days – can you believe it – oh, I'm so excited! Nolan and I had a long talk, and he invited me to meet up with him and the band in Madrid! I will also visit Nana. Oh Kayla, call me soon. There is so much to tell you!"

And then Declan:

"Kayla, I hope your trip to Belfast has been most enjoyable and your interview fruitful. I enjoyed our day in Killaloe – and am finally at a point where I've straightened out the New Irish Traveler's publicity for their schedule change. I will have to travel very soon, however, and would very much like to see you and fill you in on the band and catch up on the latest before I leave! Please text me when you return, and hope to see you before I leave – have openings on Wednesday and Thursday evenings this week. Sorry, I missed you. Have a safe trip back home."

Wow, so many new developments to process – but at first, my heart felt warm to hear Declan wish me a safe trip home. Ireland, and specifically Killaloe – were indeed now my home. And Declan was looking forward to seeing me again.

But just as I was really looking forward to returning to Killaloe, the feeling of impending loss started to sink in. Louisa, who I hadn't spent as much time with as of late and had been looking forward to seeing her again and catching up with – would soon be leaving the country! And for how long? And Declan…he was leaving somewhere…could he possibly be going to Spain too? A feeling of loneliness started to settle around my heart – I didn't want to not see Declan for too long, just as we had started to become closer – and it would be even harder with Louisa not being there to talk to.

A strange mood had settled over me – not shaken off the strange, futuristic-seeming dream and knowing I would have limited time with both Declan and Louisa when I returned home.

Cormac met me at St. George's Market to have a good breakfast before heading back on the train and to see the market, arts and crafts and do any last-minute shopping – a way to take in a little more of Belfast attractions, like the Old Belfast Fish Market Clock without having to walk a lot and put too much pressure on my left ankle. My ankle was still sore and just slightly swollen now, and I had decided to wait to have it checked out by my own doctor when I returned to Killaloe. Further exploration of Carrickfergus Castle would have to wait. Cormac assured me that Douglas was very grateful I had been willing to interview him, and even though Douglas' positive and assured outlook that Ireland would vote to become a unified country in just a few short years I found fascinating and exciting, it still felt to me there were real obstacles to getting there.

As Cormac kissed my cheek and, thanked me for coming, and helped carry my luggage onto the train platform, I had a feeling of so much still being unresolved – the future of Ireland and Northern Ireland, the mystery of Cailin's connection to my life and why it had been so strong – and so unresolved – at Carrickfergus Castle. And why really had I fallen? Something supernatural, a ghost in broad daylight? And how did the dream last night, tie into all the others that I now was convinced had to do with Cailin and her life long ago?

Even though feeling unresolved, even haunted by all this, I was still happy and almost relieved to be returning to Killaloe. When I finally sat down in the train compartment, I closed my eyes, finding some comfort among all the mystery and uncertainty by the trace of the lingering feeling where Cormac had kissed my cheek.

CHAPTER XI

It turned out that when I returned to Killaloe, the first person I heard from was not Louisa or Declan. I had slept all the way from Belfast to the Connolly station and almost missed my transfer! Somehow, I was jolted awake right as everyone who was also transferring was exiting the train and missed the first shuttle I had to take to the Heuston station in order to transfer to the Limerick train, but thankfully, they were still coming every half hour. Loving all the readily available espresso that was in Ireland now, I ordered a double latte from the transfer station café to keep me awake for my next transfer.

I'd managed to stay awake almost all the way to Limerick, and then heavy tiredness came over me a few minutes before arriving at the Limerick station, but I only nodded off for a few seconds and woke up right before reaching my stop.

The cab dropped me off around 11 PM at my apartment in Killaloe, as the sky was beginning to take on the faded twilight of the late Ireland summer nights. Of all the thoughts swirling around in my head – submitting my interview of Douglas O'Donnell to Aiden, seeing Declan and Louisa, and not knowing quite how long either of them would be gone, it was when I got ready for bed that my thoughts about Cailin consumed me the most: what just had happened to her all those years ago at Carrickfergus Castle, what had happened between her and the man that kept appearing in my dreams? A feeling of loss – I'd felt it on and off since leaving Carrickfergus Castle, but it seemed now was the first I'd defined it – loss.

Yet now I was home, and as I curled up in bed under my blankets, I felt a real sense of comfort being back in Killaloe. As I reached over to turn off my bedside light and set the morning alarm on my cell phone, I noticed I had a new voicemail.

"Kayla, Grady here! Hope you are doing well. I found out something new in my ancestry research about your great grand aunt Cailin that I think you'll really want to know! Please let me know if you can be available to discuss over tea this week."

Even though I was happy and surprised somehow to hear from Grady so soon after getting back, I suppressed a chill and pulled the covers over me more snuggly. Wow, my great grand aunt! Somehow, it felt like Cailin wanted me to discover her secrets.

Grady agreed to meet me the very next afternoon, on the first full day of being back from Northern Ireland, at the Bean & Plover. I arrived an hour before we had planned to meet at 3 PM to work on planning the rest of the week, including when I'd talk to Aiden about my interview with Douglas O'Donnell. As I ordered my latte and said "Hi" to Tori, so good to see a familiar face and be at the café again, to be home – I hadn't realized it before, but I felt more at home than I had since I had left for Belfast. In a sense, it felt like I was returning to 'me' again.

I was happy a more private table in the corner was available, and the new photographs on the wall – one of the Shannon River waterfront nearby and one that I found especially striking of Lough Derg lake – with the castle ruins nearby and a blurred-in-motion photo of a mother and two kids playing in the playground, the photographer also capturing a sparkle of the water on the lake. The photos made me think of Louisa and Moley – and their photo shoot – wondering if they would still have it now that Louisa was flying off to Madrid – or if they had already fit it in without me.

I set up my laptop and pulled up both my weekly calendar and my interview with Douglas that I had transcribed that morning, but wanted to give it a final look-over before submitting it to Aiden. I knew it would be a busy week ahead, having to make sure I saw Declan and Louisa as soon as possible and scheduling my doctor's appointment (my ankle was, to my relief, actually feeling a little better today, but still thought it important to get it checked out), and work.

After easing into getting to work by thinking about the new photographs on the wall and looking around the café, so contented to be here again as I took sips of my latte, I had become so absorbed in my work that Grady actually startled me when he arrived at my table.

"Hello there, Kayla!" Grady broke me out of my concentration, and as I looked up to him, returning his hello, he started to laugh. "No need to jump out of your seat! Sorry to startle you, lass, working on something important?"

I hadn't realized I had jumped, but I indeed stood up then, and a strange impulse came over me to hug him, not even sure where that was coming from – but alas, my shyness came over me and clasped his hand in a friendly shake instead.

"Oh, just work and things – not more important than meeting with you! Good to see you, and so interested in what you learned about Cailin."

Grady pulled out a chair to sit down and said, "Thanks for meeting with me today, Kayla, and yes, I think you'll be very interested to hear what I came to share with you about Cailin."

We both sat down then, and the first thought that came into my head was if Grady would like something to drink.

"Would you like to get something to drink too?" Grady was already pulling some notebooks and a laptop out of his satchel briefcase.

"Oh – well, a spot of tea would be nice."

"It would be nice to stretch my legs for a moment – can I go get it for you?"

Grady agreed, thanking me with a "thanks lass" and saying that he could get his computer set up in the meantime, and a cup of Irish Breakfast sounded lovely.

When I returned with Grady's tea and sat across from him, he indeed had his laptop and notepad all ready to go, the notepad one of several on the top of a stack and opened to a page about two-thirds of the way through propped open with a pen. I found myself burning with curiosity about what he had found out about Cailin.

"So, how have you been, Grady?" I started. "I'm really curious what you found out about Cailin! So my relation to her is she's my great grand aunt?"

"That's right," Grady said as he typed something into his laptop. "And right now, I'm especially intrigued by the period between the time when the photograph of her that I showed you was taken in Northern Ireland and when she married Neil O'Grady."

"What happened during that time?"

"Well…she seemed to have disappeared."

"Disappeared?"

"In the years from 1921 to 1923, I am not able to find any records from her life – except for one odd letter that was sent to her from her Aunt Mary."

"Wow, so you have the letter?"

"Yes, right here," Grady reached into a manila folder and took out a letter written on faded blue paper that had almost turned white.

Dear Cailin,

I hope this letter finds you well. Martha and I, and your father, miss you so. And just yesterday Sean finally called me from London and asked after you! No one seems to understand why you went away – and we are concerned about you. I've kept your secret, but I am not sure how long I, in good faith, can do so as the more time passes, the more your family worries. I hope you have found solace with the Sisterhood of Brigid, but in time your heart will heal.

Love,

Aunt Mary

P.S. You remember Neil O'Grady? He asked after you recently at the Ballyvourney Fall Fling – his business is doing very well and he becomes more handsome by the day.

Both a chill and an excitement came over me then – it seemed to me this letter was a big clue – we just had to find out what the Sisterhood of Brigid was! And to see Cailin's Aunt mention

Sean, my Irish great grandfather! Both reality and mystery colliding, and I felt my heart quicken. The Sisterhood of Brigid. Cailin shared a connection to Brigid! Like some of the gaps in the unknowns of the universe were starting to fill in…this had to do with Brigid coming up in my dreams, her name being called in the first strange dream I had of Inis Cealtra and also connected to the experience I had at the actual Inis Cealtra!

"Grady, you'll never believe this, but I have been having strange dreams, ones that have to do with both Cailin and Brigid."

I went on to tell him about my dreams and that after visiting Carrickfergus Castle, I was certain I had been dreaming about Cailin, and of the time she was there in the place the photo had been taken. That I felt certain the photo he showed me of Cailin was taken at Carrickfergus Castle! And I had not only somehow been dreaming of her but of her connection to Brigid too.

"The day we went to Inis Cealtra, and you showed me her grave – earlier, before we all met up at the Bargaining Stone… come to think of it, even before stepping inside the old St Brigid's church there, I was feeling Brigid's presence. I remember it seemed like I was hearing her singing on the wind while we walked over to the church, but it was when I was inside St. Brigid's church and facing the West Doorway, as Louisa was exiting, I saw some kind of apparition, with a gold sparkling, almost invisible cloak – and it made me think of Brigid somehow – and then Louisa later told me that at the same time she had been walking away from Brigid's church and heard a wail-like sound, beautiful and haunting, as I exited out of the church through the West doorway."

"Wow," Grady had a look that could only quite come from him, I thought – a little incredulous but that despite himself, he believed me, that I was convincing him… "And you think this was somehow Saint Brigid?"

"I remembered after a painting I had seen of Saint Brigid of Kildare where she was depicted with long dark hair, a gold cloak, and a green dress. I know this sounds crazy, a bit impossible – but the first dream I had of Cailin and a mysterious man, I heard him call out Brigid's name – we had just connected hands through the Bargaining Stone!"

"Kayla, this is pretty incredible! I think if you'd told me this before I'd gotten to know you a little better, I would have been pretty skeptical, but I was able to follow your thought process here, and I admit your dreams and Cailin's life do seem to be connected somehow."

"Thank you," Grady, giving credence to what I was expressing, only assured me that it wasn't just mostly my imagination and that I was really on to something. Yet the big question remained – WHY was this happening? And could someone long gone from this Earth really be communicating with me somehow? "So what's next? Have you ever heard of the Sisterhood of Brigid?"

"I have not – though there is a religious community called the Brigidine Sisters – it's been around since the early 1800s. Started by the Bishop of Kildare at that time. At the time they were reclaiming their Catholic heritage and Celtic culture, coming through the repression of the 18th Century Penal Laws. Perhaps there is some relation between the two groups."

Just then, I saw a text come through from Aiden, saying he received my interview with Douglas O'Donnell, and it looked very good. He would have time on Tuesday to give it a final read and then would run it by Liam. He also had a reminder that the Montpelier Festival started on Friday, and they would be sending me to cover it that day.

The Montpelier Festival! I'd almost forgotten with all my focus on meeting and interviewing Douglas O'Donnell! Local attractions, events of interest, my usual beat – yet interviewing Douglas had thrilled me in a way I hadn't expected. Though now everyone at the paper was to try to see their story at least partly through the angle of celebrating Irish Independence. I turned back to my conversation with Grady.

"I will start researching the Brigidine Sisters and see what I can find out. I guess we don't have any other clues or records of where Cailin was during that time."

"No, it's strange – but in the spring of 1924, I found the record of her marriage to Neil O'Grady."

"Wow."

"And Kayla, are you familiar with the Legend of St. Brigid's Cloak?"

"The legend? No, not really…though there must be some significance to her cloak since I've seen it in paintings of her."

"I'd say! Look it up, it's the story of her first miracle."

The first week that I was back in Killaloe turned out to be so jam-packed that I was lucky to fit in both a visit with Declan and Louisa. Louisa was able to meet with me first and asked if I'd like to meet at Boruma's again. To this backdrop, very much feeling some kind of residual presence of Declan and Nolan, we sat outside on a table for two that was not too far from the larger table we had shared with the two Irish men who had been growing in significance in our lives.

"So, when will you see Declan?" Louisa asked. "I had no idea he was going to be leaving the country soon too!"

"Well, it turns out the only time that will work with both of our schedules is for him to meet up with me at the O'Briens Bridge on Friday, the day I will be covering the Montpelier Festival." I looked out across the Shannon River then, feeling a new loneliness start to sink in, yet I was comforted by the view of the river. "Oh, Louisa, it's going to be hard to have you both leave just around the same time."

"Maybe you can come out to Spain at some point too!? And I will definitely keep in touch with you. In fact, I'm starting a page on Instagram dedicated to my experiences in Spain!"

"Please text me too, you know how I am about forgetting to check social media." For some reason, I had been slow to catch on to the social media craze, seeming like there was always something else to put my mind and energies to.

"Of course," Louisa said. "Maybe this will get you to finally remember to check my updates, though." I laughed, glad Louisa was lightening the mood. "Do you think Declan is going to Spain?"

We talked for a long while, thankful Louisa hadn't booked anything else after our early dinner, and we spent a long time catching up. I told her I indeed wondered if Declan was going to Spain on "band business," as he was helping Nolan and the band even more since the location of their last concert had to be changed.

Nolan and Louisa had started commenting on each other's Instagram posts more and more, and then after she had said Madrid was so gorgeous and how it had been calling to her, and she really needed to finally go visit Nana there, Nolan had called her, and they had a long talk. And then he talked her into going to visit him in Spain!

"Did Nolan mention to you anything about Declan coming out there?"

"Oh – not specifically – and Kayla, of course, I would have told you already if he did! Nolan did say Declan "saved" them by finding the other venue so quickly. And to be sure to say 'Hi' to Declan and YOU next time I see you!" Louisa emphasized 'you' in a way that communicated that I would, of course, be mentioned along with Declan. I wondered then, had Declan mentioned me when he talked to Nolan?

"Thanks, Louisa – I'm really happy and excited for you."

"And there are more exciting things that will be coming up for you, too, I expect. And you'll know this Friday where Declan is going. If he's going to Spain too, you'll have to find a way to come over there!"

On our walk back over the bridge back to my apartment, I mentioned to Louisa about my ancestry search and my dreams about Cailin. I found it curious how I hadn't brought it up much during dinner, except that it looked like the photo Grady had shown me taken of Cailin in front of the water looked just like it was taken at the part of the bay near the docks at Carrickfergus Castle.

"Wow, you didn't tell me about all these dreams you've been having! Far out. And we had that strange experience near Brigid's church on Inis Cealtra, too!"

"Yes, and so interesting. I saw something ethereal-looking, and you heard something. And now I've found out Cailin was involved in something called the Sisterhood of Brigid!"

"When I'm in Spain, I'll ask Nana about it… she is a devout Catholic and has actually studied a lot about Irish as well as Spanish Catholic Saints," Louisa said.

Louisa and I had reached the end of the bridge on the Killaloe side, and I felt such a mix of hope and loss, and something new and impactful on the horizon. It seemed as though geography and physical location had very little meaning when it came to how we were all connected. And then it hit me – perhaps neither did time!

"Thank you. It's interesting how things can be connected…" I said and thought about how when I saw Declan, I would be standing at the end of another bridge – the one that would connect us to Montpelier.

CHAPTER XII

I waited for Declan at the east end of O'Brien's Bridge, looking across the small stretch of water that shimmered as it gently lapped onto a shore that was a lighter, rich green of the Emerald Isle.

As I stood on O'Brien's Bridge waiting for Declan, calming my anticipation by thinking about the article I was writing, I thought about my very old relative, Turlough O'Brien, and his Bishop brother who helped him build the bridge. What history, the first bridge here having been built in 1506! There was so much interesting history of the area, that first bridge having been destroyed just 27 years later – thanks to King Henry VIII of England, whose Lord Deputy had destroyed it after battling the O'Briens, who had rebelled against England. What a long and often dark history the Irish had with the English! A completely different stone bridge now stood there, at the same ancient river crossing that far predated King Henry the VIII and even Turlough O'Brien – the river crossing mentioned in the Triads of Ireland.

I spotted Declan then, walking towards me, his black hair had grown a little longer, and the vest he was wearing looking like it fit into an earlier time period – and brief chills ran through me as I thought of the man in my dreams. I pushed that feeling aside as

Declan came near, so happy to see him again and to be hearing the rising sounds of the fair, the music and chatter lightening my mood.

"Kayla O'Brien – over there in O'Briensbridge, it is quite lovely too," Declan and I found ourselves in an instantaneous hug, and at first, I felt confused – over there? Weren't we standing on O'Brien's Bridge? And as we parted from our hug, and as he looked at me, I noticed that his eyes seemed to be reflecting the same sparkly grey-blue of the river. I realized he had meant the town of O'Briensbridge, the town on the opposite side of the bridge from Montpelier. And that was the first time Declan had addressed me by my full name, thinking he must have made the connection between my name and our "location of O'Briens."

"Oh – yes, I'd love to explore more over there too," I replied as we walked to the end of the bridge toward Montpelier and the faire, and even though the faire only started about a half hour ago, it was getting more populated and animated.

"It's good to see you again, Kayla," Declan said as we walked toward the children's playground that had been transformed into a fairyland and looked and made me feel magical. Declan seemed different somehow than when I last saw him, in a way that seemed like he was seeing me in a new way – a positive one – and I had felt a longing to hold his hand as we walked by little children dressed up like leprechauns and fairies, little girls with flowers strewn in their hair, running and playing in shimmering dresses. I was too shy to actually take his hand first, but I felt the warmth coming from him as he walked close to my side.

"You too! I am so glad you could meet up with me today before you go." (I still needed to find out where he was going!) "Even though I am working and covering the festival for the Munster Post, we can still enjoy the afternoon, and I'll do most of the write-up tomorrow, anyway."

"Very good – by enjoying it, I'm sure that will enhance your article."

I was relieved Declan didn't mind at all that I was working, too. "What an adorable fairyland here," I said, and as we walked through the playground, I noticed the fair was divided into several sections and what looked like a different activity in each.

"This is really brilliant – my niece would love this," Declan said. We now stood at the opposite edge of the playground from where we entered on the side of the bridge.

"How nice! How old is your niece?" I asked him. It struck me that I hadn't talked to Declan at all about our families before. This growing feeling of closeness to him felt really real, but there was still a lot more that I didn't know about him.

"She just turned nine," Declan said. "My sister and her

family live in Galway. I should tell them about this festival. They could use some encouragement to come visit me as I'm usually the one to go there."

"Good idea! Nice that you visit them there – love Galway Bay, and I've been meaning to visit the Aran Islands too."

"Ah – yes, I do love it out there – Galway City is great, too. Have you ever been out to the Aran Islands?"

As much as I loved County Clare, Killaloe, and the Shannon waterfront, our conversation was having me yearn for the sea again.

"No…I hope to soon," I instinctively reached into my purse for my notepad then, telling myself I should jot down some notes about the fairyland for my article and not get too caught up in daydreaming about the Aran Islands and the sea.

"For your article?" Declan asked.

"Yes," I smiled a bit apologetically, hoping I wouldn't be boring him. Declan then took out his phone.

I wrote notes for a few minutes as Declan did something on his phone, and then Declan said, "Look over there – a little ways up the riverbank – looks like they are jousting!"

I quickly finished the notes I was taking, satisfied I was done and ready to move on, and said, "I'm ready. Let's go check it out!"

As we got closer to the area along the river where the

jousting was taking place, the music I had heard previously became louder, and I noticed several feet away from the jousting tournament, a medieval band was playing – the musicians all dressed up in medieval clothing, and the sounds of the lute, recorders, and pipes became clear. The crowd watching the jousting tournament was a mix of people in costume and regular clothing.

When we joined the crowd watching the jousting, the tournament was in full swing, and many in the crowd were rowdily cheering. I was struck and even amused by the perfection of it all – the white horse and the black horse draped in the shapes and colors of the opposing clan symbols of the rival knights on horseback, the knights also adorned in the clothing and colors of their clans along with their protective armor and helmets.

Declan, looking like he was enjoying himself, said to me, "Look at the swords. They are actually silver-colored styrofoam."

I found his comment completely jarring, in a funny way, and it was hard to stop laughing. "I suppose they'd have to be," I said through giggles and gave him what I thought was a sly look as I took out my notebook again. I was glad he could be well entertained while I took notes.

The jousting became fiercer, the two opponents very evenly matched as they usually missed, maneuvering their horses passed each other, sometimes forcing more of an impact while hitting the others' shield. The audience was becoming more and more excited and louder, and as the intensity built, I put my notebook back in my purse and decided to join in fully with the crowd.

Declan seemed to be routing for the knight on the white horse, which I found adorable despite myself, and I joined in routing for the "white knight," too.

Suddenly, it seemed like most of the crowd, at least the people around us, were all routing for the knight on the white horse – and as we cheered him on, the white horse came up on its hind legs, whinnied, and then charged toward the opponent, and its rider plunged the sword into the other knight's shield, splitting his sword in two.

The crowd around us erupted, and the knight on the white horse dismounted as the knight on the black horse trotted toward the stands, and the "white knight" bowed to the crowd as a young woman dressed like nobility came up to him, and the winning knight took off a red scarf and handed it back to her with the lower half of his broken sword.

With the memory of Carrickfergus still very fresh and now experiencing yet another Medieval setting – I was feeling transported – and a little giddy.

"That was fun," Declan said, and as the crowd started to disperse, we began walking toward the bandstand, where the sounds of the lute were further transporting me, and I began to think of the man in my dreams – and my fascination with him and especially the man I was with who he reminded me of, and my feelings were starting to make me self-conscience.

A dance was underway on the other side of the bandstand from where we came. "The jousting, the dancing – they really transported this into the Middle Ages!" I said as we walked toward the dancing and noticed some tables and chairs available where I thought we could sit next and perhaps grab some refreshments, and just as my hand was about to reach into my purse to grab my notebook again, a shock of excitement tingled in my arm as Declan took my other hand and said,

"My lady, care to dance?"

My insides did that thing where they felt like they flipped inside out, and for a moment, I felt I didn't know which world I was in – this one or one of my dreams. I looked at Declan, his eyes looking more green in this light, twinkling with amusement and interest – then looked around me at the crowd and the others coupling up as they walked toward the dance floor and felt giddy in the knowledge that, indeed, I was awake.

"Yes, my…" Declan grabbed my hand then and led me out to the dance area, the Medieval lute playing a slow yet festive melody.

And as we danced, the magic of this world, this here and now, came into focus in a brand new way. Declan was a wonderful dancer and expertly moved in his turns – most of the dance couples were doing variations of the same classic moves. The dances were not close slow dances but a lot of coming together and apart, clasping hands while turning. Yet this kind of touch was thrilling to me and seemed just the right dance to do with Declan at this moment, at this stage of coming together.

And Declan was so enjoying the dance, taking on a fun role as a medieval Irish dancer, but when our eyes met, he had a look like growing admiration and interest in me that made me feel so alive, gave me so much hope…

Then, as we turned and our hands met up again, I suddenly felt strangely off-balance and dizzy and felt my skin prick with tingly chills – and for the briefest of moments, saw little sparkly lights out of the corner of my eye along with the skin prickles, and then the mysterious calling like as if on the breeze…

"Fi…On…"

Then, a strong, secure hand clasped mine and the band was now playing an upbeat tune, and Declan was pulling me toward the group for a circle dance.

"You ok? We were dancing like pros, and then you lost balance for a moment there, closed your eyes for a moment?"

"Oh! I'm ok, must have lost my breath for a moment?"

"Do you need to rest?"

"Um…no, I'm ok, this is fun…." I did seem ok now and wondered if I really heard what I thought I had? Again…just like I had heard at Carrickfergus castle. I felt a little weaker but wanted Declan to keep enjoying the dance, and I felt an even stronger desire than before to keep dancing with him.

As we did the group dance – in a large circle where we kept doing a turn with our partner that led us to take a new one – it was really fun, and my dizziness dissipated, but I was still out of breath. Even though there was an excitement to the group dance and even a welcome break from the intensity of the closeness with Declan when we were alone dancing, and even though I was enjoying myself, I was becoming more and more winded and felt relieved when the dance was over. I didn't end with Declan as a partner, but an older grey-haired gentleman just a tad shorter than me, who bowed admiringly as we parted ways.

I spotted Declan just as he finished up chatting with the partner he had ended the dance with and caught his eye as I walked toward them.

The woman – a pretty redhead that reminded me of Meara Moran but more full-figured, looked admiringly at Declan (I guess I couldn't blame her!) but felt relieved nonetheless when a man who appeared to be her significant other put his arm around her and whisked her away from Declan.

"Hi there," I said.

"Hi, how are you doing? Feeling better?"

"Thanks for asking, that dance was fun! But I am a bit winded…"

"Why don't we go sit down, take a break, and grab a bite to eat, sound good? I overheard some people talking about a great fish-n-chips stand and other eateries in the restaurant tent. Shall we check it out?"

"Sounds just right, thank you," I replied, and Declan put his arm around me for a few moments as he started to lead me toward the direction of what I assumed was the tent with all the refreshments.

As we walked together, I had the strangest sensation, like I couldn't believe this was all really happening. A single American woman from California, in her forties with a few relationships behind her, who had wondered what would ever become of her love life at this stage of life. This woman was me, and now I was developing a friendship with an attractive Irish man – and feeling somehow like this land was a home to me that I hadn't known how much I missed until I was here. I felt like me – but not the old me –

and the line between the dreams I'd been having and the life I was living seemed blurred.

Being with Declan now made me realize in my heart that I no longer had doubts that he had something to do with the dreams I'd been having and what Cailin wanted me to discover. Yet I really had no idea what this could be.

We arrived at the refreshment tent, and I was happy to see that there were many separate tables spaced out, and Declan led us to an empty table at the corner next to a banner with a beautiful Celtic cross. A view of the Shannon River could be seen out of an opening at that corner of the tent.

"I'll go grab us something for lunch," Declan said. "Think I'm going to check out the chipper, fish and chips sound ok?"

"Sounds great," I said, and after Declan left I realized I forgot to ask him what to have to drink. I texted him to please get me a glass of water, sparkling if they had it, repressing an urge to also ask for a latte. I felt a warmth inside that I was at the point where I felt so comfortable texting him like this, and then laughed to myself that I needed the water but wasn't sure if I really wanted the water or a latte, but really a glass of wine…

When Declan returned, he had a bottle of sparkling water, two boxes of fish and chips, and two pints of Guinness! So we were going to have lunch his way, and I felt just fine with that.

"Thanks so much," I said as Declan passed me my lunch and sat down.

"You're most welcome, Kayla! What a great festival! Glad we met here today. Cheers!" Our glass commemorative Montpelier Festival beer mugs clanked as they connected.

"I'm so glad this worked out," I said as I took a sip of my Guinness and then blurted out, "So when do you leave for your trip again?" We hadn't talked at all about his trip yet, even though we had met today originally because it was the only time we both had before he left.

"Sunday night, actually – and this is my last day of fun before I spend the next two days hectically getting ready and wrapping things up with another client before I'm completely wrapped up with Nolan and the band."

My excited feeling when Declan mentioned "his last day of fun" and a sinking feeling of recognition that Declan would soon be very far away from me mixed in a way that made me feel out of breath for a moment again. So Declan was going to Spain!

"You're going to Spain?"

"Oh! I thought I'd told you more about it already. Yes, after having a long talk with Nolan after he faced some more snags in scheduling some more shows after the concert at Plaza Catalunya, we decided I'd go there for a few weeks to help them with further scheduling and publicity."

I drank another swallow of Guinness while telling myself at least Declan said weeks…he wouldn't be gone that long, right?

"Wasn't that concert at Plaza Catalunya a smashing success?"

Declan looked as though he would laugh – or at least break into a smile – if he hadn't been finishing up his mouthful of fish and chips. When he was ready, he said, "Indeed! You'd think it would all be smooth sailing after that, right? Unfortunately, there are still permit issues for the location for their concert in Madrid."

"I'm sure he'll – Nolan and the band – will appreciate you being there! Did you know that Louisa is also going to Madrid very soon?"

"Oh! I did not. The last I talked to Nolan was Wednesday…when did Louisa decide to go?"

"About a week ago – funny, I found out at the same time you were both going on my voicemail the last morning I was in Belfast." Declan gave me a questioning look then, and I realized just then why what I had said would seem contradictory. "I mean – she left a message saying she was going to Spain, your message just said you were leaving on business…but not where."

Declan chuckled in his lovely way then and said, "Right – I must have thought it would be good to give you the details when I actually saw you. So, how was your weekend in Belfast?"

My Guinness was already half drunk, and that tipsy feeling mixed with my emotions at that moment opened up the floodgates of wanting to let Declan inside, and share with him what was most perplexing at the moment.

"It was good – intense in a way, it was a very interesting interview with someone about Irish Reunification – still waiting to see if it will run in the paper. However, it also led me to Carrickfergus Castle, which is where I recently discovered Cailin, my great grand-aunt, went and met an old love of hers – though not the man she married. I was shown a photo that looked like it was taken there, and when I saw it for myself, I knew it was the place," I fell short of saying how I also dreamed of her – and him – at this place. Yet.

"Wow, that's interesting – this is the relative you found out about recently, the one through your friend in that group you're in… Celtic Light, right?"

At first, I felt amazed that Declan said this, as I briefly couldn't remember telling him, but then the image in my mind flashed back to standing with him among the circle of trees at Brian Boru's fort, and remembered I told him about the relative in Celtic

Light there – and of my dreams.

"Yes, Sean O'Grady – it turns out his great grandmother is my great grand aunt."

"That's great, and you didn't know of this relation before now?"

"No! When I first talked more to Grady, he told me I looked a lot like his great grandmother, Cailin O'Grady. Then at Inis Cealtra, Grady showed me her grave there! And that he knew of some history with the O'Grady's and the O'Briens, which led him in doing more research. Cailin's brother, also named Sean, married a British woman, Eliza Fitzgerald – my great-grandmother!"

"Wow! They must have emigrated to America at some point?"

"Yes – I grew up hearing stories of how they couldn't stay in England – Eliza's family didn't accept him, and they couldn't go back to Ireland, so that situation led them to America."

"And you being here seems full circle."

"Wow – suppose so – hadn't thought of it like that before," And even though my Guinness was about gone, the warmth and wonder I was feeling I knew was not just from that – was genuine.

"Kayla, when we were back at Bael Boru…didn't you tell me that one of the dreams you had was at Inis Cealtra?"

So, I didn't have to broach the subject of my dreams with Declan. I had already made him think of them. And suddenly, I felt free to confide much more to him.

"Why yes – the dream at Inis Cealtra was the first dream like this I had. And the new mystery I'm trying to uncover is where Cailin went after she left Carrickfergus."

"Really?"

"I met with Grady at the Bean & Plover after I got back from Belfast, and he showed me a letter Cailin's aunt wrote to her – this is the only thing he knows that links Cailin to the years between 1921 and '23. No one knows exactly where she went."

"Well, what did her aunt's letter say?"

"It's so interesting! She says she has been keeping Cailin's secret, but her family misses her so much, and that she hopes she found peace… I think she used the word solace – with a group called the Sisterhood of Brigid."

"Huh – so some kind of religious order, maybe? Sounds like she was heartbroken."

I was so grateful Declan was following this and listening so well. "Yes – it sure seems that way. The aunt also says in time Cailin's heart will heal. And there's a P.S. – about who turns out to be the man Cailin later marries! Asks her in the P.S. if Cailin remembers Neil O'Grady, that he asked about Cailin while she was still mysteriously away, and Aunt Mary says he is a great prospect like his work is successful and becoming more handsome by the day."

"She wouldn't be the first person to seek God after a broken heart," Declan said, taking a final sip of his Guinness. "Are you familiar with St Brigid's prayer, 'I'd like to give a lake of beer to God?'"

I laughed. "Why, yes!"

Declan continued. "I'd sit with the men, the women, and God there by the lake of beer.

We'd be drinking good health forever and every drop would be a prayer."

"But seriously...I was just thinking, do you think the Sisterhood of Brigid could tie back to Inis Cealtra in any way?" Declan asked. "Seems to me, Cailin... it's hard to believe, but somehow you are dreaming of her, including that early dream you had at Inis Cealtra."

"Wow, I think you are right." My affection and attraction for Declan at that moment also became full of gratitude. I knew instantly when he said the Sisterhood of Brigid was connected to Inis Cealtra that it must be true! Why hadn't I fully realized this before? I had never dreamt that Declan would be so insightful and helpful with my search into the mystery of Cailin – and be so open-minded. And then it hit me – the man in my dreams, though I felt certain he wasn't Declan, but the man Cailin had somehow had her heart broken by before she married Neil O'Grady, nevertheless reminded me of Declan, resembled him – even those eyes.

And just like that, the rain started pouring hard outside of the tent – like it had the very first time I visited Inis Cealtra.

We were now all done with our lunches, and more and more people started pouring into the tent to get out of the rain.

"Well, I only have about an hour or so left, unfortunately, as I have a client who wants to connect with me today before I leave for Spain. Do you want to walk around now and see a bit more?" Declan said.

I did have my lightweight raincoat but not an umbrella, but the rain was already starting to lighten up a bit, and at that moment, I'd probably go anywhere with Declan anyway.

"Good idea, it would be good to check out more of the festival – looks like the rain is lightening up a bit too," I said. We both stood up then, and it seemed to be getting more warm and humid the more people streamed into the tent, so I was looking forward to leaving and stepping out into the mist with Declan.

"Turns out I have an umbrella," Declan said and opened it up to share with me as we stepped out of the tent.

This part of the festival, right outside the tent, had rows of shops with different things for sale – from pastries to jewelry to crafts – and I was reminded of the day when Declan and I went to the farmers market and walked the trail that led us to Bael Boru. We spent a little time looking at the shops, and Declan telling me more of his thoughts on going to Spain and that he would be gone for a month, and though I was glad it wouldn't be longer was feeling the little pangs of missing him already. Sharing his umbrella added to the feeling of intimacy to our remaining time together.

The rain was turning into a mist, and as we reached the end of the row of shop stands, Declan put his umbrella down and said, "Ah, just a fine mist now, do you mind?"

"No, this feels good, actually!" Standing at the end of the row of shops, I looked back and saw that the character of the festival was changing, many seeking shelter in the various shops, but glad to see a string quartet still playing, sheltered under a standing umbrella, and the beautiful music travelling through the misty air gave it a magical quality.

At this end of the festival a good view of the wide river could be seen, and a pretty tree-lined walking path that winded around the trees along the river.

I sensed Declan looking at me, looking down toward the river, and he said, "Would you like to walk down to the river? I hear this is also a popular hiking place, and the trails are quite lovely."

"Sure," I said softly, my intellectual brain telling me I had enough information at that point to do a good write-up of the festival, but it was my spirit intuition, this part of me, that was pulling me to go be with Declan in a quieter, more private place.

When we reached the banks of the river, I was struck by how completely at ease I felt being alone with Declan, but I also noticed something else I hadn't amongst the bustling of the festival – he seemed just a bit preoccupied, a little more distant than he had seemed when we were talking at lunch.

We walked along the riverbank, both just meandering without saying that we would walk back toward the direction of the bridge, at least for a while… or exactly which direction we were going.

"Kayla, when you were telling me about the letter Grady showed you, it sparked some kind of feeling like I was remembering something, and as we were walking down here it just hit me."

"Really?"

"I received an interesting letter about four months ago from my grandmother, who lives on the West Coast near a little town near

Galway, Rossaveal, close to the ferry that takes you out to the Aran Islands. It's one of the places where Irish is still spoken – her first language was Irish, actually."

Declan paused then, and his eyes had a faraway look, so I said, "That's so nice your grandmother is still here."

"Yes – she's my last grandparent left. She will be 91 in October. Her letter mentioned to me an old love she had, who she had loved most, other than my grandfather Ian. She had been thinking of him because she felt he had never gotten over an old love who had wronged him somehow – and she thinks that kept him from ever really being able to love her fully or open up to her. She thinks if he had healed, gotten over her – she might have married him – but alas was glad she ended up with Ian Maloney as she couldn't imagine life without her grandson Declan – well me," Declan's far away glance turned to his eyes looking right into mine – an intense and longing look, and his tale sounded eerily familiar.

"What a sweet letter. It does…it reminds me of Cailin's some, having to get over her lost love and then finally marrying Neil O'Grady."

"That's what triggered the memory," Declan said, then paused as we walked up into the cluster of trees a little ways from the water's edge. "At the time, I was perplexed why she shared this with me, but all I could think of then was that my relationship with my old fiancé had ended, and she was telling me I should get over her so I could move on."

So Declan wasn't that far over a broken-off relationship – perhaps that's why he was taking things slowly with me?

"That makes sense. She sounds like a wonderful and interesting lady."

"Indeed," Declan smiled genuinely at me then. "Though that relationship ended six months before she wrote to me, so thought I was moving on, well…" he trailed off like he wasn't sure how much more he wanted to say. "But hoped she was just being – well, grandmotherly, you know, protective."

"Did she say or ever tell you what happened to that first love, the man who never got over someone else?"

"Ah, no – that letter was the first I learned of him. Don't even know his full name…in the letter, she said his given name was Fionn."

We walked together in the forest of trees then, not too far into them as we could still see the river through the spaces in the trees, my heart beating fast, the significance of what Declan told me sinking in, but also seeming almost unbelievable. Fionn! That was the name I'd been hearing like carried on the breeze… that must have been the name I had heard at Carrickfergus Castle when I fell!

Somehow, improbably, could the man Cailin loved be the same man Declan's grandmother had loved? Who never could quite love her back?

I started to shiver then, realizing that when I was having the dreams, I was somehow seeing through Cailin's eyes – things she had seen all those years ago. But somehow, it always felt like me, too.

Declan came closer to me and said, "Kayla, you're shivering. Are you cold? Here," and took off his jacket to give me.

"Oh, thank you, that's really sweet of you," and took it, not knowing quite how to articulate the real reason I was shivering.

The path took us back to the same place we had started, near the bridge that connected Montpelier to the town of O'Briens Bridge. There were fewer little fairies and elves playing in the playground now. Nevertheless, a magical feeling was still very much with me – having walked a ways through the deep, rich green, shady trees until the walking path took us to where we could peak out at the Shannon again, all the while filled with a new understanding that Declan, this Irish man who had intrigued me, admittedly ever since the first time I saw him at a completely chance encounter at the Bean & Plover, who had grown in my consciousness, heart, and life ever since – it's as of now we had both walked out of the shadows together, and I was seeing the man in my life who was undoubtedly connected to my dreams, Cailin – and the name I had been hearing on the wind – Fionn.

"I've really enjoyed the festival with you today, Kayla," Declan said, holding my gaze. There were always lots of feelings I had in Declan's presence, but now I was feeling a tinge of the feelings that I had in my dreams – that longing.

"Me too. Thanks for spending this time with me here before leaving for Spain," I said.

"The pleasure is mine," Declan said, coming closer to me. "You think you got enough for your article? I hope it wasn't too much of a bypass coming back through the trail."

"Oh yes, I've got enough – and the trail was beautiful, and in a way, too, it gives me a better sense of the whole place." I just knew then I had to somehow communicate with Declan about how I'd heard the name Fionn – but was it too strange to describe to him *how* I had heard it?

"You know, that name – the name of your grandmother's old love, Fionn – it sounds very familiar to me, I…"

"Did you dream it?" Declan gave me his puzzled, intrigued expression again.

"Well…no, I don't think so – or I don't remember, but…"

Declan surprisingly hugged me then, and I felt like I just

wanted to stay there always, and I nestled into his arms.

"I really enjoy spending time with you, Kayla," he almost whispered to me, his mouth close to my ear. "I feel connected to you…in a way I can't quite describe."

"I feel the same…" and I almost told him then how before I fell at Carickfergus Castle, I'd heard a sound, a call – that at the time I couldn't quite make it out, but sounded like Finn…Fionn.

But instead, I turned my face toward Declan's and felt his lips press gently into mine, and we kissed lovingly for just a couple of moments, and it was short but felt like the most wonderful kiss I had ever had – for it was a gentle, testing-the-waters kind of kiss, and loving.

It was Declan who pulled away first and put his hand on my cheek, and his eyes showed longing, yet a type of confusion and unsettledness that didn't quite sink in until later.

"I'll miss you," I said, feeling both like me and something beyond me.

"Kayla, I'll think of you when I'm gone. At least it will only be a month," He paused, looking out toward the river. "Would you like to walk halfway across the bridge with me?"

So, hand in hand, like a couple, we walked on the bridge, and my heart was both full and sad he was leaving. He talked to me about Spain and some of his ideas for the band, and he would keep me posted and expected I'd hear a lot of what would be developing over there from Louisa too.

"Well, here we are – where we started," Declan said when we had reached the same part of the bridge, on the walkway on the opposite side as before.

"Good luck getting ready, and safe travels," I said.

Declan squeezed my hand as he looked off toward the town of O'Briens Bridge. "Thank you, Kayla – and for the amazing day," and just like that he was off, and a misty rain started up again.

That night alone in my apartment, I felt sad that I would not see Declan for what looked like at least a month, yet tingly with a kind of anticipation and excitement that I learned of Fionn, the lost love of Declan's grandmother. Even though my rational brain scolded me that it could just be a coincidence, I knew in my heart – it felt like in my bones – that Fionn was the haunting name I heard calling out to me, and it was the same Fionn Declan told me about a few hours ago.

I longed to talk to Louisa about what had happened – and that Declan and I had finally kissed – but while also a part of me feeling private about that part, I felt an ache to be able to talk to a friend. I also felt a need to do research – on the Sisterhood of Brigid, Fionn… yet I didn't even know Fionn's last name! I settled on making some herbal tea and journaling. I had bought a new journal recently to focus on my research about Cailin and my ancestry and had come up with using the back pages for research notes and the front pages for my thoughts and emotions.

Only drawn to the front pages to start, I wrote:

Tonight, I am so full of emotion, I feel like my heart is so full, and all my other possible sensations are numbed. I am falling for Declan, and today revealed what I expected – what I so much hoped – that he has interest – and attraction for me. I'm trying not to worry why he kept his kiss short – short but the sweetest and most meaningful kiss that I can remember. And in him telling me the most pivotal information – that his grandmother was connected to Fionn- I now know of the person of the name I've been hearing calling to me…

I stopped writing then, the lightning bolt of the realization of Fionn hitting me. Fionn *was* the man in my dreams, and he was the one Cailin loved before her heart was broken and disappeared to the Sisterhood of Brigid. Cailin had been the woman who broke Declan's grandmother's old flame's heart, so he could never fully love her. That woman had been Cailin!

I shivered and reached for a warmer wool sweater, pacing by my bedroom, knowing I should actually be getting ready for bed but feeling hesitant to fall asleep any time soon. A little warmer with the sweater, but chills still going through me, I wondered – did Cailin – somehow the spirit of Cailin – call out to me, feeling I had a connection to Fionn?

And then another realization hit me like a bolt of lightning – the person I needed to talk to right away was not Louisa or even Grady.

It was Niamh.

CHAPTER XIII

The Celtic Light gathering that day was at Lough Gur, a beautiful lake in the Southeast of Ireland in County Limerick, that some considered to be the most spiritual lake in Ireland. For the last two days after I saw Declan at the Montpelier Festival, I had been so consumed by thoughts and feelings, and anxiety had come over me that I had dealt with in between reaching out to Niamh and Grady by delving into my work.

I had just received a message the evening before that Niamh would talk to me after the group outing today, and though I had been so relieved, I still couldn't stop the rush of thoughts coming at me and had had a restless night's sleep. It wasn't until I was on the grounds of Lough Gur that I felt the first sense of peace and calm that I had since Declan and I parted.

We all met up by the sign describing Lough Gur and its grounds. The lake could be seen nearby, surrounded by the greenest of grasses and the enchanting hills beyond. It felt strange for Louisa not to be there since we had both made it to every other Celtic Light outing since they started up in the late Spring, and I missed her presence. I was glad, though, that Grady arrived just in time to hear Niamh introduce the guest she had invited to our outing.

"Hello everyone, welcome to one of my favorite places to bring our group of Celtic Light travelers, the spiritual Lake of Lough

Gur – which I consider the lake and sacred grounds to be one of the five places in Ireland where the veil between this world and the spirit realm is most opaque," Niamh began.

"What are the other four places?" Katie, whom I had shared the boat with to Inis Cealtra, asked.

"Ah – how about we talk about them later today, and we will be visiting them all this year! Now, I would like to introduce you to Garrett McNeill, a folk historian, author, amateur archeologist, and expert on the history and artifacts of the Ballyhoura and Munster Vales region of South East Ireland."

Grady whispered in my ear then, "Ah – he's impressive – have several of his books, and he came to talk to us last year too."

"Thank you, Niamh, and it is good to be with the Celtic Light Group again and see some familiar and new faces! First off, how many of you are familiar with the legend of Gearoid Iaila?" Garrett McNeill said.

At first, no one spoke, and then, to my surprise, Grady said, "He's the one banished to the bottom of the lake, right?"

A couple of people in the group laughed, and Garret McNeill looked pleased.

"Yes, that's right – the Goddess Aine banished him to the bottom of Lough Gur. And, every seven years, he returns to the surface in order to try to break the curse. The legend goes that once the silver wears down enough on his shoes, he will escape and walk amongst us again…"

"So when we walk up to the lake in a few minutes, see if you can feel their presence – the lake sometimes even has a silvery mist," Niamh said. I thought it was interesting she said "their presence," like Gearoid and Aine were just different sides of a coin…

Garrett McNeil went on to describe some of the natural features of the lake, how it formed a horseshoe shape at the base of Knockadoon Hill, and the rugged, elevated ground at the base of the hill. And despite Gearoid being banished at the bottom, the lake was actually not that deep, 3.5 meters at its deepest point, fed by underground springs. So it was not flowing anywhere – no Shannon connecting it to other lakes or out to the sea. He also spoke of Lough Gur and the surrounding area being one of the most important archeological sites in Ireland, humans having lived there since Neolithic times, and the only place in Ireland where human remains of every age throughout the centuries could be found.

As we all walked toward the lake, with Grady by my side, I realized not only did I feel more peaceful there but also much more introspective – even more introverted – and in touch with my inner spirit. Grady, too, was uncharacteristically quiet as we walked toward the lake, and I just heard a splattering of quiet conversation among the group.

Then, as we reached Niamh and Garrett, who headed up the group (somehow, Grady and I were the ones who reached them first, when they were close to the edge of the lake), I heard Niamh and Garrett speaking Irish together and longed to understand them.

I walked past the group across a lovely medium shade of green grass, that grew taller and mixed with reeds with reddish buds as I came closer to the water, as the water seemed to be drawing me to it. I had never seen a lake that reflected the sky and land around it so perfectly. Like a mystical mirror image. The sky was a beautiful and mysterious mix of white and darker, greyer clouds and patches of sun here and there, and the pristine lake not only mirrored this back in a crystal-clear way but also the green of the hills across the lake and the scattering of trees around it.

I just stared into the water, mesmerized, and I heard Niamh announce to everyone to wander around and have some personal time to contemplate and absorb the energy of the place. At that very moment, it felt like all the pressing things in my mind could wait, this sacred lake before me seeming to already have wisdom beyond all the mysteries that had been swirling through my mind.

"Kayla, looks like you have found a new peace here by Lough Gur," to my surprise, it was Niamh's voice, somehow at the same time startling and gently pulling me out of my trance.

I turned to face her, seeing she had now come to stand at my side. "Yes – thank you. I've never experienced the feeling that this lake is giving me before."

"Yes – I've always felt something unique and very sacred here too. No matter what myths and legends there are, there is something undoubtedly here."

"Thank you for being available to talk to me later on," I said.

"Of course, and I know you were interested in talking to me sooner, but I sense you've come to a new inflection point on what you've been experiencing?"

I looked at her humbly and in awe then, always impressed by how she sensed what was happening.

"Yes, you're right. And I appreciated our phone conversation when we were in Northern Ireland, that helped, too."

"After our tour today, I'm inviting Garrett up to my house. It's very close to here – to meet Cormac too."

"Oh, Cormac is in town?"

"Yes, my dear – he will be happy to see you too. He has been wanting to meet Garrett for some time now – he's very impressed with his books. I was thinking I could let them talk and we could have our own talk while I let them get a chance to get acquainted. Does this sound good to you?"

"Yes, that sounds perfect. Thank you so much!"

"I'll leave you this thought until then; the time we experience, the feeling you get from the lake – does it seem to be in the present, or like there is more than today here?"

I thought I was getting the gist of what she was conveying. "It feels ancient – yet new too. Like there are many layers…"

"Ah, so you see – this is also true of everything in our lives – time, the present, and the past. It's all here. It just sometimes takes a beautiful, sacred spot like Lough Gur to sense it."

After Niamh walked back toward the rest of the group, I stood looking at the lake for a few moments more, contemplating what she'd said, watching the perfectly reflected, ever-changing sky ripple in the water, a soft yet indistinguishable hum on the soft wind blowing up against my back. Even though I was told the lake wasn't that deep, it gave me the sense that it could go on forever. Time! I had felt like the gap between present and past had been narrowing in my experiences lately, waking and dreaming. But could reality really be so?

I said a short thank you to the lake, surprising myself with the gesture but feeling like it was gifting me a wisdom that I still didn't fully comprehend. When I turned around to walk toward the group, people were still exploring the area on their own, and Grady walked up to me.

"I saw Niamh come over and talk to you," Grady said.

"Ah, yes – I wanted to talk to her later – about the strange dreams I've been having…that I mentioned in the Bean & Plover to you about. When we met and, you showed me the letter."

"Ah, a good idea to talk to Niamh about these kinds of things. She may know something about the Sisterhood of Brigid, too."

"Niamh also shared with me something about time – the present and past both existing together…" I struggled at that moment to articulate it exactly.

"Like non-linear time?" Grady raised an eyebrow to me.

"Yes – I think so! Think that's the concept…"

"It's all interesting. Yet when you find yourself with not enough time left for what you need to do…it seems irrelevant in a way."

Grady's comment perplexed me, and I looked at him intently then, wondering what he exactly meant and why he was feeling like he didn't have enough time. For what? I hoped he was ok.

I was about to ask him more when he suddenly said, "Look, they are all gathering in the circle now."

Grady quickened his pace and I followed, and we joined the circle, with Niamh also linking hands in the main circle and Garrett

McNeil in the center.

"Have you enjoyed your time at this ancient lake, and has the energy you felt been more positive or negative?" Garrett McNeil got a resounding "positive" from the group, with a few disclaimers:

"It has a very old, mysterious quality."

"It feels like…if I don't keep aware of my surroundings, it may just pull me right into it…"

"It's very peaceful…but also feels like it has deep secrets," I added.

"Yes! Great observations. And interesting Meara about the feeling like if you don't keep your awareness up, the lake could claim you – as legend has it, the Goddess Aine, the White Lady, will pick someone every seven years and take them to her realm below."

Garrett went on to tell of the lake to be believed to go all the way back to the pre-Celtic Tuatha Dé Danann, belonging to its leader, Fer Fi, the brother of the Goddess Aine.

"I heard a tale that Geroid returns on horseback – on a white horse?"

"Right out of the lake?"

The group explored the folklore and tales of Lough Gur and Geroid back and forth with Garrett, and my mind wandered to the white horse at the jousting match that Declan and I watched. I felt some pangs of missing Declan, though it hadn't been that long since he left. I then made an effort to listen more intently to Garrett again, who was now describing the more natural and archeological elements of the lake and its surroundings. How the lake itself was shaped like a horseshoe, about the base of Knockadoon Hill and the surrounding elevated countryside, and about the ancient castle ruins nearby, Bourchier's Castle and Black Castle.

Next, we were off to the ancient stone circle of Grange to continue our spiritual and archeological journey. As we walked away from Lough Gur, I looked out across the lake again and listened to the wind rippling across the lake, feeling like even with how fascinating the area and the stories Garrett told of it were, the lake's knowledge was so much deeper than any of them – and somehow, incredibly, applied to what I was yearning to know since the visits by Cailin began. Be it her essence, her spirit…

And in no time, we arrived at Grange Stone Circle, with the sun high in the sky, and as I caught sight of the wide stone circle through the trees, I became excited by the mysteries to come.

I felt a similar wonder when I arrived at Niamh's house. It was located at the edge of a forest, a hike to Lough Gur Lake in one direction and a longer one to Glenstal Abby in the other. I was still feeling full of wonder from just having walked and danced around the stones at Grange Stone Circle, and I had an impending sense that a lot was about to be revealed to me. And even though most of it was positive excitement, I felt a tinge of foreboding, too.

After Garrett had told us about the history of Grange Stone Circle, Ireland's oldest standing stone monument, built around 2,200 B.C. soon after the bronze age began, Niamh followed by describing the many rituals that took place there from the ancient past to the present.

Another time of quiet and contemplation was granted to us then. I walked around the stone circle contemplating each stone, and then looked more closely at what I had just heard was the largest stone there called Crom Dubh, named after the God Crom Cruach, which meant black, crooked one.

The stone was four meters or a little more than 13 feet high, and as I approached it, I noticed how it was so much taller than all my fellow Celtic Light travelers who passed by or stood looking at it too.

Even though everyone I noticed stopped to observe the large stone as they walked by, I then found myself alone facing it. The branches of the large tree behind it casted spidery and wispy shadows in the front of the stone. It seemed to me the strongest stone I'd ever been near, the most grounded, and its energy not only radiated strength but wisdom. And like its ancient memory, the stone stretched back thousands of years.

The Mist and the Wind

As I respectfully turned my head to my left and mused about the very interesting stack of much smaller stones next to Crom Dugh, wondering what the meaning was of stacking the stones one on top of another with several even smaller stones on the top, I heard a text come through on my phone. It was from Aiden.

> Kayla, I have good news!
>
> Your interview with Douglas O'Donnell
>
> will be published in this Friday's edition.
>
> I made a few edits at Liam's suggestion
>
> and sent you the copy before it goes to press.
>
> Great job! This interview is sure to inspire
>
> a lot of discussion!
>
> Best, Aiden

A thrill came over me then, and I had a strange mix of excitement from Aiden's news and feeling humbled and reverent to the stones all around me. I wanted to share my news with someone, but all was still quiet and contemplative there. I silently thanked the spirit of the place, and then, as the wind picked up and the leaves began to blow around behind the stones, including behind Crom Dubh, a sensation came over me of things set in motion, a big change on the way.

I had told Grady my good news right before Niamh led us on a sacred circle group dance inside the stone circle, and he had given me a "congrats!" and high-five right before we took hands for the dance getting underway. And now, as I stood inside Niamh's home, near the glass doors that led out to her back patio, I saw Cormac and felt the excitement to tell him wash over me.

"Kayla, it's so nice to have you over here for the first time," Niamh said as she led me out the glass doors near the kitchen to the back patio. The view of her pretty backyard there was bright and welcoming, especially as the sun had come out after a mostly cloudy morning, and it reminded me of a fairy-tale in the way it was a little clearing bordered by a forest.

Cormac and Garrett were sitting at a small white table on the far end of the patio, near the corner of the house that was set up with stone patio tiles and three different areas to sit, with two small round tables and a larger, rectangular one. Cormac stood up when he saw me, and Garrett said hello to me with a smile but stayed seated while taking sips of his tea.

"Kayla, so good to see you again!" Cormac said and, to my surprise, gave me a light hug with a tender pat on my back.

"Cormac, you too!" I said, feeling a bit flustered with his affection and my excitement in telling him the interview would be published. "I have good news, the interview with Douglas

O'Donnell will be published in this coming Friday's Munster Post!"

"That's fantastic!" Cormac said. Niamh had just put out a pot of tea and scones at the other smaller round table, far enough from the table Cormac and Garrett occupied to have a private conversation, and Cormac walked over and poured a cup of tea, and brought it over to me.

"*Slainte*!" Cormac said as he clicked his teacup to mine. "Such great news. I will let Douglas know right away. And I have some other important updates to discuss with you, Kayla."

Niamh, who had walked up to us a moment ago, said, "Congratulations, Kayla! I am so happy Douglas' views will be shared with the Irish people in this way. Let us have our discussion now, Kayla, as I know you have some important personal things to make sense of in your life now."

"Very well," Cormac said. "I will resume with Garrett – and Kayla. We will talk more later on, ok?"

"Of course!" I said, wondering what Cormac was wanting to update me on so much – was it all related to Douglas O'Donnell? His tone was different than I had heard him use before, more commanding and urgent. Niamh and I walked over to the table where she had laid out our tea, and it felt like her energy was pulling me with her.

We sat down, and I said, "This is really good tea! Irish Breakfast?"

"Yes, it's from my old friend Tara's tea shop. She makes these scones too – so everything's Irish!"

I laughed, remembering the "English teas" my friends and I occasionally went to in the States, with steaming pots of teas, scones, finger sandwiches, and pastry for dessert.

I looked out onto the trees bordering Niamh's backyard for a moment, then, just past some pretty white flowers Niamh had planted, noticing the wind blowing the tree branches around. I heard a faint whispering sound then and told myself not to let my imagination get carried away with me, that it could be anything more than just the sound of the wind.

"So Kayla, tell me what happened recently that was so significant? Is it connected to the dreams you've been having?"

"I…found out who the man is – the name I've been hearing sometimes, the one I heard right before I fell at Carrickfergus Castle – he's an old love of my friend Declan's grandmother!"

"This man is the same one that has been appearing in your dreams?"

"Yes! I think I've pieced it together. Declan, he shared with me when I last saw him that his grandmother sent him a letter, about six months after Declan broke up with his fiancé, that she had an old love that she had to get over – a man she loved deeply, but could never really love her fully because he had never gotten over another woman."

Niamh got right to the point. "So, you think that woman is Cailin?"

Niamh's directness took me a little by surprise and, at the same time, gave me even more confidence that I had myself reached the right conclusion.

"Yes... I do. I'm just a bit confused...well, what Cailin wants from me."

"I'm getting the sense," Niamh began. "That this was set in motion a long time ago."

I was thinking about what she said, feeling like I was on the threshold of understanding, as amazing as this seemed.

"It was set in motion when she was still alive?"

"Yes...I'm sensing that. You know our conversation just a couple of hours ago when we were looking out at the lake?"

Understanding was dawning on me. "About time – or timelessness?"

"Yes. It may be, that when you are seeing Cailin's visions in your dreams, you are meeting her in one of those places – thoughts and desires she already had, but they are not constrained by time. You have met her in the timeless place, so to speak."

Wow. This seemed so amazing. So was it still possible I was being visited by Cailin's ghost, or something else entirely?

"Niamh, I'm wondering if somehow this is connected to a time when Cailin 'disappeared' for a while, and all I know about this so far is she spent time with the Sisterhood of Brigid. Have you heard of them?"

"I...I believe I have. There was an offshoot of the Brigidine Sisters, interestingly, I just heard about them around a year ago – it was last summer about this same time – when I was taking a walk with my friend Thomas from Glenstal Abbey. He said right after the War of Independence, a friend of his father who had studied religion with him had been dissatisfied with the Brigidine Sisters and started her own order."

This was it! This had to be.

"I just bet this is where Cailin went! Was this around the same time Cailin 'disappeared' between the years of 1921 and 1923?"

"Yes, the timeline fits – he told me she broke off from the Sisterhood during the final years of the war. I'll get a hold of Thomas and see if he can confirm the name of the order and anything else that could be helpful."

"Do you remember if he said her name, the name of the woman who started the new order?"

"I don't recall – I'll ask him that too."

The thought nagging at the back of my mind surfaced. "Niamh, if somehow I am connecting with Cailin in the "space beyond time," so to speak, is it also possible her ghost – or perhaps I should say spirit? Could still be visiting me, too?"

"I do think it's possible, as I fully believe our souls pass on. But I am getting the strong sense that somehow her communicating with you was set in motion when she was still here on this earth plane, and I'm beginning to think it was when she spent those years in the Sisterhood of Brigid. And I also have the sense Thomas can help us shed more light on this as well."

Chapter XIV

After my talk with Niamh, which put me in such an elevated mood, closer to discovering what Cailin was doing during her time at the Sisterhood of Brigid, which was somehow connected to why she was contacting me – and Cormac's enthusiasm about my interview with Douglas O'Donnell being published – I'd almost forgotten the peculiar vibe I'd gotten from Cormac earlier in Niamh's backyard when he invited us all to celebrate at Dougal's Pub.

The plan became clear as Cormac drove us all there, me sitting in the left front passenger's seat and Niamh and Garrett in the back – that Niamh would leave by 9 PM to get Garrett to his train back to Dublin, and then she would return home, and Cormac and I would get separate cabs back later. Cormac, right off the bat generously offered to pay for my cab back home.

"Glad this worked out for everyone, I'm so happy to be celebrating with four of my favorite people," he'd said.

The pub was a bit more upscale and somewhat larger than most other Irish pubs I'd frequented so far, yet it still had that warm, welcoming vibe that I'd experienced at all the pubs I'd been to in Ireland so far. When we arrived, a fair-haired man behind the bar waved at Cormac and found us a lovely table near the stone fireplace and a lot of interesting framed Irish posters on the wall, and Cormac pulled my chair out for me and put his hand gently on my back while talking to the fair-haired man like old friends.

It seemed as though Cormac was going to pull out his aunt Niamh's chair, too, but Garrett was already on the other side of the table following Cormac's suit by pulling out hers. As everyone got settled and Garrett finished up talking to his friend who worked at the pub, an old sign made of a mirror caught my eye that read "Maloney & O'Toole – Galway Bay Distillery, Est 1824 – and thought instantly of Declan, Declan Maloney – and how his grandmother lived near Galway! Could it be the same Maloney family?"

"Oh!" Cormac said as his friend looked like he was about to go back to his restaurant duties. "Mícheál, you have met everyone here but this lovely lady why we are all here celebrating – this is Kayla O'Brien, the adventurist American journalist who now lives in Ireland and writes for the Munster Post – in whose interview with the great Douglas O'Donnell will be published." I stood up again to shake Mícheál's hand.

"Kayla, great to make your acquaintance," he said, his Irish accent rather thick and seemingly different from Cormac's and Niamh's. "O'Brien, you say? Sounds Irish to me." There was something about him that reminded me of a younger Grady, too.

"Yes – Irish American – Irish in Spirit," I replied and got

chuckles all around. I sat back down then, along with Cormac, and Mícheál asked us what he could bring us back to drink.

"They are famous for their cider, Kayla," Cormac said.

"Oh, sounds good!"

"Ok, two ciders for Kayla and me," Cormac replied for the both of us.

"Just sparkling water for me," Niamh said.

"And for you, Garrett?" Cormac asked.

"I'll try the cider, sounds great."

"Straight away," Mícheál said and walked back to the bar area.

"Is he the owner?" I asked Cormac.

"Yes, indeed – and we've been friends since college and haven't seen him since I've been stationed up in Belfast. It's great to connect with him again."

"I took Meg and Lucas here two weeks ago, to celebrate moving into their new place – and so wonderful to see Mícheál doing so well with the place. And Kayla, they are practically your neighbors now!" Niamh said.

Cormac raised an eyebrow and looked at me with interest.

"Oh yes! I bumped into Megan and Lucas at the Bean &

Plover a couple of weeks ago. They decided on the house in Ballina. It's close to where Grady lives," I said, looking at Niamh, which was much more calming than looking back at Cormac.

"They did indeed! They mentioned they saw you at the Bean, they said they were looking forward to getting together with you again, invite you over," Niamh added.

"Excellent," Cormac said. "Now I have yet another reason to come visit here more often."

I looked at him and smiled, feeling a confused attraction mixed with trepidation.

I was thankful when it was Garrett who decided to steer the conversation.

"So Kayla, it's great to hear the Munster Post will publish your interview with Douglas O'Donnell! I personally think it will be hard to convince Unionists in Northern Ireland to be behind a vote for Unification."

"I wonder too, Garrett," Niamh added. "Though I think it's been a long time coming."

"What are your views, Kayla? It would be interesting to get your perspective, having moved to Ireland from the States."

"I'm still learning a lot about it myself," I started. "But I see how with Brexit looming, there is – real concern about what happens when the Irish Republic stays a part of the EU, and Northern Ireland leaves it, and the problems that creates at the border, and with the Good Friday agreement…"

"Exactly, Kayla," Cormac said.

"Yes, good points – though we don't know exactly how Brexit will unfold yet – perhaps a trade agreement will be reached," Garrett said.

Niamh looked at me then, like she was interested in how I would respond. "And…and listening to Douglas reinforced to me how pressing this is… and the question has, it seems to me, been in the hearts and the minds of the Irish people for a long time."

"I agree, Kayla," Niamh said.

The drinks arrived, and we ordered our meals. I took a few sips of the delicious cider after we all toasted "*Slainte.*" I pondered how these two aspects of my life were merging – my connections with the spiritual Celtic Light group and my work as a journalist – and somehow feeling it would all soon collide with the mystery of Cailin, too.

A lively conversation ensued, with Cormac and Niamh very sure that Douglas was right – that Irish reunification was coming – and Garrett skeptical but not completely ruling it out.

"How are you liking Mícheál's favorite cider?" Cormac

asked me after a waitress brought out all of our meals. Mícheál was attending other pub business elsewhere.

"It's so good. I can't remember trying a cider I liked so well." I preferred it to beer – even Guinness, I thought.

The conversation moved to Garrett's current research and newer book about the tombs in the area, including the fascinating Lough Gur Wedge Tomb, also referred to as Giant's Grave.

"This is a fascinating area. In addition to Giant's Grave and, of course, the Grange Stone Circle, where we visited today, I am fascinated by the stone forts of Knockadoon on the top of the hill and the castle ruins nearby," Garrett said.

"There's a lot to see around here! I'm finding it all fascinating," I said.

"Excellent, Kayla – the tomb is very fascinating. We must make a point to go with the group," Niamh added. "There is a lot to fit in in this area in just one afternoon."

We all talked more about the area and Garrett's fascinating descriptions of the sites of archeological interest, and Garrett promised to keep us all posted on when his book would be released. We didn't come back around to discussing Irish Reunification or Douglas O'Donnell, but I sensed in the air it was still fresh on everyone's minds, altering the mood.

Soon enough, it was time for Niamh to take Garrett to catch his train, and as I hugged Niamh goodbye, she said quietly to me, "I think your friend Declan will have more answers for you."

"Thank you so much," I replied quietly, avoiding the curious look Cormac was giving us, and to my surprise, Garrett also gave me a hug. "So great to meet you, Kayla."

Now, it was just Cormac and I left from the group.

"Would you like anything else?" he asked. I was almost done with the fish and chips I ordered and had finished off the delicious cider.

"Hmm…I think I'm good. Something hot to drink, perhaps?"

"Oh, great idea! The Irish coffees here are great, Mícheál, back in the day, he used to make the famous Shannon Airport ones when he worked there."

"Sounds good, thank you," I felt like I didn't really need more alcohol, but I was feeling a bit chilled and admittedly antsy being alone with Cormac now, especially with his new way of interacting with me this afternoon and evening, and felt not entirely opposed to some liquid courage.

Cormac waved the waitress down, who had just come around to check on a nearby table, and ordered two Irish Coffees.

"So Kayla, I really appreciate you interviewing Douglas O'Donnell and writing up such a great interview."

"Oh, of course! I'm really fascinated by the subject. I hope it is received well – we will find out Friday," I said lightly.

"Ah – I expect it will have some varied reactions – indeed many positive. And you will become a much better-known columnist yourself, Kayla."

I felt a little self-conscious then and felt my cheeks starting to become flushed, and all I could think to say was "Thank you," and held Cormac's gaze for a few seconds before looking away.

"So Kayla, you told us some of your interesting thoughts on Reunification earlier, but I want to ask, how do you really feel about it? After talking to Douglas, did you feel inspired by the vision of a Reunified Ireland?"

I thought I saw in the expression on his face the same one he had earlier when we were in Niamh's backyard, and he told me he had an important subject he wanted to talk to me about. But I didn't hesitate in my answer. "It seems like it's so tied into the long-term Irish struggle – since Ireland got independence from England after the War of Independence, even before that – with strong feelings on both sides. But yes, I do support it – I just have this feeling that Douglas is probably right. It will happen. I'm just not sure when."

"Great, Kayla! I had a feeling you would be supportive, even inspired."

At that moment, the waitress came back with our Irish Coffees, and I took a big sip of the sweet and strong delicious mix of coffee, rich cream, sugar, and whiskey – the sweet sting a welcome sensation for the mix of fascination and nervousness I felt for what Cormac was about to tell me.

"So Kayla, you think Unification may take longer than Douglas is predicting by 2027?"

I thought about this for a few moments. "Honestly, I'm not entirely sure. I think it depends on what happens with Brexit and how the final Brexit deal will affect the border between Northern Ireland and the Irish Republic."

"What if I were to tell you, Kayla, there is a way to start working for Irish Reunification now, that what we do even before Brexit will help pave the way?"

"Really?"

"Kayla, I want to offer you an opportunity to help us."

So this is what Cormac had wanted to tell me. They somehow wanted to recruit me for the cause. I took a couple more sips of Irish coffee. "Wow, is this to help make the prospect of a United Ireland more likely? What are you looking for, exactly?"

"We are looking for a few more people to help promote the Sinn Féin party – ideally, you would come to work with me, and Douglas, to do this. Now, I realize you wouldn't want to entirely give up your journalism…"

"Yes – well, as a journalist, can I help in a way? Like with the interview of Douglas O'Donnell?"

"Yes – but I would like to invite you to take an even stronger role. Are you familiar with Gerry Adams?"

"I have… until last year, he led Sinn Féin , right?"

"Yes, and this October, he will be called as a defense witness for a legal action in the case of the killing of Jean McConville during the Troubles."

"I did read something about this – she was a widow who was abducted by the IRA in the 70s, left behind a lot of children?"

"That's right – I expect him to be cleared of any legal problems and association with the murder, but we also expect that it will stir up memories of The Troubles, and some people will think of the IRA when they think of Sinn Féin again."

"Ah."

"So we are planning to ramp up efforts to promote 'today's Sinn Féin' party, give it a more positive image, and both Douglas and I agree that you, with your excellent writing skills and what we think, is the ability to connect with younger voters in their 20s and 30s – and 40s as well – I would like to ask if you would like to join us."

I was flattered that they wanted to offer this opportunity to me. At the same time, even though it sounded very interesting, my gut feelings were warning me it would change my life in a way that would not be right for me at this time…

"So what would I be doing, exactly? To write to appeal to these potential voters?"

"You would be writing recruitment newsletters, distributing pamphlets in the same neighborhood where I first introduced you to Douglas, near the peace walls and the O'Connor Hospital.

A strange, strong déjà vu sensation came over me then, and I felt a bit shaky, seemingly out of nowhere, yet somehow the area he mentioned felt eerily familiar, not just from the brief time we spent there…

Another sip of Irish coffee, and I bluntly brought up what I felt was "the Elephant in the Room."

"Thank you for thinking of me for this – and I feel like I'd like to help somehow – but would I be able to do this and still write for the Munster Post? And stay in Killaloe?"

"Perhaps there is a way, but we would need you up in Belfast a good majority of the time. Though since the Munster Post is publishing your interview, perhaps they would be open to you writing more articles related to Irish Nationalism and Reunification?"

I was feeling quite overwhelmed, like large ocean waves were pushing my ship in one direction, yet my destination – even my destiny – seemed to be in another.

"Perhaps."

"Yet there is something else too, Kayla. Douglas and two of his colleagues are looking to expand the newsletters – to turn it into a weekly paper – so we would very much like that to be an opportunity for you."

The waves pushing my boat were getting only bigger, prompting me to go a way that I felt a little intrigued to explore – but very treacherous as well, and not where I thought I'd be headed at all…

"Cormac, thank you – and Douglas – for wanting me to be part of this – and believing in my ability to help you with the cause. I…I am not sure if I can contribute this much – there are things in my life I am figuring out now, right in Killaloe – and I am not sure if I'm ready to look to moving on from the Munster or rocking the boat there…"

"Kayla, please take a little time to think about it then. And you wouldn't necessarily have to leave the Munster Post, perhaps you could even combine them somehow. These things in Killaloe you are figuring out – is this related to what you were talking to Niamh about back at the house?"

"Yes. Has to do with an Irish relative I recently discovered I had."

"I'd love to hear more about this sometime, too, Kayla, if you wish. May I say one other thing to leave you with as you think about it?"

"Sure…what is it?"

"I would very much – like you to be up in Belfast for a chance to spend more time with you," Cormac unexpectedly took my hand then, but perhaps not as unexpectedly as I had kept telling myself, and I felt a wave crashing inside, a pull and a tug of desire, but not the pull of my heart that I felt for another, and it felt like my boat had capsized.

I looked into Cormac's eyes briefly then, feeling like it was time to pull my hand away, but completely overwhelmed with the moment. Then, an entirely new thought came to me that added to my nerves.

"Cormac…what about me being an American? Do you think

I would be perceived as butting in – overstepping the bounds of interfering with Irish politics?"

"Yes, this could be – Douglas and I discussed that too, actually. But Kayla, I would protect you." I averted my eyes away from his intense gaze and wanted to pull my hand away then, but I felt so stunned it wouldn't move. Then, a few moments later, I was saved from the situation by Mícheál coming back to our table. This prompted Cormac to give my hand an affectionate squeeze and release it to a curious glance from Mícheál. Cormac then talked to Mícheál about how it was great to be in the South again and visit Niamh – though so many interesting and important developments in Belfast and the North, and how it was great he could introduce him to me. When we stood up and walked with Mícheál to the bar area, I felt a little off balance and giddy, the cider followed by the Irish coffee making me more tipsy than I realized, and I felt completely flattered by Cormac's attention and that he was interested in me too, but still hearing my inner voice tell me that it wasn't right to explore more than friends with him, when my heart was with another…

"Can I get you both another drink?" Mícheál asked.

"No, thank you but I should be getting back," I failed to suppress a yawn then, which at the moment struck me as funny. "It's been a long day."

"Kayla's right. I should really be getting back to Aunt

Niamh's for the night, too. Want to be up for visiting with her more before I head back up to Belfast tomorrow in the early afternoon. So great to see you, Mícheál." The two men gave each other a "man-to-man" hug and pat on each other's backs, and Mícheál gave me a hug too and told me that it was great to meet me, and gave Cormac a look like he approved, which made my face flush a little, feeling both flattered and confused.

Mícheál then called our cabs for us, and Cormac and I waited outside on the lighted patio for just a few minutes. The sun was setting a little earlier, a little short of 10 PM now – and something about this almost twilight seemed especially mysterious.

My cab arrived first, and Cormac hugged me goodnight. Right before he pulled away, he whispered in my ear, "Please have a serious thought about my offer, Kayla – I think being in Belfast would suit you," and brushed his lips lightly on my cheek.

"I will think about it…thank you, Cormac. Safe travels," and Cormac opened the cab door for me, I got in and then was off to my Killaloe home.

PART III

CHAPTER XV

The water in the bay is choppy and restless, invoking Fionn's mood as he walked by my side with some distance between us.

"It's too late," he says quietly.

I want to shout, "It can't be! It is all a misunderstanding. Why can't you believe me!?" But the words catch in my throat, and I catch a glimpse of the ferry from the islands, panic setting in.

Tears are rolling down my cheeks now. "Why won't you believe me, Fionn? I love you."

"Too much was rushed - you were too foolish. I've lost trust. I...a part of me still loves you. And – even though I must leave you now – somehow, we will be reunited. I foresee, if not in this lifetime, sometime in the future, what has been done will be righted, and our hearts will find our way back together again."

"Why not now? If there is still some love between us to be saved?"

The red and blue ferry landed at the dock, the one that would be carrying my love away from me.

He pulled me with one strong arm to his shoulder and placed a gentle kiss on top of my head. For a brief moment, I hoped.

"I'm leaving – I barely came out alive, and I need to have a fresh start, to connect to all the good of my Irish roots. I just was not leveled with enough – I can't be certain it is different this time."

He stepped onto the boat. Was it really going to end this way?

"Slán, a ghrá until we meet again."

I watch the boat start to depart, and I almost jump into the cold, choppy water – wanting it to transport me to when Fionn and I can be together again – alive or not. Instead, I lean over the ledge and wave to him as the boat becomes more and more distant, my face getting wetter and wetter with salty tears.

I wake up suddenly, crying into my pillow.

Very early in the morning, the sun barely peaking over the horizon, the first thing I did when I had gathered my emotions enough was to write down the phrase in Irish I had heard in my dream.

"Slán a graw…gra… ghrá?"

I think I knew already, but to be sure translated it on my phone – words I had heard in the beginning of studying the language.

"Goodbye, my love."

Back at the Limerick offices of the Munster Post for a meeting, I was in a giddy daze from the publicity the paper was receiving after the interview with Douglas O'Donnell was published barely a few days ago.

It was a Tuesday afternoon, and Liam had called a special meeting to discuss the next issue and how he wanted to expand on the anniversary of the Irish Independence theme.

Douglas O'Donnell's interview was not printed in my usual local happenings section but in the front page section, on the very second page!

Is a Vote on Irish Reunification Closer than We Think?

An Interview with Douglas O'Donnell

By Kayla O'Brien

When I had made my way to the Bean & Plover Friday morning, for the first time ever, I heard people discussing one of my articles – and Tori, the barista that I seemed to be becoming more and more friendly with, glanced at my full name on my credit card before saying, "My goodness, Kayla! Your interview is quite the topic of conversation here at the Plover this morning! I can't wait to read it after my shift."

Most of what I heard being discussed at the Plover while I sipped on my morning latte, at a table I chose near the ordering counter to admittedly hear as much as I could from the patrons, was quite positive: "I knew this was coming all along," "Well, it only makes sense with Brexit looming," with only one skeptical comment and one negative, though even the negative one had a kernel of positive within it: "Well done interview, but Douglas O'Donnell is naïve if he thinks those Unionists in Ulster are ever going to go for it – no matter how much a debacle Brexit is."

And it seemed like all weekend, as I tried to make more progress on learning more about the Sisterhood of Brigid, I kept getting calls about the Douglas O'Donnell interview – including from Megan, who congratulated me and said it was being talked about on her side of the river in Bellina too – and from Grady, who I learned for the first time was very pro-Unification, which surprised me a little but wasn't altogether sure why.

And here at the Munster Post meeting today, Aiden made a point to congratulate me on writing such a thought-provoking interview, and most of the staff joined in to congratulate me.

I had felt since Cormac made me the offer to work with Douglas and him for the Unification cause up in Belfast, I would turn them down, but the praises and support from Liam, Aiden, and the staff were making me feel even more certain that I needed to prioritize my work with the Munster Post. And just as I was thinking about this, but how I could also stay on good terms with Cormac – and even find a way to still help them to a lesser degree with the cause – Aiden leaned in closer to my ear and quietly told me,

"Kayla, I wouldn't be surprised if a promotion is coming – you really nailed this one. Impressive for a Yankee," which made me giggle softly as Liam was making some announcements for the next edition, but also filled me with a new confidence and happiness.

Refreshments were provided after the meeting had adjourned, and as I was chatting with Aiden and a couple of other reporters, Liam came up to us.

"So Kayla – it turns out your article got in the hands of a reporter at RTE News – I just got a message that they want to get in touch with Douglas O'Donnell for a television interview!"

"Wow! That's amazing."

"I think this calls for a toast," Aiden said, who was in a very lively, almost mischievous mood. "Here's to Kayla O'Brien and furthering the cause of a United Ireland!"

We all clinked our cups then, and I felt high with how taking a chance on interviewing Douglas O'Donnell had turned out so well.

As the conversation started to turn to other things, I found my mind starting to wander, and I stepped away, grabbed a new sparkling water, and went to look out the window onto an industrial street in Limerick. My career was going better in Ireland than I'd ever imagined, especially this soon, and I had two Irish men interested in me when I had been going through a spell of singlehood before coming to Ireland after my last relationship had ended. Yet there was still that empty space in my heart of the distance from Declan and the mystery of my connection to Cailin always with me.

I looked at my phone absent-mindedly then, and to my surprise, I had a voicemail. My heart started beating faster when I saw who it was from.

"Kayla, this is Declan. It has been going great in Madrid, but it turns out I'm at the airport now and flying back to Ireland – and then straight to Galway. My grandmother is not well, and I need to be back with the family. I wanted to let you know... I'd be back, hope to see you in not too much longer."

Declan was coming back to Ireland! I felt a rush of being so pleased he was coming back, and a sadness at his news, and a little guilty for feeling happy about his return under those circumstances. I said a silent prayer then that his grandmother would be ok and he would get to see her soon.

The meeting was starting to wind down, and I grabbed my coat and thanked Liam again and said bye to Aiden, who said he'd be contacting me soon about my next assignment.

As I stepped out the door to the moody Irish sky, streaks of gray and white clouds mixed with spots of sunshine, I took a deep breath and resolved to contact Cormac that afternoon to turn down his offer – and hoped the news of RTE wanting to interview Douglas on TV would make him happy and soften any disappointment. I could help them with the Irish Reunification cause in another way and wanted to – but I belonged in Killaloe, staying with the paper and in my heart with Declan.

CHAPTER XVI

Preoccupied with thinking about Declan returning from Spain, I was grateful for the distraction but, at the same time, having trouble focusing on what Niamh was saying as I drove back to Killaloe and took her call on speaker phone. It felt like suddenly everything was being speeded up – my career at the paper, my seeing Declan soon, and letting Cormac down (I wondered if Niamh knew anything about Cormac's offer?) And finding the truth about Cailin's past – and why she was visiting me from beyond– which I felt I had to know, whether I wanted to or not.

I pulled over when I reached the waterfront next to Flanagan's on the Lake restaurant so I could talk to Niamh without the distraction of driving and in a more calming setting.

"So Thomas knew a little more about the Sisterhood of Brigid, but the most interesting part is he was able to get in touch with Alannah, the granddaughter of Aibreann Addis, who founded the order, and Alannah had the most revealing information of all!"

"Thank you so much, Niamh," I walked close by to the outside dining area at Flannagan's and toward the Shannon River. "What does she know?"

"Apparently, they used to do a ritual, and its purpose was to find their way to a loved one they wanted to be with again – whether living or passed on – and no matter how long it took," Niamh said. "In other words, it was a way to bypass time really, to ensure the love would endure despite time."

A strange sensation came over me, almost feeling like déjà vu, and I remembered what the tall, dark-haired man – Fionn – said in my dream.

"Niamh!" I let my thoughts pour out of me. "I dreamed that Fionn told Cailin this. I was seeing through Cailin's eyes, but I'm sure this was Cailin – and I'm sure… at least the essence of it! Really happened. He told her he must leave her then, but somehow they would be reunited, if not in this lifetime, sometime in the future! And what was done will be put right – and their spirits would find their ways back together again!"

"Ah. Yes, Kayla, I've felt for a time now that you and Cailin are truly connected. She must have taken part in that ritual at the Sisterhood of Brigid."

"Niamh, do you think Fionn led her to do this – I think he must have told her this before she joined the Sisterhood! In my dream, it felt like the final parting – they were at the port of Rosaveel, I believe, and he waved goodbye as he sailed away – I think toward one of the Aran Islands."

"I think you are absolutely right. When Cailin learned of the ritual, she must have known she must do it, after what Fionn had told her."

"Niamh – Declan, his grandmother lives in Rosaveel, and she grew up on one of the Aran Islands, on Inis Meain – and he is coming back. Declan called me to let me know he's coming back to see his grandmother, who is ill. He's…he's always reminded me of this man in my dreams…well, Fionn. Do you think there is really a connection here?"

Niamh sighed, and it flashed through my mind briefly if she then knew Cormac would be disappointed. But when she spoke, her voice was warm and wise. "Yes, Kayla. And I think in your heart you already know there is."

CHAPTER XVII

It felt both eerie and strangely familiar to be walking next to Galway Bay in the port town of Rossaveel, walking along the pathway on my way to meet Declan.

The night before, Declan had called just after 8 PM, and right away I heard the distress in his voice. He said his grandmother refused to go to the hospital, though she had her old family physician visit there, who told Declan that currently she was stable. But that,

"She told me something pretty shocking – I'm having some trouble processing it. Can you come to meet me at Rossaveel if it's not too much to ask?"

"Of course! Are you ok, Declan?"

"I… will be, I think. I just have a sense you will understand and even offer me some insight. And it will help to confide in a friend outside of the family. And…"

"Yes, of course. I'll leave early tomorrow morning and meet you."

"Thank you. And Kayla?"

"Yes?"

"It will be really good to see you."

The waterfront park and Rossaveel seemed both similar and

a little different than it had in my dream. A few of the boats looked more modern, but the whole feel of the place seemed about the same. I mused that I hadn't – or hadn't through Cailin's eyes – looked around that much in my dream, consumed with Fionn, the movement of the water, my (her?) emotions, and watching the boat – which was indeed a bit different than the large ferry passengers that were lining up to take passengers to one of the islands – to take Fionn away…forever?

Declan said to meet him at the Two Friars Restaurant, a seafood restaurant across the street from Galway Bay that had great outdoor seating where we could talk privately. I had been following the map directions from my phone but also saw the sign above three other similar signs, all in Irish, that showed the restaurant's image of a banner with two friars and 'The Two Friars Restaurant,' in English pointing in the same direction as I was walking.

I arrived before Declan, and for a brief moment, I remembered how I had waited a while for Cormac at the Barge restaurant in Belfast, it nagging at me that I had been putting off telling Cormac I would not be taking him up on his offer.

I didn't have to wait for long, Declan arriving about ten minutes later, walking out the door to the patio, and as he came toward me, I caught my breath – he looked even more handsome, with a subtle tan now and his black hair longer and very ruffled, though when he arrived at my table saw the wrinkles in his shirt and the dark circles under his eyes.

I stood up to greet him, and he encircled me in a warm hug, like he also needed comfort and affection himself.

"Welcome back," I said softly, and he squeezed me a little tighter for a few moments before we sat down.

"It's good to be back and see you again, Kayla."

The waiter came straight away, and Declan ordered an Irish coffee. He asked me if I wanted one, and I nodded.

"Their Irish coffees are strong here – need something a bit stronger than a Guinness today," he said in his sheepish way, yet he looked haunted and unsteady. What had he just found out?

"I'm here to listen. When you're ready," I added.

"I am in… a few moments. I think I need some of that whiskey to hit me first," the waiter came back with the Irish coffees, and Declan ordered some oysters and potato fritters.

He turned the conversation to me then. "How are you doing, Kayla?"

"I'm well – the interview with Douglas O'Donnell was in Friday's edition, and it went over really well. People are really interested!"

"I bet they are," Declan took another drink. "That's fantastic, Kayla! I come from a very pro-Republic family it turns out. Always thought reunification was going to be Ireland's destiny, eventually." Declan expressing this gave me a warm feeling inside.

"How was Spain? I've been so busy and preoccupied with other things, I haven't looked up about how the concerts have been going in the last few days."

"That was all going splendidly – we have the next five concerts lined up, and they will also have two concerts in Portugal next month."

"Wow, that's great!" I felt a little worried Declan might be going back there for a longer stretch next time but was happy for the band. Interestingly, Declan calmed me right away.

"I had to come back and see my grandmother – but as it was, I left them in a good spot, so not sure they'll need me back right away."

"Well, at least that gives you more time with your grandmother." I hoped Declan would be back for a while. "How is she doing today?"

"A little better, she's sleeping less, and talking a little more…she actually kept asking me about who I was meeting, and when I told her it was you, she was very curious…"

"Really? Well, I'm really glad she was better today."

The food came, and Declan and I both helped ourselves first to a fritter.

"Kayla, I'm just going to come out and say it – my grandmother told me something that…I may not be who…exactly who I thought I was."

A strange sensation came over me that this was somehow fitting into the puzzle I was trying to solve – and making Declan all the more a part of it…

"Oh dear, what did she say?"

"That I, my grandfather, may not be who I thought he was – that it's possible my grandfather was that man she loved, the letter I told you about – and not my grandfather that I have always known."

"Your grandfather might be Fionn?!"

Declan gave me a startled look. "Why yes, you remembered his name! My whole family tree could be different now. But she doesn't know for certain, and it wouldn't have been any of my father's younger siblings…but my father could be Fionn's son."

I could hardly believe this was happening and knew I would not – could not – hold back what had been happening to my life from Declan any longer.

"Declan – I'm so sorry you just learned this under these

circumstances. Not to lay even more on you – but I am almost certain that other woman – the one that your grandmother said Fionn never got over…"

"Yes?" Declan sounded puzzled and curious, a haunted look in his eyes.

"She was Cailin, my great grand-aunt."

We talked a long time then, and it poured out of me about my more recent dreams, including the one I had most recently at the port of Rossaveel, and that even though Fionn never got over her, he could never quite forgive her either, and from all I'd pieced together, I still wasn't quite sure from what.

"It was during the war, right?" Declan asked me, now on his second Irish coffee, and even though I'd never been around Declan when he'd had more than one Guinness, I could see why he was drinking more tonight. How would I feel if I found out my biological grandparent was someone different than I'd known all my life? I never knew about Cailin until I came to Ireland, as amazing and unreal as her discovery was and my uncanny connection to her. Yet, nonetheless, knowing of her helped fill in the puzzle of my life, not undid it.

"Yes, that's right, when I was visiting with Grady – when he first told me about my relation then – he showed me a photograph that he said was taken by a man she was involved with who he thought had been in the IRA. Now I know that man must have been Fionn."

The dream I had at Carrickfergus castle, that that photo so reminded me of, flashed in my mind.

"Declan, in one of my dreams – I think I mentioned it to you a while back, at Carrickfergus castle – the man in that dream… Fionn told me to hurry to him, that every minute counted in freeing Ireland!"

"Wow. Kayla – so strange you could actually be dreaming of the past like that."

"There was this tension in that dream, a guilt I was feeling…"

"I have to admit, Kayla – before, I would have had trouble believing all this."

"I have trouble believing it too at times, but it seems so far to all add up. When I dreamed of Fionn saying goodbye to Cailin at Rossaveel harbor before he sailed away, he said that if it couldn't be in this lifetime, one way or another, they would find their way to forgiveness – and back to each other. And then Niamh found out Cailin went on to do some kind of ritual when she went to the Sisterhood to make time not a barrier in finding their way back together again."

Declan and I met eyes then, and he seemed incredulous, and yet a glimmer of understanding where I already had gathered this could be going…

"You just said in your dream…he was taking a ferry to one of the islands?"

"Yes – I – Cailin was so sad. He must have been going to one of the Aryan islands – it felt like she wasn't going to see him again…"

"Kayla, my grandparents – they didn't move to Rossaveel until my father was almost eighteen. They lived there on the islands, on Inis Meain."

Chills went through me, and just for a split second, I saw the image from my dream of Fionn on the edge of the ferry, looking back toward me, his long black hair blowing in the breeze.

"This is just a lot for me to absorb right now," Declan said, looking toward the direction of the bay.

"I understand! It is for me, too. I'm sorry you just received that news from your grandmother."

"My sister was there too. She thinks it might be my grandmother's mind, fantasizing since she hasn't been well…"

"Oh, my goodness. What do you think?"

"My grandmother has held secrets – but she's very direct and honest when it comes to it. Well, I should be getting back," Declan said.

"Do you want to walk part way together?" I asked, wanting to be with him some more, try to soothe him more…

"No…Kayla, thank you for meeting me, and confiding in me this incredible experience you've had – I think I just need to be alone for a few moments with my own thoughts. We didn't finish our appetizers either, why don't you stay and enjoy them and the view." He stood up then and kissed me lightly on the cheek.

"I understand. Please let me know if I can do anything to help," I felt uncertain at that moment where I stood with him, but his touch still held affection.

"Thank you, Kayla. I'll keep you posted."

The next morning, after grabbing a latte to go at the Bean & Plover, I walked to St. Flannan's Cathedral, feeling drawn there – for some solace, feeling a little uncertain at that point what would happen with Declan. I had faith that after he processed everything, he would still want me in his life, but I couldn't help letting my insecurities creep in. And somehow, I thought being in the presence of the cathedral would give me courage and strength (spiritual strength seemed to be what I needed) to finally call Cormac and let him know I couldn't come up to Belfast and dedicate myself as much as they wanted me to their cause.

I arrived at the cathedral's entrance and called Cormac. It rang several times, and as I contemplated whether I should leave a message or not to deliver my news, he picked up.

"Hello, Cormac speaking."

"Cormac, hello! This is Kayla."

"Well, hello," Cormac said. "Good to hear your voice again. How are you?"

"I'm…I'm doing ok. I'm sorry it's taken me some time to get back to you."

"No problem at all. You've been giving my offer some serious thought, then?"

"I have thought about it. I really appreciate the offer, but I am going to have to decline at this time. I feel like I belong in Killaloe, and with more time to dedicate to the Post and this part of Ireland, my community."

"I see. I think you would have found the work – and life – fulfilling here too."

"I would still like to help with the cause in other ways. I have good news, RTE wants to interview Douglas O'Donnell after reading the interview in the Munter Post!"

"Very good news – I admit I just found out and was going to call you soon. They contacted Douglas, and he told me. He also told me to say 'hello' to you, how grateful he is to you, and he hoped you'd come to work with us…"

I felt a tinge of guilt and feeling bad that I was disappointing not only Cormac but Douglas, but I was still firm that I was making the right decision.

"I'm sorry to disappoint Douglas – disappoint both of you," I said. "I'm happy to help as I can, from my 'neck of the woods,' so to speak."

"I understand. You feel you have a different calling now."

"Yes! Thank you, Cormac, for understanding."

"I'm very busy, as you know. I would, however, still like to see you when I can, get to know you better."

I felt a flush of excitement then, but it felt strange – like it was detached from my spirit – my destiny – like it belonged to a different me.

"Cormac, you are a great guy and I have enjoyed your company and knowing you very much – and appreciate collaborating with you to get Douglas' vision out," I decided all I could do at that point was come out and say it. "Cormac, I… I have feelings for another."

"Ah. I see. Is it serious now?" His voice was sounding more detached, business-like now.

"Honestly…I'm not sure. I thought it was going in that direction. He's part…of what I've been seeing Niamh about – he's involved in this search to find out more about my Irish relative Cailin, and – she has something to do with that strange experience I had when we were at Carrickfergus Castle."

"Really?" Cormac laughed softly, but it wasn't mocking, more like awed and a bit dumbfounded. "That sounds right up Niamh's alley."

I laughed then. "Yes…"

"Well, Kayla, sounds like you have a lot of – well, I'll just say soul-searching to do, whether that sounds like it implies a double meaning or not." I felt impressed with his insight and humor. "I do actually have to finish some work for the embassy now, but thanks for letting me know."

"You're welcome. Thanks again for your offer, and I do appreciate it even if it doesn't feel like the right thing for me at this time."

"My loss, Kayla. Best of luck to you."

I wandered into St. Flannan's after Cormac hung up, feeling dazed – a mixture of relief, a sadness of saying goodbye, and like I had a fresh start in going toward what felt like was the right path for my future – still as uncertain as that seemed.

I walked past the ancient Romanesque archway and up to the Ogham stone and felt comfort in the energy there. Somehow, it felt that I was much closer to coming to a resolution – of Cailin finally finding some peace as well as some more for me. I thought about Fionn in the dream, playing the lute – that dream had seemed more ancient – but the man had looked and felt like the same man in my other dreams.

I walked up to the pew in between the rows of seats and sat in the front, on the very end of the left row of seats, in front of the beautiful Great Oak screen, with its sun and flower-like carvings, the light streaming through the stained glass windows on the other side.

As much as I felt closer to figuring out the mystery of Cailin's otherworldly presence in my life – in my dreams – there was still so much I didn't know. What did Cailin do that Fionn would not be able to forgive her for, at least in time for them to be together? And if Declan was really Fionn's grandson…and then it suddenly dawned on me. Was Cailin…was Cailin trying to lead me to Declan?

And I supposed it was going to take a while yet to learn more about what happened. And would Declan really believe this – or accept it?

Somewhere in my heart, I felt faith that Declan would not

just run away from it all.

I sat there for a few minutes – almost alone at that time in the chapel except for an older woman I saw sitting further back on the other side of the pew. I closed my eyes and meditated – and for the first time, I prayed to Cailin.

"Cailin – if you can hear me, I hope somehow in my lifetime I can bring you the peace that you so wanted." And then I meditated on the images I saw in my dreams, and then in my mind's eye of the photo Grady showed me of Cailin, which was also the place of my Carrickfergus dream, by the water.

When I opened my eyes, it seemed the sun had come out, and more light was streaming through the beautiful spheres that resembled flowers on the oak screen.

Then, I felt a gentle breeze on the back of my neck.

I felt like peace was to come.

Then, just a moment later, my phone rang. I thought not to answer – but a worried pit suddenly formed in my stomach – and I turned my head, seeing that the older lady was now gone.

Alone in the pew, I answered.

"Hello?"

"Hello, Kayla?"

"Yes?"

"This is Ide. Sean O'Grady's sister."

"Oh yes! How are you? Is everything all right?"

"Oh, Kayla, I am so sorry. Grady passed away last night in his sleep."

CHAPTER XVIII

The next three days were the most trying I had all summer –
it seemed that all my preoccupation with the mystery of Cailin, my
feelings for Declan – all the ups and downs of this amazing summer
in the home of half of my ancestors – should not have consumed me
so. I grieved for Grady – who had been becoming a better and better
friend – a relative I hadn't known I had. He was who I discovered
Cailin through; we had a shared family connection. Ide said he'd
had a stroke and unfortunately passed away soon after. He had some
health issues, high blood pressure, and mysterious headaches as of
late.

"The night before he passed Kayla, he told me how happy
he was to be discovering more about his ancestry and that he had
met you, and you really inspired him in his family research."

A memorial service was being planned for Grady on Inis
Cealtra, and though he had wanted to be cremated, he had asked for
a ceremony near Cailin's grave and his ashes to be scattered in
Lough Derg Lake, right off the island.

So I was still very sad about Grady as I arrived at Declan's
grandmother's house in Rossaveel.

I never realized so many emotions could go through me at
once. Declan had called two days before; I had been invited by

Megan and Lucas to visit them at their new home in Ballina, and I had paused on my way there to look across the Shannon on the edge of the footbridge when Declan called.

"Kayla, this is Declan. Sorry it's taken me a few days to be in touch again."

"That's ok. I know you have so much to sort through – to think about. How are you doing? How is your grandmother?" My heart felt tight.

"She's doing better, actually! Her cancer is regressing – there was finally a turn for the better."

"Oh, Declan! That's wonderful news!" I tried to keep from crying – I had lost Grady, but Declan still had his grandmother.

"Thank you, sweetie."

"That must be such a relief!"

"It is."

After a brief pause, I asked, "How have you been holding up?"

"Better – I feel a lot more grounded than I did."

"I'm glad to hear that."

"Kayla – besides wanting to tell you the good news about my grandmother, there is another reason I called. My grandmother

– she'd like to meet you."

***

So there I was, standing in front of the lovely cottage in Rossaveel, about to meet Declan's grandmother. Declan had said he told her about me, and she kept asking him more and more until he finally told her about the 'fantastic dreams' I'd been having, that I'd discovered Cailin was my Irish great grand aunt and that I thought she was the woman Fionn had never gotten over. Declan's grandmother insisted on meeting me then.

When I knocked on the door, Declan answered and I was happy to see he looked much more rested and in better spirits. The noticeable dark circles under his eyes that I saw last time had faded significantly, and he looked freshly showered and dressed, his slicked hair combed back attractively.

He led me into a tidy living room – the place was just as I imagined an Irish cottage should look like, but even more charming and cozy. Declan's grandmother sat in a pale yellow chair that had a kind of soft-looking light tan fur over the back. The walls were painted a warm yellow, as well as the brick of the fireplace, that I imagined would make the cottage extra-cozy in the winter. The back of the adjacent couch was adorned with a subtle red, green and yellow plaid tartan throw, and several vases with wildflowers in a variety of colors were displayed on the mantel and antique wooden coffee table. Yet the lighting in the room was on the dim side, and the sunlight streaming through the windows gave the welcoming room also a mysterious quality.

I was then pleasantly surprised to hear Declan and his grandmother converse in Irish for a few minutes; the thought also passed through my mind that I hoped he could help me learn the language sometime.

"Mamó – this is Kayla," Declan said.

I noticed the resemblance right away. Her hair was dark like his, though greying now, with several streaks of light silver mixed in with the black, more elegant than faded – and their eyes were similar, but hers a bluer grey.

"Kayla, and indeed it is!" she said. "So good to meet you. You look just like her."

Declan and I looked at each other, and his expression seemed as surprised as I felt, so I knew this was the first time he'd heard this, too.

"Oh! So lovely to meet you too," I walked over and grasped her hand gently, and she kindly took it – she seemed friendly but resigned somehow – like she'd finally found her peace.

"She looks like who, Mamó?"

"Like Cailin," she must have seen the stunned expressions

in both mine and Declan's faces, and she softly chuckled.

"Yes, Declan – she is indeed related to Cailin, and Cailin is indeed the woman Fionn loved – though he told himself he was done with her for a while – but she sadly always had a hold on his heart."

Declan rubbed his forehead then, but I thought I saw in his face a glimmer of acceptance.

"Oh…oh my goodness! I'm – sorry…" I stammered, and this caused Declan's grandmother to chuckle again.

"Mamó…"

"Oh Declan, yes I'm your grandma, but I do have a name too – Kayla, I'm Deidre," and she stood up slowly. Then, with the aid of her walker, Declan rushed to her side, and she shooed him off a little.

"I'm so happy to meet you, Deidre. Thank you for letting me know that Cailin was the woman in Fionn's life. It's good to learn more about my family history – Cailin ended up marrying Neil O'Grady, that is how I found out about her through Neil's great-grandson, Sean O'Grady. But from what I've learned, she never got over Fionn either."

"Oh yes – I'm sure that's true," Deidre said. "And I have gathered it's more than just family history you're piecing together, right?"

I moved through the sadness I had been feeling when thinking about Grady again to an amazement at what Deidre had just asked.

"Why, yes." I looked at Declan, wondering how much he had told her – but could tell he was puzzled too, there was a lot he still didn't know.

"Follow me, you two," Deidre said as she slowly walked with the aid of her walker to a neighboring room. I noticed she had a nice, two-piece royal blue dress on – she was quite old and, at the same time, very elegant and dignified. I also noticed the beautiful Celtic cross necklace in a glittery copper color she wore.

Declan and I followed her into the room, and she opened up a desk drawer, the second from the bottom left, and pulled out an old, faded, silver-colored envelope that looked like it belonged to what was once nice stationery, and handed it to me.

"I've had this letter for a long time now, and I often wondered why I even kept it. It's from her to him – and just why Fionn left it here I never quite understood. He left me soon after he read it."

Deidre must have seen my expression as she said, "Oh – don't feel bad – I did eventually move on and had many happy years married to Ian Moloney. "He," (she looked at Declan then) "was the true man, the true head of this family, no matter what my heart thought it knew at the time. I think this will answer some of the questions you are still looking for."

She handed it to me, and I looked at Declan and he nodded, and I was grateful when he came to stand with me, to come read it with me.

And what completely caught me off guard was the photograph that almost fell out in between the folded-up letter.

There she was, looking so much like in the photo I saw of her at Carrickfergus – and she was standing with Fionn, who had some resemblance to Declan for sure, but the lines of his face a bit more angular, his chin longer – but in the photo, even though it was black and white, I saw the similarity of the shape and intensity of the eyes.

"Wow, she really does look like you," Declan said to me softly.

Dear Fionn,

I hope you will find it in your heart to read this and that it will finally have you believe, or at least start to believe, that I sincerely never betrayed you or carelessly put you in danger.

When you saw me talking to the British soldier, I was

working undercover for the IRB, trying to obtain information so their offense could be thwarted. The reason I was late to meet you at the castle was not because I was trying to delay you – I regret every day that you may have been put in danger and had to flee – but I had to make sure they did not suspect I was undercover for the IRB and had to cover my tracks.

I've spent the last year doing much soul-searching, and as much as I will always love you, I realized I should set you free. I have been seeing someone who has recently proposed, and though I have not quite answered him – as I guess my heart, ever so much as it has healed, is still holding out hope that I will be reunited with you again.

Do you remember when we visited the fort, when I first met your mother afterward in Killaloe? I always felt connected to you there… and I'll just say that in my time away from you, my spiritual sisters and guides lead my heart there once again. And it was there that I saw that you were right, that if not in this lifetime, somehow our hearts will find a way to each other again.

And now that you are safe and Ireland is free – it is truly only the beginning for our blessed country, blessed Éireann .

Yours always,

Cailin

The fort…Cailin must have done the ritual at Bael Boru! She even mentioned Killaloe. Feeling unsteady, like I was falling as the mysteries were falling into place, Declan steadied me by putting his arm around my shoulder. I looked at Deidre then, who had a mystery in her smile as she looked at us, and she said, "Now I know why I held onto it all these years."

I then handed Declan the letter with the photo, and I looked into his eyes and felt like I'd truly come home.

CHAPTER XIX

Declan and I walked together hand in hand after the sun had just set, having come from the pub after an evening of sailing in Dromineer at Lough Derg.

"Sailing with you, enjoying the music tonight at the pub – it's all so great, but just being with you, enjoying our time, makes me feel all right again," Declan said as he gave my hand a gentle squeeze.

"I feel the same. And you know – I've been thinking, no matter who your grandfather – biological grandfather was, Ian Maloney will always be your grandfather too. You might just have two grandfathers – but Ian is the one that was with you as you were growing up, so he's really…"

"Thank you, Kayla. I understand – it's hard to know. Perhaps there is a test…to know… and then do I really want to know? It's peculiar how I look like both of them – Fionn and Ian – in different ways. Whereas you," he gave my hand another squeeze, a deeper squeeze this time, "Really do look like her. No mistaking the relation there." He led me to the edge of the lake, and it being early September, it had already started the descent into darkness, the sunset a little before 9 PM that we had watched together outside at the pub. It was now close to ten and dark, many stars already visible in the sky, and the reflection of the crescent moon was shimmering on the water. The stars I could see were breathtaking.

"This is one of my favorite spots along Lough Derg," Declan said as we stood looking out at the lake, the ruins of Dromineer Castle behind us, the restaurant and club house part way across Lough Derg to our right. The largest lake in Ireland stretched out before us as far as the eyes at night could see, the stars endless.

The wind picked up then, and for a faint moment, I heard a sound like laughter, a woman's laughter – I turned my head to see where it had come from, and my hair blew around, and the wind gently whistled – and I didn't know if I'd heard laughter or just the wind.

And then Declan was brushing my wind-blown hair from my face, and his lips were on mine, and sparks – the sensation of the wind, and heat, and melting with him – and he was not holding back this time – and my heart was bursting.

We were together again.

"You're lovely," he said when we came out of our embrace, and he held my hand and led me to sit down in the grass.

We sat close together, looking at the stars, and he said, "I believe there is a lot more to time that we do not know yet, have yet to discover. When telescopes look far out enough into the night sky, they see not where we are but eons ago. So in that sense, we can already time travel. Perhaps when we pass away, we are not constrained by time the way we are when we are living. And as they say…love never dies."

I leaned my head on his shoulder then. "Declan, I feel a sense that Cailin is – well, much more at peace now. I think…"

Declan gently interjected and took my hand. "Well, if Fionn had to give up Cailin, and Cailin never got the chance to make right the great misunderstanding between them – in time – I will make it my mission to not give you up, Kayla."

And then I felt happier than words could describe, that somehow Declan and I were a small yet solid part of the universe before us, as a shooting star delighted us, streaking across the sky.

Epilogue

Three Months Later

Declan and I watched the beautiful lights of the Magic Fountain in Barcelona, Nolan and Louisa to our right – two couples enjoying the magic lights where the New Irish Travelers played a concert the night before.

"Kayla, I am so glad Declan finally got you over here!" Louisa said. I held Declan's hand and felt so happy for Louisa – and Nolan – and all of us…I almost thought I must be in a dream…

But this was real. Now and fresh – really happening in this lifetime.

And perfect.

"I'm so glad too," I said, watching the lights in the fountain turn to yellow, to red, then to blue – to music that we could all enjoy on Nolan and the band's well-earned night off.

"Do you think you'll stay awhile? It's so good to see you again," my friend Louisa was beaming, and it was more beautiful than the new sparkling engagement ring she wore.

"Well – a week or so," I said. "We are definitely ready for a vacation!"

"Indeed," Declan said.

"We're so happy for you," I said. Nolan then spun Louisa into a kiss.

"I'm so happy for you both – even more than for how great the tour has gone," Declan said, and I gave Declan a gentle shove, and we all laughed.

"You should stay a while!" Louisa said. "Declan, you are so helpful with the tour, and we love having you both around."

"Indeed," Nolan said, and the way he said it reminded me of Declan and made me laugh again.

"It's good to be here, but we will head back to Ireland after some time off – back to Killaloe," Declan said, holding me close.

"Yes – back to Ireland. To home."

"I hear you – that's where your heart is," Louisa said, coming around. "And we will come back to visit you – after we woo more of the world with Nolan's playing," Louisa said.

And we all became quiet then, content with our place in the world – and watched the fountain, the lights and water, dancing with the music.

A Note from the Author

Thank you for reading my first novel, that was much inspired by my trip to Ireland in 2019. A writer all my life, I was touched in a way by the trip to the Emerald Isle that stayed with me. Even though I started writing the novel before Covid led us to stay in and away from others, at least physically, the time we were staying in and safe gave me the perfect opportunity to explore the affect my trip to Ireland had on me, and to challenge myself to explore my main character's connection to Ireland and her ancestry, which in turn, inspired me to connect more with what I was learning about my own ancestors.

The magic realism genre calls to me, as I've always been fascinated, and felt very comfortable with, exploring spiritual experiences, heightened feelings, and things I don't quite have an answer for, but feel real nonetheless.

I'm also intrigued by the nature of time, and how so much of how we experience life is not based on "linear time." A memory from long ago in the past can come to us in a flash, yet we are unsure why his memory is coming to us now.

Thank you so much for spending time in Kayla's world, and whether you enjoy the novel with a cup of tea, Kayla's favorite, a latte, or curled up in bed before a good night's sleep – my wish is for my story to engage you and to inspire you to feel the comfort of the unknown.

About the Author

A native of the San Francisco Bay Area and a longtime resident of San Diego, California, no matter what else I have had going on in my life or career, I have always loved writing. Many of my long-term friendships have revolved around writing, and helping their writing shine as an editor. I have always written stories since I was a young child and learned to write well enough, and continue to love escaping into a good novel that helps expand my life perspective after each good read. I find the same with travelling, when I look back on the experiences, whether to Ireland, other parts of Europe, Southeast Asia like the magical world of Cambodia, or even trips throughout the United States like to Michigan where I also have family. On these trips I learn and grow as a person. And since most of us will never go everywhere on planet Earth, books are a magical way for us to travel to places in our minds to enrich our lives. Also a great lover of music, I've always been awed by my friends with great musical talent and enjoy concerts of all kinds, and enjoy being the editor for the online music and concert magazine Pow.

Currently I am back in the Bay Area connecting to my roots, and enjoying having just adopted a sweet Havana Rabbit I call Mocha.